TIME'S HOSTAGE

HIGHLAND TIME-TRAVEL PARANORMAL ROMANCE

ANN GIMPEL

CONTENTS

Copyright Page

A witch with no loyalties… A Druid with a life-shattering secret…

Part witch, part demon, Sorcha's been on the run ever since she escaped Hell's gates. Bouncing through time, she's managed to stay one step ahead of Rhea Roskelly, blackest of Black Witches, who wants her for her demon blood. Constantly looking over one shoulder is annoying, but freedom is worth any price.

Tavin used to be a Druid. Actually, he still is, but his magic took a decidedly unDruidlike turn a few years back. Rather than deal with his kinsmen, who'd be convinced he sold his soul to evil, he drops out of sight.

Things have changed since he left. A lot. Roskelly witches are part of the Druids' community. To his dismay, another witch appears out of nowhere, except this one is half demon. Certain he must be mistaken, he drops his invisibility illusion to take a closer look. If Druids have been corrupted by Black Magic, he'll have to intervene. The odds are hideous, but he has no choice.

*P*art witch, part demon, I was born in Hell. Most demons get their start in Hell's halls. Not true of witches, but I'm one of the unusual ones. Notice I said unusual, not lucky. My mother is a Roskelly witch. Because evil was hardwired into her, she fell hard for dark enchantments, sucked them down like nectar. I have no idea if she knew she'd be trapped behind Hell's gates forever when she sashayed through them, but even if she'd entered the Dark Realm with full knowledge, she'd like as not have made the same choice.

I'm getting ahead of things, though.

This isn't about Yanna, my mother, but about me.

The thing about being born somewhere is it's all you know. I don't exactly remember playing like little kids I've run into since I found a way out of Hell, but nor do I remember being miserable.

Not as a youngster.

No. That part came later when my demon father—a handsome fellow if you discounted his amber eyes and horn stumps—told me the time had come for me to earn my keep. I might have been five then, or as much as six or even seven.

Everyone's childhood ends somewhere, but mine crashed off a million-meter cliff when I ended up siphoning blood from things that weren't quite dead yet. In a backhanded way, it was perfect since I wasn't very tall, and my victims lay on the ground. Easy enough to reach, but I felt their pain—and their horror. Like I said, if my youth held anything in the way of innocence, it departed damned fast.

Mom was no help at all. She loved Black Witchcraft more than she loved anything or anyone, including me. Like as not, she never even noticed I wasn't around much. Hell's not all that clean, but it has kitchens just like everywhere else. And a laundry. Eventually, I was assigned to both. An improvement from harvesting lifeblood from the dying.

I've never minded hard work, and I put in my time cooking and washing robes and capes. I was lonely, but no one else in Hell saw things that way, so I didn't have words for what was missing. Elements like friendship or simple conversation weren't valued. Mom stewed in her own demented world, only occasionally surfacing to glance at what went on around her.

Time passed, long enough for my body to take on a woman's shape. There's a lot of sex in Hell. Not much to do there besides eating and fucking, but demons don't appeal to me. Don't get me wrong, some of them, like griffons and satyrs, are beautiful, but I ran the other way when they tried to herd me into a corner, cocks swollen and sexual heat blasting from every pore.

I think I'd decided even then that I needed to leave. It was just a matter of how and when. Lots of reluctant recruits get stuck in Hell. Most of them don't take to it like my mother did. Of course, she'd signed on of her own free will. I suppose it made a difference.

Regardless, punishment for attempted escapes was swift and sure.

Not death. No, that would have been far too easy. Hell's punishments were sophisticated, like reliving your worst fears over and over until you lost what little mind you had left. My strongest asset was blended magic. Something about witchy power mingled with my demon blood gave me an edge. The demons and sprites and monsters thought twice about messing with me after I surrounded myself with magic.

Once I figured out they were afraid of me, I grew bolder. Daring enough to watch from the sidelines while demons came and went. The first time I saw a demon open Hell's gates, I got ridiculously excited, so much so my warding failed and my hiding place was discovered.

I paid for that.

A hundred lashes that flayed skin from my back. Good thing for magic. It heals and heals fast, but I'll carry scars forever. They're not a bad thing, though. The slight tightness across my shoulder blades is a reminder, one that's stood me in good stead.

It took a long time, years, until I succeeded in leaving Hell. No one counts time in the Dark Realm. It's one of many differences between it and Earth. I planned and planned, holding back until I was certain I could pull things off. If I tried—and failed—the demons would have made certain I'd never get close enough to the gates for a second attempt.

Demons.

My blood, but not who I am.

Not sure quite what that makes me since Mother's Black Magic gives me the creeps and makes my skin crawl with disgust. I grew to hate her, and the demons too, but Hell was the only place I'd ever known. Homes are weird like that. No matter how awful, they're a macabre comfort zone.

Once I understood I'd become complacent, that my scheming and planning to escape were a hedge against boredom, I made my move. I was terrified if I didn't do something, I'd never gather the moxie to leave at all.

I'll spare you the details, but one dark day, a day like any other in Hell, I put my plan into action. It went off without a hitch. After shaking off shock I wasn't being wrapped in chains and dragged to one of Hell's fiery pits as punishment for insubordination, I ran through those high gates into rain and cold.

I was surprised I had the presence of mind to shut them behind me.

Barefoot, shivering, without so much as a cloak to drag over my head, I pressed forward, and the next part of my life began. It's when I met my bird. My familiar in witchy terms. I'd been free for all of maybe an hour. Soaked and chilled, I diverted magic to protect my feet from the cold, rocky ground, when an enormous black raven flew in front of me. Wings spread, it blocked my path.

I may have left Hell behind, but I recognized magic when it slapped me front and center. For a long, hideous moment, I was certain one of Hell's denizens had tracked me and was intent on dragging me back.

"Look deeper," it cawed and showed no sign of moving.

I could have feinted to one side, could have run away, but something about the raven drew me. With a deeply sinking feeling, certain I was making a mistake, I looked right into its amber eyes.

"*You are mine, witch,*" the bird said. "*I have waited long for you.*"

"I don't understand." My words sounded thin, hollow, scared.

"*No, you wouldn't. Follow me, Sorcha Roskelly, and I will explain everything.*"

CHAPTER 1

Music pounded through the smoky, crowded bistro. Drums, lutes, lyres, and the inevitable bagpipes. Sorcha made her way through tight knots of men, tray balanced on her shoulder. The raven that never left her side clung to the other shoulder, talons digging deep for purchase. Laden with tankards of ale, the tray was heavy, requiring both her hands to hold it steady, one beneath and one clutching its rounded edge.

Hands groped her as she passed, but men were pigs, and it went with the territory. Serving wenches were fair game. So far, she'd escaped being tossed onto her back for sport, but only because of her magic.

And her bird. It snapped its beak sharply if a man's hands grew too familiar.

"Aye, lassie. Bring that here," a man with matted

red hair boomed. Swathed in a spotted tartan, Liam was one of the regulars, showing up most nights for food and drink.

"Och, but ye dinna order it. If ye want some, be quick about it, and have your money out," she retorted and twisted to drop the tray onto a nearby trestle. More hands shot out, grappling and slapping as they fought to take possession of one of the dozen jugs of spirits.

The tray emptied fast. She collected coins, dropping them into her apron pockct. A tall, dark-haired man swathed in a filthy cloak grabbed a jug and headed for the door. "Not so fast," she called after him, but he kept right on walking.

Sorcha shrugged and whistled once, high and shrill. It was an agreed-upon signal and guaranteed the ale thief wouldn't make it out the front door. Not in one piece, anyway. A muffled shriek, followed by a thud, confirmed he'd been caught.

The bird squawked in satisfaction from its perch.

"Ye're a hard woman," Liam muttered and held onto her hand a few beats too long as he placed grimy coins into it.

She tossed her head back. "And why should the innkeeper foot the bill for those who wish to drink for free?"

Liam didn't answer, just laid claim to the last

tankard. She beat a retreat to the low-ceilinged kitchens toward the rear of the *Wild Pig Inn*.

"Back for another round?" The proprietor transferred more ale onto the tray. Burly and blonde with kind, dark eyes, Karl was one of those rare married men who wasn't constantly on the lookout to exercise his cock. He offered a sliver of meat to the bird, who picked it up daintily, careful not to poke a hole in his hand.

Sorcha arched her back, rubbing the lower portion, and shouldered the tray again. No reason to say much. As jobs went, this one was decent. She had a straw tick upstairs in the stable, and no one bothered her after she crawled into it each night.

She ferried another load of spirits to the common room, and then one more. As she worked, she thought about the last year. She'd been in Glasgow longer than she'd been anywhere in a long while. She'd picked 1870 on a whim, and so far it was working for her.

She'd had to do a smidgeon of work to alter her speech to blend in, but at least no one shot her odd looks anymore.

A wry smile twisted one side of her mouth downward. Men with grubby, grabby hands were an inconvenience, one she'd put up with forever if it shielded her from the Roskelly witches. After bouncing from spot to spot, traveling through time, she wasn't under any illusions. She'd only managed to escape detection because of her demon blood. It cut both ways, though, since it made her that much more attractive to the Roskellys. Once they'd discovered her —a few months after her egress from Hell—they'd hunted her through time and borderworlds with no signs of giving up.

How long had that been?

She narrowed her eyes in thought. Maybe fifty years, but it might be as much as seventy or even eighty. She'd never totally moved beyond her tendency to ignore days, months, and years as they clipped past.

Her mother, a Roskelly witch steeped in Black Magic, had become a demon's paramour. Sorcha had been the result. Nothing quite like being born in Hell to make her nimble—and cautious. She'd been staying one step ahead of demons since before she could walk. Lucky for her, her mixed-blood magic was more robust than theirs.

Stronger than the Roskellys' power too, but she'd had a few very close calls. Witches were smarter than demons, by a good big bunch...

"So are ye planning to turn loose of yon tray?" Karl's voice broke into her thoughts.

"Aye. Sorry." She dropped it, waiting for him to fill it once again. The raven clucked quietly, sounding more like a chicken. Karl obligingly fed it more scraps.

"Ye're shameless," she told the bird.

"Nay. Practical," it replied, sounding smug

This time, Karl added baskets of coarse brown bread to the tray. Good. It wouldn't weigh quite as much. She dug through her pockets, emptying them of coin. She'd often considered hanging onto one or two, but it was bad luck to cheat those who fed you. Karl's good nature would evaporate in a heartbeat if he suspected her of double-dealing.

And then she'd be out of both house and job. Glasgow might be sizeable as towns went, but the innkeepers all knew one another. If she dealt dirty with one, she'd be unlikely to find another position. Not without casting spells, and any obvious use of magic might give her away.

She could always set herself up selling charms and potions, but that would alert any nearby witches, something she couldn't risk. Rather like innkeepers, witches all knew one another. And right now, the Glasgow witches had no idea she even existed.

She had a good thing going at the *Wild Pig*. It had provided a lengthy break from leaping through time, trading one spot for another like an escaped hostage running for her life.

"Are ye feeling a mite off?" Karl closed a hand around her upper arm to get her attention.

"Nay. Just tired. We're near enough to closing, I'll

be fine." She snatched up the tray and shouldered back through the wooden, swinging door and on into the common room.

No one else had tried to make off with their food or drink, no doubt deterred by the thief who'd been clubbed in the head earlier. Half a dozen more trips, and Karl strode into the common room alongside her. Raising his deep voice, he told the men they'd be closing in a quarter hour.

Last call for spirits was always busy. Breath hissed from between her teeth as the beefy Scott who guarded the door barred it for the night. Sorcha carted her empty tray back into the kitchens and stood over the sink washing tankards in tepid water.

Rather than remaining on her shoulder, the raven perched on the edge of the sink. Its presence steadied her. Normally, familiars only presented themselves after much ceremony, but this one had been earmarked for her, had somehow known when she'd slipped her bonds and left Hell. She'd been so delighted to not be alone anymore, she hadn't questioned it. Some boons were like that. You welcomed them, accepted their presence in your life.

The bird had a good heart, and a pure, clean spirit. It had proven its worth many times over, and she'd done her damnedest to be a worthy partner.

Once she was done with the dishes, she took her

food basket and nodded goodnight to Karl. Head bowed, he sat at a table totaling up the night's take in his ledger. A lantern shed a feeble, yellow light over his efforts.

Sorcha hesitated. It would take very little to make his light shine brighter, make it easier for him to see. She hurried away before temptation got the better of her. He was human. Any display of supernatural power would scare him, and men who were scared reacted badly. He trusted her, and she'd be wise not to rock that particular boat.

She hustled out the back door, dipping her head to avoid the low lintel. The yard was always muddy because it never stopped raining in Scotland. Behind her music played, sometimes deft, sometimes halting, as tonight's musicians experimented with new songs or different renditions of older ones. They always played for hours, sometimes all night. She'd often wondered how they got by on no sleep, but it wasn't any of her affair.

Besides, she was worried if she dug too deep, she'd find magic of a different sort. Power that might bite back if she unearthed it. It took magic to know magic, and she kept her ability concealed.

As was its wont, the bird launched itself off her shoulder for its nightly hunt. Or perhaps it went elsewhere. It would return before morning. It always did. "Good hunting," she called after it, keeping her voice soft.

The high, strident cries of a raptor on the move blasted her before the raven vanished into the night sky and was lost to sight.

She let herself into the stable amid the scents of horses, cows, goats, and hay. The animals kept the stout, wooden building warm. When she'd first come to live with them, they'd been restless, no doubt sensing her demon side, but she'd soothed their fears with gentle magic, and now they accepted her as one of them.

Tucking the cloth sack with her day's allotment of food beneath one arm, she climbed the ladder to her spot under the eaves. The scents of buttered bread and roasted meat made her mouth water. Karl was liberal with what he gave her. Most nights, she ate until she was stuffed and still had something left over for the next morning.

She sat cross-legged on her bed—straw tucked into rough, cotton sacking—and dug into her meal. As she ate, she thought about...everything. Her life. Her plight. Should she remain? Should she leave? If she left, where would she go? What would happen if the Roskellys captured her?

Rhea, their *de facto* leader, had nabbed her once. Sorcha wondered how Rhea and her mother were related, but she'd never know, not for certain. Shared blood was the only logical explanation for how the old witch had zeroed in on her, though. That little incident had happened only a few years after she'd made good on her escape from Hell.

Aye, my escape from Hell.

She finished the first piece of bread, chewing and swallowing before starting in on a hunk of roast pork.

Her mother was almost less than worthless. She'd lost her mind, wandering in dark places Sorcha could only guess at. The few times she'd commanded Yanna's attention and asked how to leave Hell, her mother had first shushed her and then laughed like a mad thing.

Sorcha's take-home message had been that no one ever left Hell, except maybe the demons who ran the place. It had given her an idea, though, a starting place. She'd taken to shadowing a few of them, watching how they came and went.

She'd been patient, spent time practicing their incantations. Her hated demon blood had been her salvation. She'd needed it to cast the same spell, the one that opened Hell's gates. The day they'd parted at her behest, she'd stood before them, dumbstruck, losing precious moments before running like the wind, not caring what was on the other side.

Free. I'm free. I'm free, had blasted through her mind.

She reached for a waterskin and took a deep drink, washing her food down. She'd indeed been free, but she hadn't actually expected her ploy to work. She hadn't had the presence of mind to bring anything with her. Not even her other frock. When Hell's entry clanged shut behind her with a shot of black lightning to add drama, she'd stood barefoot in the coldest place she'd ever been.

Rain sheeted from dark skies, and she'd begun to shiver.

She had no idea how much harder things would have been if her bird hadn't shown up an hour into her freedom and demanded she follow it. If she hadn't been so lonely her bones ached, she might have walked away from what had turned into her staunchest ally.

Good thing she hadn't.

Even with the raven, everything had taken forever, but she'd figured out her new life in bits and pieces. Magic kept her warm and helped her find shelter. She hadn't known it for a few weeks, but Hell had spit her out in western Scotland in the 1960s. The whirr of machinery and the stench of pollution became constant companions as she solved the problems of how to get what she needed to stay alive.

Taking her clothes off in a strip club where no one asked any questions about where she came from, or why she had no shoes, meant money. Money meant food—and lodging in a fleabag boarding house. When men accosted her, intent on satisfying their lust with her body, the bird stepped in. If it wasn't enough, she flattened the horny bastards with magic.

That turned out to be her first serious mistake.

Her first brush with the Roskelly witches.

Why the hell had her mother left the fold? Dark enchantment called to its own, and Yanna's power was as black as magic came.

The stable door creaked open.

Sorcha extended a slight thread of magic to see who it was. No one went riding in the middle of the night. Or milked cows or gathered eggs. The bird was more than capable of leveraging power to open a door, but it usually cruised through a perpetually open window near her sleeping spot.

She detected familiar energy and frowned. "Rose?"

"Aye, mistress," Karl's twelve-year-old daughter replied in a soft voice.

Sorcha laid her food bag to one side and pelted down the ladder, facing outward in her hurry. "What is it, dear? Is aught amiss?"

Rose's dark eyes rounded into small moons. Long straight brown hair fell to her waist, and she was wrapped in a cream-colored wool cloak. "'Tis Mum. She's bad off. Da, he said to ask you to come. Ye've the healing touch, he said."

"Take me to her." Alarm bells tolled. Karl was a proud man. For him to request assistance meant his wife was in serious trouble.

Sorcha rushed out of the stable after Rose. The raven materialized out of nowhere and took up its customary spot on her shoulder.

Karl's wife, Daria, was deep into her latest pregnancy. The bairn should have been born by now, at least by Sorcha's estimates, but Karl and his family weren't her concern, so she'd kept her misgivings to herself. Rose was the oldest of eight. Sorcha assumed after that many children, Daria knew what she was doing.

She entered the inn and followed Rose up a back staircase. She'd been in the family's rooms above the inn a few times to clean, so she was familiar with their layout. Below her, the intrepid musicians played on. Their attention was elsewhere, so she felt safe enough questing forward with a splash of magic. She was still gathering information about Daria's condition when Rose held a door open.

Sorcha walked into the combination kitchen and living area for Karl's family. The children slept on the far side of a curtain to the left of a coal-burning stove. Karl and Daria's bedroom was behind an identical curtain on the right. A muffled moan was followed by a sharper one.

Sorcha didn't waste time asking permission. She pulled the thick, cotton curtain to one side and closed the short distance to where Daria lay on her back on a feather bed. Karl sat next to her. Worry streamed from him in dark-gray waves of distress.

Sorcha dropped a hand over Daria's rounded abdomen. The muscles were knotted, and not moving. Power flowed from her splayed hand, gentle, encouraging, as she felt for life within.

"How long has she been lying here?" she asked Karl.

"Doona ken." His voice was raspy and harsh. "I found her like this. Goddammit. Why dinna she come downstairs for me? Or send one of the bairns?"

"Maybe she dinna wish to bother you." Sorcha aimed for soothing. "She knows how busy ye are every night." Bending forward, she added her other hand and a staunch bit of magic. Between the two, she felt the faint flutter of the baby's heart.

"Och aye." She fed more magic into Daria's womb, willing the babe to live.

"What?" Karl dropped a heavy hand atop hers. "Is—?"

"Nay, the babe lives. Bring me a kettle of hot water and let me work."

"Will Mum be all right?" Rose asked from where she'd taken up a vigil next to the curtain.

"I hope so, dear. Help your Da. I need water and clean towels or sheets. And tea. Get my herbs. They're at the head of my bed."

"Of course." Karl sounded pathetically grateful to have something to do. "Aught else?"

"A few moments alone with Daria."

"Ye'll have that while we're hunting your requests."

As soon as Karl and Rose had cleared the sleeping area, Sorcha dropped all pretense of normalcy. Reaching into Daria's mind, she established a connection and drew the woman toward consciousness. The raven wove its magic in with hers, strengthening it.

"Sorcha?" Daria's voice was thin, thready.

"Aye. I need ye upright, walking. The bairn will be here afore ye know."

"Nay. 'Tis dead," Daria moaned, and her blue eyes filled with tears. Lank black hair fell around her thin shoulders and milk-swollen breasts.

Sorcha gripped both sides of her face. "Look at me. I wouldna lie to ye. The babe lives. On your feet. I need ye walking."

She half carried, half dragged the other woman until she had her feet beneath her. Arm around Daria's waist, Sorcha walked her from one side of the small enclosure to the other, all the while urging the unborn child with magic. Encouraging it to fight its way out.

A muted whoop escaped Daria. "'Tis working. The child is moving. I was certain when I quit laboring the babe was done for, and me along with it."

"None of that," Sorcha said, her tone sharp. "It tempts fate, and not in good ways." She placed a hand over Daria's stomach, gratified to feel the muscles flowing, laboring to expel the baby.

"It's coming. I feel it."

Sorcha eased Daria back onto the feather bed with her knees bent, legs spread. Sure enough, the child's head was crowning. Karl and Rose rushed back into the alcove in time to see the baby slither into the world. Sorcha gathered it close, still deeply immersed in the power she'd summoned to ensure no one died.

Not here. Not tonight.

The sound of Rose's soft sobs was joined by Karl's rough words of thanks. The baby's first cries woke something primal in Sorcha. She'd been afraid she was too late, that her magic wouldn't be enough.

But it had been.

She'd used her ability—her tainted combination of demon and Black Magic—for good, and it gave her hope. She'd controlled the outcome here, which might mean she could do the same in any situation.

Later, she'd ask the bird how much it had helped. Its power still thrummed within her, warm and glowing like strands of quicksilver.

Sorcha kept one hand firmly on Daria's stomach. "One more good push, dear." Smiling through tears, Daria complied, and the placenta emerged. Sorcha severed the cord and laid the squalling infant into Karl's outstretched hands. He wrapped his son in a length of blanket and took another rag to clean him.

The sounds of sleepy children's voices reached her.

"Rose, tell your brothers and sisters all is well," Karl instructed.

Sorcha rooted through the herbs they'd brought and selected black cohosh and raspberry, mixing them in an infuser in a cracked ceramic teapot. Once the tea had steeped, she poured a cup and handed it to Daria. "Drink it all. 'Twill help ye heal."

"Thank ye a million times over," she murmured before draining the cup.

Sorcha got to her feet. "I'll be in the stable if ye need me."

Karl scrambled to his feet with his son in his arms. "I canna thank ye enough, Sorcha. Ye saved my son's life. Mayhap my wife's as well."

She patted his arm. "Take good care of them." Before he said anything more, she slipped around the curtain and out of his rooms. Tonight had helped her, taught her the full brunt of her power wouldn't sweep her off balance, make her plummet into a darkness not unlike the Hell she'd run from.

She was outside the inn, one hand on the stable's side door, when she felt witch power closing on her. A dark, malevolent cloud, it pounded against her. The raven screeched outrage. Sorcha threw up wards. All she needed was a few moments. She'd escape into a time vortex. She'd done it before. If she constructed it right, no one could follow her.

It was how she'd escaped Rhea Roskelly a few other times, and she was almost certain the canny old bitch was bearing down on her again. No doubt drawn by the magic she'd expended.

She tossed prudence aside. She'd been discovered; no more need for caution. Nay, what she required now were speed, cunning, and as much magic as she could command. Sorcha reached deep. The bird helped, forming a crucible to concentrate her ability. Demon power boiled from her guts, joining witch magic. Working fast, she pried open a time portal and beat a path to the future. Maybe if she went far enough forward, Rhea would be dead.

The thought pleased her. Of course, Rhea was just one Roskelly, but the others didn't seem so hell-bent on capturing her. She sealed her casting to ensure no unpleasant surprises on her journey and settled in. Karl and Daria would wonder what happened to her, but it couldn't be helped.

Eventually, the black of her travel portal shaded to

gray, and she prepared to exit. Where would she emerge this time?

Aye, and how long will I be able to remain?

Sadness filled her, but she pushed it aside. If bouncing from one corner of time to another was the price for leaving Hell, she'd pay it a thousand times over.

CHAPTER 2

Tavin Shaw willed himself to silence, keeping his power as unobtrusive as possible. Druids were gathering on South Ronaldsay Island in the Orkneys. More Druids than he'd seen in one place in the last hundred years. Only thing he couldn't determine was why.

He lived near the standing stones at Callanish on the Isle of Lewis during the spring, summer, and autumn months. He didn't need money, but he maintained a blacksmith shop to keep busy. The forge was honest work, and it lent him a revered position in the small community. Over time, folk had grown used to him leaving toward the tail end of the year. For some unexplained reason, time had gotten away from him, and it was well into January. He should have been gone long since, but just because his annual pilgrimage south was late wasn't a reason to not go at all.

He'd been back on the mainland and on his way to Glencoe intent on catching a train when an outpouring of magic caught his attention.

More than an outpouring. A veritable flood. He'd learned long ago to live and let live, but he couldn't ignore such an obvious summons. What if Druids were under attack? He'd been one of them long ago, before his magic took an unexpected turn. So unexpected, he hadn't wanted to explain himself—or become a petri dish for the others to pick apart—so he'd faded from view.

It happened with long-lived mages. Many wearied of their long lives and vanished. Insofar as he knew, no one had wasted time or energy searching for him.

Rather than leave his aging Renault in long-term parking at the train station as he'd planned, he nosed the vehicle north toward Inverness and John O'Groats. Druid power thickened around him, seeded with anger and desperation. It wasn't until he pulled up in a deserted parking area near the ferry terminal in John O'Groats that he sensed witch magic.

Witch enchantment. What the fucking hell?

Tavin got out of his car and rocked back on his heels, scenting the air. He was certain he had to be wrong. Except he wasn't. Since when did Druids parlay with witches? Things might have changed since he'd extricated himself from his Druid kin, but he didn't believe they could have changed all that much.

Despite the power eddying around him, he was alone. He took a few more minutes to dig deeper into the witch scent. A harsh breath swooped through him.

Roskelly witches, blackest of the black.

He'd assumed they'd all died—or left the UK. And he hadn't worried overmuch about which it was. Them being gone had been an enormous relief.

"Aye, except it appears I was mistaken," he murmured, his brogue soft and thick—and troubled.

He scanned the harbor, intent on commandeering a small boat and motoring out to South Ronaldsay. It was the Druids' traditional meeting place. They were still using the same cave they'd gathered in for at least a millennia. Blessed by Danu, the cavern was safe, protected. He spied a likely skiff and started toward it but then changed his mind. From the looks of things, the meeting would likely last days, not hours. The skiff's owner might well need his boat long before Tavin returned it.

He balanced from foot to foot, weighing his options. Only three presented themselves. Teleporting, stealing a boat, or the reason that had driven him away from Druid society. He scratched teleporting off the list. It held an obvious magical signature, and he aimed to remain as invisible as he could. Minutes dribbled past. A familiar blast of power edging closer got him moving.

Druids, maybe as many as half a dozen, would be here in short order. He could pop out of the shadows like a long-lost relative and greet them, but then he'd be stuck either lying or relaying his eerie detour through decidedly unDruidlike magic.

He edged inside a covered marina. No reason to reveal himself.

Not yet, anyway.

Not until he had some idea what in the unholy hell was going on.

He picked a protected corner and undressed fast, shrouding his clothing with a "don't look here" casting, so his things would be waiting for him when he returned. Naked, he resisted the urge to shiver. It was bloody cold in northern Scotland in January.

Instead, he spread his arms, shut his eyes, and reached for power hidden deep in the earth beneath his feet. It rushed to his command, thrilling as always, and his human body fell away.

In its place, wings sprouted. His nose turned into a hooked beak. Feathers cut the chill until he no longer noticed it. He shook himself, arranging his mottled golden plumage. He'd always loved falcons, but the day he'd turned into a peregrine was blazoned into his memory.

Thank every goddess in the pantheon he'd been by himself. He'd felt off that day. Odd and unbalanced, somehow. Overly sensitive to smells and sights and sounds. He'd been living in John O'Groats at the time, earning his living as a musician. He had several hours before he was due at the local tavern with his lute, so he'd gone for a ramble across barren moorlands.

No trees grew this far north. Not new ones, and not anymore. They'd been cut down for houses and firewood centuries ago. The odd hawthorn and yew remained, though. They were revered, so the government built fences around groves and posted harsh warnings to leave the trees alone.

He'd been drawn to a gnarled stand of ancient hawthorns. Druids had strong links to the natural world, and Tavin trusted his instincts, so he'd wandered through the trees, listening to their spirits, their voices. Usually, they soothed him, but their message held a different quality. It urged him to open his magic and wait.

So he had.

The same sensations he'd just summoned had been far sharper, more urgent. He hadn't undressed since he had no idea what was about to unfold. Even in all its glorious reality, the falcon was far smaller than his human form. He'd ended up shrouded in clothing that he pecked his way out of.

It was the pecking that made him half crazy. He'd felt stretching, tearing, breaking as his body found the raptor's shape, but it was the pecking that slapped him hard, made him pant through a beak that snapped open and shut.

He loved birds, but he'd never fancied being one.

Or any other creature besides human.

A hideous squawking had filled his keen avian ears. For the longest time, he didn't realize the noise was coming from him. Once he did, he shut up fast. Whatever had happened to him, miracle or disaster, he'd see it through.

"Better." A numinous voice had eddied around him.

He couldn't talk, so he experimented with telepathy, relieved beyond belief when it worked. *"Who are you?"*

Rather than answering, the silky voice, low and creamy, said, *"Ye've been given a gift, Tavin Shaw. Use it wisely."*

Before he could sift through the million questions churning through his mind—to be certain to ask the most important ones—the same ripping, tearing, breaking sensation swept through him. This time hurt far more than the first had. What was left of his clothing ripped as an arm poked through here, a leg there.

Magic had pounded around him that long-ago day, slick with the scents of wet greenery and verdant moors. Druid magic smelled like that at its finest. He'd crouched on Scotland's perpetually wet earth and wondered if he was losing his mind.

Or if he'd fallen into a bizarre trance.

A quick examination of his shirt, rife with vertical rips from the beak that had graced his face, laid waste to his trance explanation. Around him, the trees soughed, wind whooshing through their branches. They seemed to approve of whatever had just transpired.

He'd taken a deep breath, and then another, emptying his lungs.

Could he manufacture the transformation on his own?

No time like the present to find out. First, he'd stripped out of the ruins of his clothes. It had taken him a few tries to replicate the change, but once it happened, he spread his thickly feathered wings and flew, soaring above the gnarled trees.

The sense of awe and wonder that filled him that day had never truly left. The god or goddess who'd said he'd been given a gift had spoken true.

By the time he landed and regained his human

form, he'd made a few decisions. The primary one was he'd drop out of sight. He had no logical explanation for what had happened, and he didn't want to turn into an experimental subject.

Arlen MacGregor, Arch Druid in the UK, wouldn't rest until he'd sliced and diced Tavin's newfound magic. The man was a cultural anthropologist, steeped in ancient rituals and customs. He'd do his damnedest to pigeonhole what felt like a miracle to Tavin...

Voices reached him. The Druids he'd sensed nearby had arrived and were discussing the best way to move themselves to South Ronaldsay. Teleporting seemed the clear winner, but Tavin didn't stick around to hear the rest. He spread his wings and flew out of the boathouse and thence over the restless dark waters of the North Sea.

"Och, just look at yon falcon," a woman's voice called out.

"Sure and 'tis a beauty," a man agreed.

If Tavin had been human, he'd have smiled. The tang of salt water filled his nostrils. Everything smelled far more intense as a falcon. Riding the night wind, he caught a small fish unwise enough to venture close to the surface. And then one more. Once he'd determined he could switch from human to bird and back with little fanfare, he'd spent a lot of time as a falcon. Maybe months. Birds didn't mark the passage of time like humans did.

He enjoyed the freedom of flight. Of catching food on the hoof. Of not bothering with the trappings of keeping up a home. He could perch anywhere and be comfortable. Sometime during those early months, he'd ended up near the Callanish stones. He'd liked their energy and chosen the Isle of Lewis for his next home.

He rode the ground cushion of air that created an easy zone for flight and put his back into covering the kilometers to South Ronaldsay. He wanted to get there in time to hear everything. As he flew, he reviewed his information about Roskelly witches.

Gaps peppered his knowledge, but he'd come face-to-face with Rhea—their *grand dame*—and two of her sisters in the middle of the 1800s. A shocking amount of power bled from them, so much he'd never have escaped with his magic—or his life—intact, if a pack of Druids hadn't responded to his distress call.

The old witch had shaken a fist in his face and said, "Ye've not seen the last of me, Druid. I loathe your kind."

"Aye, we're none too fond of you, either," he'd shot back.

Later that evening in a smoky alehouse, he'd laughed about his narrow escape, but the laughter held sharp edges. He'd taken care to ward himself better after that, trained himself to run at the first hint of Roskelly stench.

Despite Rhea's threats, he'd never crossed paths with her again. As he thought about it, he hadn't sensed any witches, Roskelly or otherwise, in his part of Scotland for at least the last fifty years.

The island formed ahead of him, a dark lump against a slightly lighter sky studded with clouds. He banked right, intent on approaching the cave from a tunnel behind it. If the goddess blessed him, he'd manage to conceal himself near enough to listen to what transpired with no one being the wiser.

The small, narrow passageway that was originally designed as an escape route was right where he remembered. Rockfall had partially blocked the entrance, but he was small enough to slither through. He flew as far as he dared and then stood near an earthen wall, inviting the earth's power to shield him from discovery.

Arlen's voice chimed a greeting in Gaelic.

Tavin bobbed his head. He'd arrived in time. He had no idea what he'd do if the Druids had somehow fallen beneath Black Witchcraft's heels, but he'd cross that bridge when it found him. The next nearest Druid enclave was in the Pyrenees. If his worst fears were realized, he'd drive there and talk with Europe's Arch Druid.

Maybe the UK Druids were so far gone there was no retreat from evil.

He shook himself, keeping his feathers quiet. He was making assumptions. Never a sound move. First, he needed to listen. Then he'd determine if they even required his help.

He hated to admit it, but he'd enjoyed his solitude.

And his freedom.

Was all of it about to crash down on his head?

If it did, he'd take the necessary steps to manage things. He may not have lived hand in glove with the Druids for a long time, but he was committed to wiping out wickedness wherever it reared its misshapen head.

The rustle of bodies and soft conversation filled the neighboring chamber. Tavin hopped forward a few feet and peered at a crowd. At least a hundred Druids, many of whom he'd never seen before, milled about. And three Roskelly witches.

Two had flame-red hair, and one looked disturbingly like Rhea with midnight locks. How fitting. She had green eyes, though. Rhea's had held a bluish cast. As he took stock, he realized the redheads both had Rhea's unusual eye color.

Not just Roskellys, but direct relations, apparently.

One of the redheads hovered next to Arlen with a hand tucked possessively around his arm. The dark-haired witch seemed glued to Sean Weatherford, the

Druids' longtime money-magic man. A deeply sinking feeling made Tavin ill. Was this how the witches had inveigled their way in?

Sex was a tried-and-true element in witchy arsenals.

Arlen and Sean knew as much, though. Why had they fallen for the oldest trick on a witch's dance card?

Guess I'm about to find out...

"We all seem to be here." Arlen's deep, rich voice rose above multiple side conversations. Tall and spare, he had shoulder-length black hair, austere features, and shrewd dark eyes. Tonight he wore a cream-colored shirt, gray pants, and a thick, blue plaid woolen jacket.

A chorus of "ayes" followed his pronouncement.

"For those of you who don't hail from our local Druid group, let me catch you up," Arlen went on.

A collective sigh followed by indulgent chuckles circled the cavern. Perhaps fifty meters across, it was so tall its ceiling disappeared from view above. Rush lanterns shed wavery illumination, and many of the Druids had kindled mage lights that bobbed by their sides. Though Tavin couldn't see it, he remembered a tarn at the cavern's far end. Water ran down over rocks, creating an aquamarine pool that had once hosted odd little fish with bug eyes, well adapted to seeing in the cave's perpetual gloom.

"I'll be sure to keep him on track," Sean cut in.

"But if you don't quiet yourselves, we'll never get started." Shorter than Arlen, Sean moved with the grace of a jungle cat. He had curly dark hair and brown eyes that always looked as if he were laughing at a private joke.

"You do that." Arlen sent a pointed look at his second in command.

He cleared his throat. "Sparing the grisly details, Katerina"—he dropped a hand on the redheaded witch's shoulder—"came to Inverness on a lecture tour about two months back. She's a cultural anthropologist just like me. I sensed fell forces had her in their gunsights. Took me a while to tease out why. She's Rhea Roskelly's great-great granddaughter—"

A hiss started in one corner of the room, rising in volume to the accompaniment of fingers forked in the universal sign against evil.

Sean clapped his hands together so hard magic shot from his fingertips. "Silence," he roared. "Katerina not only knew nothing about the Roskelly witches, she had no idea she was one of them."

"But what about her magic?" one of the Druids in the crowd called out. "Surely it manifested."

Katerina, a tall, stately woman wearing black trousers and a green jacket let go of Arlen's arm. "No. It never did. When my great-great grandmother began following me, I figured I was going mad."

"Circling back to the point," Arlen continued, "Rhea Roskelly shanghaied Kat into the past twice. She's now my wife, and we've been working hard to catch her magic up to snuff."

"Her mother, Liliana"—Sean took advantage of Arlen stopping to draw breath to speak—"is mated to me. These might be the only White Witch Roskellys in history, but go ahead, use your own magic to test them. You'll see they carry no dark taint."

"Where does she fit in?" A burly man with blonde curls pointed at the other redheaded witch.

"I'm Gloria Roskelly," she said, stepping forward. "Liliana's mother and Katerina's grandmother. I've been working on defanging Rhea for years. When it was just Liliana and me, we had little chance, but there's enough magic in this cave to get the job done."

"What's in it for us?" A bald Druid with bright blue eyes, decked out in an old-fashioned tartan, strode toward Arlen until only a meter separated them.

"Aye, excellent question," several other Druids yelled from all corners of the cave.

"I'm afraid we managed to piss Rhea off," Arlen said, keeping his voice soft. "As in really piss her off. She blames the three witches here for the death of the Roskelly witch line, and she's not going to slink away with her tail between her legs. So far, she's borrowed demons and dragons from Hell and dragged them across the veil."

"She canna do that," the bald Druid said, outrage lining his tone. "'Twill upset the natural balance of the world."

"Which is why all of you are here," Arlen pointed out. "I told you I'd spare you details in the interest of developing a plan rather than hashing over history, but Sean nearly died. Rhea embedded a splinter of darkness in his magical center. Liliana and Gloria saved him."

"But first I had to escape." Liliana's raspy contralto rang through the cave. "Rhea ditched me in a whirling cylinder. I still have no idea where I was. If I hadn't brought spell accoutrements along, I'd still be there."

"And I'd like as not be dead," Sean added sourly.

Tavin had moved closer as the tale unfolded. It was fascinating in a grisly, macabre kind of way. He'd also tested the women with his own magic and verified Arlen's pronouncement about them being White Witches. Enough Druid power was bouncing about the cave, he'd felt safe tossing his into the mix.

"I get that ye need our help." A Druid with brown braids crossed her arms beneath her breasts. "What, precisely, did ye have in mind?"

"'Tis exactly why we're here." Arlen turned to face her squarely.

"Aye." Morgan, their antiquities librarian, supported Arlen's statement. Silver hair was wound into a bun low on her neck. Her slight form was wrapped in a black wool cloak, and her dark eyes burned with keen intelligence.

"We've come up with an idea or two," Sean said, "but with so many of us, I'm certain we can fine-tune a bulletproof—"

Air sizzled through the black-haired witch's teeth, and she spun in a circle. "What was that?"

"What was what, darling?" Sean asked.

"Ssht." She jerked her chin toward the rear of the cave. "Something's here. I felt it."

For a long, heart-stopping moment, Tavin feared he'd been discovered, but then he realized Liliana had pointed away from his hiding place. He sent power spiraling out, intent on discovering what she'd sensed, and muffled a squawk.

Witch, but demon too.

Holy hell, could this get any more disconcerting?

I'm out of practice, he told himself. Running a forge wasn't exactly the same as facing off against evil. Once he'd been a warrior, but that had been so long ago he barely recalled the difference between an inverted wedge and a frontal assault.

Arlen and Sean spun and faced the direction Liliana indicated, hands extended and power arcing from their fingertips. "Show yourself," Arlen bellowed. "Now."

More invested in not missing even a second of what came next than remaining undetected, Tavin moved into the cavern and fluttered to a high vantage point. No one noticed him since they were all just as intent as he was on the tableau unfolding a few meters away.

Magic fizzled and sputtered over by the pool. Colors rose and fell.

The witches joined Sean and Arlen. Magic thickened and pulsed, filled with compulsion. Just as a sheet of undulating red was shading to violet, the kaleidoscope frittered to nothing.

A tall, curvy woman with blonde hair that fell past her ass punched through whatever she'd been hiding behind. Her patchwork skirt, homespun tunic, and ratty jacket suggested she'd come from another place in time. A large black raven rode on her shoulder, cawing at them.

"Who are you?" Arlen's voice carried through the cave. "I command you—"

"Stuff it." She waved a dismissive hand and narrowed blue-green eyes. "Goddamned Druids. You could have left well enough alone, but did you? Oh hell, no."

Gloria stepped toward the newcomer, eying her intently. "You're one of us," she pronounced.

"Us as in?" The blonde quirked a sarcastic brow. "Look, I have no idea where I am. I was running from one of my relatives who has it in for me. The best way to do that is time traveling. I wish you no ill will. Just let me leave, and—"

"Christ on a crooked cross." Gloria closed the distance to the blonde. "I'll be goddamned. You're Yanna's daughter."

"You win a kewpie doll. Now can I leave?"

Gloria shot out a hand and gripped her arm hard enough the blonde winced. "You're my sister." She shook her head, disbelieving. "You must have been born after Mother ended up in Hell."

"That would explain the demon blood I sense." Liliana had joined Gloria. She drew her dark brows into a single line. "Whose side are you on?"

"My own. Can I leave now?"

A large black raven took shape over Gloria's head. It flew to the raven on the blonde's shoulder and touched beaks. The other bird rose into the air, and they circled the room in a graceful aerial ballet.

An owl rose from Liliana, joining them. And then an eagle emerged from Arlen's wife and winged toward the other birds.

Tavin blinked hard. Witch familiars. He'd heard of them, but never actually seen one.

"No one is going anywhere," Arlen said in a no-nonsense tone. "Not until we sort this out."

The ravens flew to Tavin's perch, cawing at him. He cawed back, but the jig was up, and he knew it. Sean's sharp gaze settled on him, followed by a blast of seeking magic. The other Druid's eyes widened.

"Tavin?" Incredulity underscored his name.

He needed his tongue. It took less time and magic than telepathy. Power sizzled and simmered as he shifted back to human. Standing buck naked in the middle of people he used to know wasn't high on his list, so he raised his voice and asked, "Could someone toss me a cloak?"

CHAPTER 3

Sorcha remained in her time portal until her magic was too thin to support her there for much longer. As usual, she had no idea where she'd come out, but she'd landed in enough spots, blending in shouldn't prove a problem. She'd have to find clothes to match wherever she was, but at least Rhea hadn't followed her.

And she'd done a good thing, saved Daria and her babe. The expenditure of power had been her undoing, but it had been worth it. A frisson of sorrow tracked down her spine. She'd miss Karl and his wife and children. Hell, she'd miss her job at the *Wild Pig*.

I was thinking about leaving, she reminded herself.

Yeah, but not seriously.

Besides, leaving under her own volition—as opposed to being forced to flee—held an entirely different flavor. Coercion left a bitter taste in her mouth, not that she'd ever had the luxury of leaving anywhere because she wanted to.

Except Hell.

Her casting developed grayish edges. Time to prepare for the inevitable. She cloaked herself in magic to ensure she was invisible. Nothing like popping into the middle of a bunch of superstitious humans. She'd only made that mistake once. It had cost her six months in a dungeon. One of the jailers had taken pity on her, and she'd struck a bargain.

Her body for her freedom. He'd thought she'd stick around forever, but she'd run as soon as she'd fulfilled her end of their pact.

After all, she was nothing if not an honorable demon.

She cut her journey through memory lane short and concentrated on cushioning her fall with still more magic. Her entry was all but silent; she was certain of it. A quick glance revealed a sizable cavern.

Filled with Druids.

A closer appraisal revealed three witches.

Sorcha shrugged. Better than a cave full of clerics by a country mile. The Druids' garb and speech patterns were modern, which clued her in which accent to use—assuming she found a way out of the cave. The group appeared intent on a discussion involving Roskelly witches.

Sorcha swallowed a snort. What a surprise. Her kinswomen were known far and wide as badass bitches. If they weren't after her, too, she'd have taken a wee bit of pride in being one of them.

And now, I'm just wasting time.

She eyed the cave's entrance. She might have half a chance of sneaking out, but it meant threading through small groups of Druids with little room to spare. If any of them were sharp, they'd pick up on her magic as she slithered past. Her bird tightened its hold on her shoulder but didn't say anything. It understood full well squawking would be a very bad idea since it would crack her invisibility illusion.

Telepathy would probably give them away too, with its expended magical signature.

She blew out a quiet breath, weighing her options.

She could remain until the Druids—and witches—left. Surely, they didn't live here. It was the wisest course, the most prudent, but she'd never had much patience. Besides, remaining in one spot held its own set of problems. If anyone was quick on the uptake, they'd recognize her small area of the cave felt different.

The witch with coal-black hair twisted to stare

right at her out of green eyes. She hissed menacingly before gritting out, "What was that?"

Sorcha cringed. She shouldn't have remained still so long.

Too late now. If she feinted in either direction, the witch who'd zeroed in on her would cut through her warding like a hot knife through wax.

"What was what, darling?" the male Druid next to her inquired, not sounding overly worried. He had a head full of brown curls and whiskey-colored eyes.

"Ssht." She jerked her chin at where Sorcha stood. "Something's here. I felt it."

The male Druid who hadn't sounded concerned spun to face Sorcha. Another man joined him. Both cast magic right at her. It stung when it connected. "Show yourself," the dark-haired Druid bellowed. "Now."

All her senses on high alert, Sorcha pumped out power. Not that she had much left after her precipitous flight through time. From the corner of her eye, she saw a peregrine falcon fly out of a tunnel and take a ringside seat. A quick blast of power confirmed it wasn't really a bird.

If she hadn't been trapped, she'd have been far more curious. As it was, the falcon could have been the devil incarnate. It wasn't her primary problem.

She eyed the tunnel. Was it a way out? Continuing

to produce diversionary magic shot with color, she edged toward the passageway. If she could only reach it, maybe she could outrun this bunch.

Maybe.

Her magic fizzled and sputtered. Colors rose and fell. She was tiring fast, but the Druids couldn't know that.

When the witches joined forces with the two Druids targeting her, Sorcha understood she was outgunned. The power bombarding her thickened with compulsion until she had a tough time breathing.

She was beaten, but she'd be damned if she'd cower before these uptight bastards. They weren't monks. They had magic of their own. Perhaps they'd let her walk out of the cave. The more she thought about it, the more likely it seemed. After all, they had bigger problems to solve than her.

"Ready?" she asked her familiar. No reason to waste magic on telepathy.

"Never readier," it cawed.

Sorcha dropped the tatters of her illusion and strode forward, standing tall. Shoulders straight, breasts high.

"Who are you?" The dark-haired Druid's voice carried through the cave. "I command you—"

"Stuff it." Sorcha waved a weary hand and narrowed her eyes to annoyed slits. "Goddamned

Druids. You could have left well enough alone, but did you? Oh hell, no."

The second redheaded witch stepped toward her, eying her closely. "You're one of us," she pronounced.

"Us as in?" Sorcha resisted the temptation to roll her eyes. "Look, I have no idea where I am. I was running from one of my relatives who has it in for me. The best way to do that is time traveling. I wish you no ill will. Just let me leave, and—"

"Christ on a crooked cross." The witch who'd identified her as "one of us" ran right up to her, probing with magic all the while. "I'll be goddamned. You're Yanna's daughter."

Sorcha swallowed shock but recovered fast. "You win a kewpie doll. Now can I leave?"

The witch moved with ungodly speed and gripped her upper arm hard. "You're my sister." She shook her head, disbelieving. "You must have been born after Mother ended up in Hell."

"That would explain the demon blood I sense." The dark-haired witch joined the one who had Sorcha's arm in a death grip. She drew her dark brows into a single line. "Whose side are you on?"

"My own," Sorcha replied tartly and jerked her arm free. "Can I leave now?"

A large black raven took shape and flew to Sorcha's bird, touching beaks. Both rose into the air and proceeded to circle the room in a graceful aerial ballet.

An owl joined them. And then an eagle emerged and winged toward the other birds. Sorcha tried not to stare. She'd never met another witch familiar before, and here were four in the same room.

"Get back here," she ordered her bird, still intent on leaving.

"Soon." It flew near enough to brush her cheek with its wingtip. *"These are old friends."*

"No one is going anywhere," the dark-haired Druid said in a no-nonsense tone. "Not until we sort this out."

Sorcha sent an appraising glance his way. He was clearly the group's leader. Would fucking him be her ticket out of here? He was comely enough, it wouldn't be a chore. Not at all. Judging from the way the one witch clung to him, though, that might not work. Both wore shiny new rings, which didn't bode well. New loves were the worst. No time to become disillusioned.

The two ravens had flown to where the peregrine perched, cawing at it. She made a rude, snorting sound. Of course the familiars would recognize the falcon for what it was.

Not a bird.

She stole a glance at the tunnel. Maybe now was a time to make a run for it, while everyone's attention was on the falcon.

"Tavin?" The curly-haired male Druid sounded skeptical.

What happened next was even more astonishing. Sorcha didn't know what she'd expected, but she didn't anticipate the magic sheeting from the falcon would spit out a man. Druid by the feel of him, his copper hair was braided close to his head in many small plaits that fell to mid-chest level.

Tall and broad-shouldered, he had muscles to burn. They slabbed his chest and shoulders and wound down his arms. A flat stomach led to powerful legs with a deliciously shaped phallus hanging between them.

Sorcha shook herself. She should be making good on her escape, not staring at the best-formed man she'd seen in years. Just looking at him made her juices flow and her nipples harden.

Colorful magic had no sooner stopped pulsing around the man who could shift into a falcon when he stood tall, surveyed the crowd with green eyes, and asked, "Could someone toss me a cloak?"

"Aye, but only if ye tell us how ye ended up able to shapeshift," the dark-haired Druid said in Gaelic.

Several garments flew through the air, landing at the man's feet. He selected a dark green cloak and slung it around his shoulders, pulling it together in front.

Sorcha wanted to scream at him not to cover

himself. She'd been enjoying the play of muscles beneath tanned skin. His hands were large and calloused, working man's hands. But why would he need to work? He could hunt and eat as a bird.

As a laggardly afterthought, she focused on what the one redheaded witch had said. Apparently, Yanna was her mother too.

Which meant she had a family. She'd never considered such a thing. All her demon father had done was donate sperm—and put her to work. Yanna had been worthless from Sorcha's earliest memories of her.

The thought of family was tantalizing and disgusting at the same time. Sorcha cleared her mind of all of it. So what if the witch was her sister? It took more than blood to create family ties.

The Druids closed ranks around Tavin—assuming the other Druid got his name right—peppering him with questions. It looked to Sorcha like a good time to leave. Magic would draw attention to her, so she edged nearer the tunnel, stopping every few steps. The raven would follow her. It always did.

She was close now. Only a few meters to go, and she could duck into the dark passageway. She mouthed a small prayer—odd for a demon—she'd locate an exit point. Even if she didn't, she could teleport out of most anywhere.

Light flashed and flared, and the scent of witch magic, bursting with vanilla, musk, and herbs surrounded her. She blinked against the sudden glare. When she opened her eyes, all three witches blocked her path.

The one who'd identified herself as Sorcha's sister extended a hand. "I'm Gloria."

"And I'm Liliana, her daughter," the raven-haired witch said.

"Katerina here. Liliana's daughter," the other witch with russet tresses chimed in.

Sorcha stared at Gloria's outstretched hand. Was it a trick? What would happen if she touched the other woman?

Gloria dropped her hand to her side. "We won't hold you against your will." Her tone was brisk. "But I'm excited to know I have a sister."

"How'd you escape from Hell?" Liliana cut in.

Gloria shot her a sharp look. "Mind your manners. We don't even know her name yet."

"Yeah, like comportment has ever been one of your long suits," Liliana carped back.

Sorcha smothered a grin.

"Would the two of you stop it?" Katerina rolled her eyes. Leaning closer to Sorcha, she said, "They're always like this. One-upmanship to the max. You came a long way. My guess is nineteenth century, maybe around 1865 or thereabouts."

Sorcha sucked in a startled breath. "Close, but how'd you know?"

Katerina shrugged. "Your clothing. I'm an anthropologist, and I've studied Scotland nine ways from Sunday. This isn't your first trip to modern time, is it?"

Sorcha shook her head. "Nope. When I first escaped Hell, I ended up in 1962. Been bouncing around ever since."

"How long is that, dear?" Liliana asked.

"Not sure. At least fifty years. Maybe a little more."

"What's your name?" Gloria asked.

"Sorcha." She hesitated before adding, "Roskelly."

The birds fluttered near, each taking up a position on the witch they belonged to, cooing like a flock of doves.

Her bird was happy, and its joy thickened Sorcha's throat with emotion.

"Well, Sorcha Roskelly, sister mine, how'd you end up here?" Gloria's voice was softer. She may have added a touch of compulsion, but Sorcha wasn't certain.

"I used my magic to save a woman and her baby. It must have acted as a beacon because when I was walking back to my bed, I felt Rhea shooting toward me really fast. All I had time to do was cast a spell and run."

"Mmph." Katerina snorted. "She wants me to serve as a broodmare and perpetuate the Roskelly witch line. Why does she want you?"

Sorcha snorted right back. "Why else? For my demon blood. It's quite a draw. They assume I'm even blacker than they are."

"But you're not. Not if you used your power to save two lives," Gloria said.

Something about her words, their warmth and supportiveness, caught Sorcha by surprise. She'd been on her own practically since birth. Emotional validation was a foreign concept. She inhaled sharply, nostrils flaring. "What do you want with me?"

"To get to know you," Gloria replied in the same sincere tone.

"Why? I'm nothing to you."

"Not true." Liliana beat Gloria to the draw. "We"—she made an inclusive gesture with one hand—"are the only White Roskelly Witches in existence. You make a fourth. I'd say it's a pretty important discovery."

"One worth exploring," Gloria added, "since it increases our numbers by 33 percent."

"We'd love you to consider being part of our family. I mean, you already are since we share blood, but it takes more than blood to create family bonds. I'm sure we'll seem strange to you at first, but our hearts are in the right place," Liliana said, punctuating her words with a warm smile.

"Besides, you'd be our guest, and you could leave anytime," Katerina chimed in. "Won't you please stay a little while? We're here to hatch up a plan to wipe Rhea and her hideous sisters off the map once and for all. I bet you'd be quite an asset in our fight."

Sorcha had stopped listening after Katerina's bald assertion about leaving anytime. "Say that again. The part about me being free to go." She planted herself in front of Katerina and draped a truth spell between them. It shone and shimmered, floating in the air.

A surprised look bloomed on Katerina's face, but she nodded and said, "I make you a vow you can leave anytime you wish. Arlen is the Arch Druid and my husband. I'll make certain he honors our agreement."

The silvery netting brightened, reacting to truth in Katerina's words.

Sorcha reeled in her casting. Confusion reigned. She'd always worked alone wielding power. Always. She'd never been part of any group magic by design. Always an outsider. Always hanging about on the sidelines. It kept things simple. No one had ever disappointed her since she'd kept her expectations nonexistent.

"I don't know." Her gaze swept from one witch to

the next. Sincerity shone from them. It felt genuine, and it kindled an odd sensation behind her breastbone. She'd stopped hoping for breaks before she was five years old, yet these women were willing to take a chance on her.

"You don't know me. At all. Why would you risk it? For all you know, I'm masking my true intentions with demon magic."

"You could be," Gloria agreed. "But if you were evil, you wouldn't have a familiar. They don't bind themselves to darkness."

Sorcha cocked her head to one side. She hadn't known that little tidbit. Probably a whole lot about being a witch she didn't know. It wasn't as if she'd had much of a teacher.

"Is our mother still alive?" Gloria asked, the corners of her eyes pinched with pain.

"She was when I left, but she might not be now. For all I know they killed her for letting me escape."

Liliana dropped a hand on her mother's shoulder in wordless support. The simple gesture underscored the wasteland Sorcha's life had been. She'd told herself she didn't need anyone, but it was a reaction to being alone. It made her solitude if not palatable, then at least bearable.

Arlen hurried to where they stood. He extended a

hand in Sorcha's direction. "I'm Arlen MacGregor. Pleased to meet you."

Sorcha hesitated before grasping his hand. "Sorcha Roskelly."

His eyes widened, and he directed his next words at Gloria. "So you were right about her being your sister?"

Gloria thinned her mouth into a harsh line. "Of course I was."

Arlen held up a hand. "Sorry. No offense meant. The goddess dropped Sorcha into our midst for a reason. Tavin as well, but we need you to join the group discussion."

"Tavin is the one who was a peregrine falcon?" Liliana asked.

Arlen nodded. "Aye. Tavin Shaw. He's also a Druid, but rather than disclose his unheard-of shifting ability, he dropped out of sight and has been working as a blacksmith over on the Isle of Lewis."

"How come you never saw him there?" Katerina asked. "You've visited the standing stones."

A corner of Arlen's mouth twisted downward, and he replied in Gaelic. "I dinna see him because he dinna wish to be seen." He draped an arm across Kat's shoulders. "Come on. We need a bulletproof plan. Everyone gets a voice."

He walked back toward the center of the cavern with Katerina by his side.

"Well?" Gloria caught Sorcha's gaze and held it.

The raven bent and stroked its beak across her cheek, its way of urging her to say yes. Maybe it was her bird weighing in that turned the tide, but she nodded once, sharply. "So long as we're clear I can be gone whenever I wish, I'll give this a chance."

Gloria smiled softly. "You won't regret it."

"No way for you to know that," Sorcha shot back.

"She's a hell of a one for making assumptions," Liliana agreed. "Damnable part is they almost always come true." She patted Sorcha's upper arm. "Welcome to the Coven, Auntie."

"What Coven?" Gloria looked askance at her daughter.

"Why the one we're about to form," Liliana answered blandly. "Looks to me like there are enough of us, and the familiars all know one another. There's power in conjoined magic, and we'll need every edge we can lay our hands on."

"Liliana!" A man's voice rose over the din of many voices.

"Chop. Chop." Gloria clapped her hands. "Your beloved calls."

Liliana mock punched her mother's shoulder. "You're just jealous."

"Hell yes, I am. I'd love a young stud gracing my bed."

"Christ, Mother. He's older than you by a couple hundred years."

"Figure of speech my dear."

Hooking a hand beneath Sorcha's arm, Gloria walked toward the sprawling group. Sorcha's first impulse was to pull away. She didn't like people touching her, but Gloria was her sister.

I don't have to be alone anymore. Not if I don't want to be.

The realization was heady. Almost as heady as her brief glimpse of Tavin's sculpted body. What had Arlen said? That it was divine intervention—the goddess's will—that had landed her in this cavern with these people. She'd never believed in such things. Always considered them so much tripe.

For the first time ever, she let herself hope he was right.

But if he wasn't, she could always retreat to the tried, true, and familiar. Being alone would be harder, though, if she spent any amount of time with the other Roskelly women.

She stood straighter. She'd work things out. She always had.

If there weren't advantages for her here, she'd strike out on her own. Get a job. And spend the next few centuries dodging Rhea and her malevolent witchy kin.

It was wise to have a Plan B, and she felt more settled as she found a spot to stand between Gloria and a small knot of Druids buzzing like a hyperactive beehive about Tavin's startling magic.

She wanted to know more about it as well. Demon shapeshifters were common, but she'd never heard of a Druid who could alter his form. She focused a thin beam of power to make certain she heard every word. If he were truly a demon, masking evil intent, she'd ferret it out soon enough.

CHAPTER 4

Tavin answered the same questions until he ran out of patience. This was precisely the reason he'd chosen to go his own way. He could tell that the Druids—some of them anyway—were trying to trip him up. Make him contradict himself.

In between questions, he'd sorted the witches' names. Katerina was married to Arlen, Liliana to Sean. The third witch was Gloria, mother to Liliana. Until recently, she'd resided in 1890s Glasgow. And the blonde demon-witch combo was Sorcha. That last brought a smile to his face. If ever a name were fitting for a witch, Sorcha nailed it.

Matt, a tall slender Druid with dark hair, was still grilling Tavin. He'd known the other man most of his life and didn't think twice about cutting him off abruptly.

"I've answered the same question at least six times. Let me recap what I've said, and then if we don't move on, I'll be on my way." Tavin took a tight breath and held it before exhaling noisily. "I have no idea why or how I developed the ability to shapeshift. I never asked for it, and it scared the stuffing out of me the first time it happened. I pecked so many holes in my shirt, I chucked it.

"I heard someone or something—I always assumed it was a goddess, not sure why—tell me I'd been given a gift. Immediately afterward, I was human again." He angled his head to one side. "I've always had more than a healthy dose of curiosity, so the first thing I did was see if I could recreate the transformation. It took me a few tries, but soon enough, I was flying above that grove of hawthorn trees just west of town."

He shrugged. "I wanted to avoid what I just fell headlong into—interminable questions—so it seemed simpler to move on. No matter what I say or do at this point, some of you will always view me with suspicion at best and outright hatred at worst."

Arlen screwed his face into a disapproving grimace. "So you exited stage left, leaving the rest of us to rot, eh?"

"You don't look particularly rotten to me," Tavin countered. "Hell, you're the last Druid I ever expected to see wed, yet here you are with a blushing bride."

"My fault, entirely," Katerina said with a grin. "I seduced him, and he had to make an honest woman out of me."

Tavin wrapped the borrowed cloak closer about himself. It was none too warm in the cavern. He longed for the winter clothing he'd stashed in the boathouse back on the pier in town.

"So?" He swept his gaze through the assemblage. "Which will it be?"

"Which will what be?" Arlen stared at him.

"If I rejoin your merry band of outlaws, you have to agree not to question me or dissect my magic hoping you'll figure out how to shapeshift yourselves."

"Ha!" The blonde who'd sashayed through time stepped forward. "How do we know you're not a demon? They're famous for shapeshifting."

"You won't. Not for certain, but maybe it takes one to know one." Tavin turned his hands palms up and sent an appraising glance that scanned her from head to toe and back again. Damn, she was nicely put together. Only a few inches shorter than him, she had full breasts that pressed against a patched tunic. A long skirt covered her from waist to feet, but he'd bet his last pound note she had an ass to go with her tits. Firm and high and inviting.

A blast of magic hit him from behind, knocking his lascivious thoughts aside. Tavin spun and locked gazes with Sean. "Couldn't resist checking, eh?" He clamped his jaws together. "Last warning. If any of you can't take me at face value, accept I'm the Tavin you always knew, I'll be gone." He paused for emphasis and crooked two fingers in a come-along gesture. "Going once. Going twice—"

Arlen sliced a hand downward. "No one will challenge you. I'll see to it. We'll need every scrap of magic at our disposal in the days to come. Apologies for doubting you, and I'm verra glad you've returned."

It was a nice, neat, politically correct speech. Tavin figured it was the best he could hope for. Time would take care of those who doubted him.

Or not.

The blonde was looking at him, scrutinizing him through narrowed eyes. He turned away. She was hotter than hot, but he'd never had any use for witches. Of course, all the ones he'd run across had been of the Black Magic variety with their curses and nasty, dirty hex bags.

He swallowed a snort. This one was only half witch. He wasn't certain if her demon portion made her better or worse. He'd never known any demons.

Aye, and I'd be wise to keep it that way.

He caught Arlen's eye. "I'll return in a quarter hour. My clothes are back at the pier. I'll teleport, so it won't take long."

Arlen opened his mouth but shut it quickly. He'd probably been about to ask if Tavin were really coming back but decided trust would buy him more than doubt.

Druids had always been self-managing. They remained within the fold because it was warm and nurturing, not because they feared consequences for leaving. Arlen was a decent leader. The Druid before him had been far more heavy-handed.

Times had been different then, though. Bloodier and more brutal.

Tavin walked purposefully toward the cave's entrance. Before he left it entirely, he leveraged its power to fire his teleport spell. Between two breaths, the dank, dripping boathouse shimmered around him, the scents of mold and saltwater thick and acrid.

He dressed quickly, tossed the cloak over everything, and summoned power to return him to the cavern. Questions bounced from one side of his mind to the other. Naturally, Sean and Arlen would wish to protect their mates. But they should have thought of the ramifications before they married Roskelly witches, even ones who'd chosen White Magic over Black.

Surely, some of the problems in such a union must have occurred to them prior to making a lifelong commitment. Druids lived through several human lifetimes. Witches too. Plenty long enough to wish they'd done things differently.

If they hadn't mated with witches, they wouldn't be square in Rhea's gunsights, wouldn't be involving other Druids in a dangerous war.

He emerged outside the cavern on purpose. Shameless of him, but he spent a few moments eavesdropping. If his erstwhile kin were going to talk shit about him behind his back, he wanted to know about it.

They weren't.

The topic of conversation was Rhea Roskelly and how best to lure her to a spot where she'd be vulnerable. Tavin stomped inside, making enough noise they'd know he'd returned. For the next half hour, he listened to one bad idea after the next.

When he couldn't stand it any longer, he walked toward the center of the group. "She's not going to fall for anything I've heard yet."

"Ye canna know that," Arlen protested in Gaelic.

"Aye, but I can," Tavin replied in kind. "Look what happened to your last scheme. Sean and Liliana almost died, and ye dinna get within spitting distance of the witch."

"Does that mean you have any better ideas?" Sean's usually pleasant expression was nowhere in sight, replaced by worried furrows across his forehead.

"Wish I did," Tavin countered.

"Are you inferring nothing will work?" Liliana tucked a hand beneath Sean's arm and stood very straight in obvious support of her mate.

"Not what I said." Tavin raked a hand through his hair, snagging fingers on his braids. Working with a group to develop consensus decisions was a skill, one he'd let lapse while bent over his forge. A spot where he held sole responsibility for his successes—or failures.

"In for a penny, in for a pound," he muttered so low probably no one heard him. He aimed his next words at Sorcha. "Were you the only unwilling resident in Hell?"

She spat grim laughter. "Of course not, though most were at least resigned to being there. Why?"

"Simple logic. Someone in Hell might want to help us—if we found a way to free them. You got out, so I assume 'tisn't impossible. The Hell angle is a longshot, but there's nothing any Roskelly here can do to lure Rhea or any of her dead sisters. They may well materialize, but they'll have a plan. One that trumps ours. Rather like the one they launched that ended up with Liliana in a whirling-dervish prison and Sean immobilized."

"I suppose you're like as not correct about her writing all of us off," Katerina said. "Particularly after our last go-round where Mother used a glamour to pretend she was me and borrowed my familiar."

"Aye, and she's seen enough Druids here of late, none of us would work, either," Morgan muttered.

"Particularly in light of the two of you"—Gloria stabbed her index finger at Katerina and Liliana —"being married to them. Rhea's always hated Druids, and now she has even more reason. To her way of thinking, they've co-opted witches who rightfully belonged to her."

"We need a different approach." Tavin grabbed what was looking like an advantage to pound home his earlier point that they were a long way from anything resembling a solution.

"Doona take this wrong," the bald, tartan-clad Druid said, "but there's naught been a dish too many cooks couldna ruin."

Tavin searched his memory banks for the man's name and finally came up with Niall. He started to voice agreement, but Arlen beat him to it.

"Hate to admit this," Arlen was saying, "but you're like as not correct. When I summoned all of you to a war council, my motives were twofold. I wanted to make certain everyone knew to exercise extreme caution. Remain alert and warded whenever it's possible."

He rolled his shoulders back. "I admit to thinking

we'd use brute force to storm the fortress, but since none of us know exactly where Rhea is, all that would do is spawn a wild goose chase.

"Though we'd take every precaution, some of us would die. Possibly for naught since Rhea seems to know where we are most of the time."

"She has spies." Gloria bit off the words.

Matt pushed his slender shoulders forward, followed by the rest of him, and squared off in front of Arlen. Dark trousers hung off his thin hips, and a too-big plaid lumberman's shirt was zipped to his chin. "I ken why ye'd be worried about your wife, and her kinswomen. Beyond that, I appreciate your warning to the rest of us. If ye truly have need of us, we'll stand behind you. 'Tis the Druid way, but I canna see how this is our battle. Not yet, anyway."

"I disagree." Morgan's clear, ringing voice rose above many side conversations. She stepped away from a rocky pillar she'd been leaning against and went on. "Rhea has breached veils that must remain closed, dragging Hell's minions with her. If she persists, she'll upset the balance point that allows human life to exist on Earth."

Morgan closed her teeth over her lower lip and bit until a drop of bright blood welled. "If Earth is overrun with demons—and it could happen if Rhea opens a gateway—we will have missed a critical window to intervene. Now is our time. And our window. If we walk away, dust our hands together, and state it isn't our problem, we're lost."

Something about her tone, rhythmic and hypnotic, caught Tavin's attention. She'd either seen something in trance or read something in the old scrolls she loved so much. Her next words clinched it.

"Earth may be on its last legs, anyway," she continued. "The damage done by men has weakened the psychic barrier protecting it from borderworlds and Hell."

"You sound certain," Arlen observed. "Are you?"

Morgan nodded until long strands of silver hair escaped her bun. "I wasn't until Gloria and I sat and compared witch lore with ours. To see the same prophecies in two places was unsettling, but it was why I didn't argue you out of today's meeting.

"We all need to work together. Probably the Druids across the English Channel as well, but that's a task for another day."

"Try this on," Arlen said, picking up the mantle of command. "Now that you know to look for subtle anomalies, return to your homes and your lives, but report anything unusual, no matter how small. It could be the leading edge of something much bigger. Sean and I will look for patterns, and Sean"—he eyed the banker who was his second in command—"will do whatever it takes to scry the future."

"Will ye let us know what ye find?" Matt asked Sean.

"Of course. Assuming visions come when I call them. It doesn't always work that way, all nice and neat and tied with a bow."

Tavin debated his next moves. He could return to his forge, but no one was expecting him back until late in the spring. Besides, it flew in the face of working together. "If it's all the same to you," he addressed Arlen, "I'll do a wee bit of scouting. No one pays the slightest attention to a falcon, and I might discover things others would miss."

"My familiar knew what you were right off," Gloria pointed out.

He shook his head. "Nay. It merely recognized I wasn't a bird. That's why both ravens chivied me to show myself. They're curious bastards, and I wasn't interested in them pecking me full of holes, so I gave them what they wanted."

"Not my point," Gloria persisted. "You're vulnerable to anyone who holds magic, not just witch familiars."

He offered her a rakish grin. "Noted. I've managed to elude discovery for the better part of half a century. I'm confident I can maintain my record for a few more weeks. If the birds hadn't pulled my cover, the rest of you would never have noticed me."

"I did. Detected you weren't a bird right off," Sorcha spoke up. "But I wasn't in a position to point it out."

"Thanks. Good to know I'm not exactly invisible to demons." Breath whistled through his teeth. "If I run across any, I'll be extra careful." He didn't bother adding he'd been so fascinated by her unexpected appearance, he'd tossed caution aside, trading it for a better vantage point.

"You needn't ask my permission to go scouting"—Arlen inclined his head in Tavin's direction—"but I appreciate the courtesy. I also welcome you speaking your mind. I sometimes get tunnel vision, and it takes a good, solid whack to bring me around."

"You're welcome to stay at my home. It's a long way back and forth to the Isle of Lewis," Sean said.

"Thanks. Still live in that renovated castle?"

Sean nodded. "Aye, and it still has thirty rooms, most of them empty."

Tavin wanted to wait around long enough to see where Sorcha would light, but it was better if he didn't know. Usually, steering clear of women didn't pose a problem, but something about her drew him, fascinated him. To avoid dealing with any of it, he slipped out of the cave and set about brewing up a teleport spell. He'd take Sean up on his offer of hospitality, but he'd look around a bit first.

Perhaps he'd get lucky.

The rustle of footsteps made him glance over a shoulder. Sorcha was striding purposefully toward him. No mistaking her intention. She had something to say.

He balanced power between his hands, watching it arc to avoid getting lost in the sway of her hips and bouncing breasts.

"Mind if I come with you?" she asked brightly and crossed her arms beneath her breasts.

Of all questions, he hadn't expected that one. "Uh, why would you want to?" He winced. It hadn't been a particularly cordial answer. He'd never valued social skills enough to cultivate them, and his lack was painfully obvious.

She didn't seem to notice because she shrugged. "Makes sense. We're the two outsiders here. Besides, my bird likes you. I don't often question it when it suggests I do something."

"It told you to follow me out here?"

She nodded. "But I wanted to, or I'd have ignored it." She laughed, a silvery chime that made him think of summer breezes and bevies of wildflowers. "It would have given me grief, but I'm my own demon—most of the time." She stood straighter. Her stance accentuated the swell of both breast and hip. "Well? We could at least take a shot at teaming up. If it doesn't work out, we'll go back to working alone."

He dug beneath the surface of her words. Like him, she'd probably spent most of her life—her post-Hell life, anyway—on her own. Maybe it had cost her to approach him.

Just like it cost him to rejoin his Druid kin.

Her smile faded. "Didn't mean to put you on the spot. It's okay if you want to think about it. I'll be at Sean's too. Once I know where it is. My, erm, sister —" She rolled her aquamarine eyes. "Damn, but that will take some getting used to. Having any family, that is. Anyway, she'll be there too, along with Liliana."

"Don't apologize. You caught me by surprise." He'd long since relinquished his teleport spell. "I'm used to being alone, but then I expect the same is true for you. Maybe we could work together." He took a deep breath. "I'm willing to give it a try." He held out a hand.

She clasped it. Heat from her touch rocketed through him like high-octane fuel. He had to remind himself to let go. The temperature of his face and body had escalated several degrees. He silently blessed the dark night. It would hide the worst of his red face.

"Where do you want to go first?" she asked,

seemingly oblivious to the emotions roiling through him.

His fingers still tingled from her handshake. "We'll start in John O'Groats and work our way south. Might take a couple of days to reach Inverness, and that's if we don't turn anything up."

"Sounds good to me."

He let magic bubble around him. She fed her own brand of power into his spell, experimenting with blending their ability to maximize it. "We have to start somewhere," she said briskly. "Better here than when we're on the run."

Puzzle pieces clicked together. "Earlier, you said you were escaping a relative. Was it Rhea?"

Sorcha nodded. "Yeah. I'm like a fucking magnet for that bitch. Ever since she discovered I'm half demon, she's wanted to stake a claim to me. Pfft. Like I'm going to roll over and let that happen."

He kindled their joint magic. The wharf formed around them almost before he visualized it. "That was fast," he muttered.

"Blended magic. Works like a champ every time."

"My car is this way." He pointed. "How would you know about blended power since you've worked alone."

"Lots of downtime in Hell. Lot of books too. I read. A lot. No one to talk with. No television. No Internet."

He wanted to ask how she'd escaped, but it was a question for farther down the road. Once they knew one another better.

"Do you know how to drive?"

She nodded. "I've had a license a few times. If I'm here long enough, I'll get another."

He unlocked the Renault and opened her door. "How do you get around providing identification?"

"You really asked that?" She turned the full force of her gaze on him, and his chest tightened. "Not much magic can't solve, and that problem is trivial." Before he could respond, she hopped into the car and closed her door.

He went around to the right side and got behind the wheel. "Has Rhea located you—?"

"Nearly every place I've been." She cut him off, anticipating his question. "Sometimes it's taken her a while. I was at the last place for almost a year."

"So, it's a good bet she'll show up here."

Sorcha cupped her chin in an upraised hand. "Maybe. She knows the Druids are out for blood. It might slow her down."

Or have the opposite effect, Tavin thought. Not that he nurtured anything like a hero complex, but wouldn't it be convenient if the old bat placed herself close enough for him to behead her with one of the iron blades he kept with him?

Sorcha was on her knees, surveying the back of the old station wagon. "Oooh, look at all those swords. Doesn't the iron bother you?"

He grinned at her. "'Tis my own special blend. I'm a smith. And I've had years to perfect a mixture of metals that's toxic to dark power but not to me."

Before he could caution her, she reached out a hand and touched one of the longswords. He waited for her to shriek and draw her hand back. Instead, she turned back around in her seat.

"Excellent. I can use them too." She hesitated before adding, "I used to worry I was wicked, but here's one more confirmation I'm not."

Something about her words, plaintive and determined rolled into one, tugged at his soul. He nosed the car to the highest vantage point in John O'Groats. If there was aught to find here, their magic would locate it.

If nothing showed itself, they'd drive south.

"Thanks." Her voice was soft.

"For?"

"Giving me a chance. No one trusts demons, and I understand why."

Her forthright manner touched his heart, but he didn't know what to say that wouldn't sound schmaltzy, so he muttered, "Don't make me sorry."

"I'll do my damnedest." Peals of throaty laughter

filled the car, and soon he was laughing right along with her. He, who'd almost forgotten how to laugh. Maybe their unlikely partnership would work out better than he thought.

So long as I treat it like a partnership and nothing further.

He parked and killed the engine. By the time he scrambled out, she was standing next to the car, power deployed like a beacon as she searched for anything that shouldn't be there.

When he threaded his magic with hers, the two fit together as if they'd always worked as a team. Alarm bells tolled. Unlike her, he'd worked with plenty of magic wielders, and the joining shouldn't be this easy.

Did she have ulterior motives?

Something she'd neglected to mention?

Caution tinged with distrust urged him to run as fast and as far as he could, but a much bigger part of him didn't give a good goddamn what she'd done. Or if she'd done nothing at all beyond being herself. Working alongside her felt good, and he'd ride this horse until it bucked and threw him. Or until he figured things out.

She sent a penetrating look his way. "Everything okay?"

"Couldn't be better. Let's examine the area toward the east, and then we'll have covered things here."

CHAPTER 5

Sorcha had sensed Tavin's ambivalence after she girded herself to approach him. It ran deep, and he'd come within a hairsbreadth of telling her to get lost. She'd played up her assets to give him a push, but she had no idea if it was what made the difference, or if he'd grudgingly accepted her offer for reasons of his own.

Reasons she wasn't privy to.

Most men were suckers for a pair of tits, but somehow Tavin didn't exactly fit that mold.

Regardless, it was good to be busy, and she was fascinated by his shapeshifting ability. Unlike her familiar, which was a separate entity, he and the bird were an either-or proposition. He maintained his human consciousness while in bird form; his comments had clinched it.

Shapeshifting demons were the same.

Did it mean Tavin had demon blood? Something he either didn't know about or had been hiding forever? He'd been telling the truth when he told the Druids he had no idea how or why the bird had become part of him.

Still, demon blood was the most logical explanation for why she'd sensed the falcon right off and recognized it as something other than a garden-variety bird. Demon essence called to its own.

Sorcha was grateful to be in work mode. She'd jumped out of his car ready to keep her part of their bargain. She scanned an area and started to move on, but something made her do it again.

And then, once more.

"Aye," Tavin murmured from where he stood near her. "'Tis subtle, but something is a wee bit off just there." He followed her power with a beam of his own.

Sorcha hesitated. Did she dare focus more magic at the offending place? If she did, she'd give herself away to anyone with a child's grasp of enchantments.

Tavin must have read her thoughts because he said, "Sheathe your power, lass. Let's move closer."

Protective warding enclosed them. She liked being surrounded by the feel of Tavin's power. It held a characteristic Druid scent, but with undernotes of musk and rosemary. She threaded her magic along the underside of his to keep it better hidden.

The slight flaw that had alerted her might be an iteration of dark power. Or it could be nothing. It sure as hell wasn't White Magic. Pockets of that, a surprising number, had been scattered through the northern port village. She hadn't examined them, but assumed hedge witches, mages, and the odd sorcerer lived here. Along with a resident Druid population.

Tavin shepherded them through a warren of narrow alleyways.

"You know your way around," she murmured.

"I should. I used to live here. 'Tis the same, yet not."

"What do you mean?"

"'This hamlet is verra small. Only about 300 people reside here. 'Tis a jumping off spot for the Orkneys, but other than Druids, I don't recall other magic-wielders living in John O'Groats."

Sorcha tallied up what she'd found from the vantage point where they'd left the car. Before she jumped to conclusions, she asked, "How many Druids?"

"It varied. Not more than ten, though."

"Mmph."

He turned to look her way. "What does that mean?"

"I found double that number of people with magic when we were back up there." She jerked her chin in the direction they'd come.

"As did I, but only a handful were Druids, and they were on their way back from our gathering in the cave."

"You can sort Druid power from other types?"

"Of course," he replied. "I'll wager you can do the same for both witch and demon magic."

She felt stupid. She'd just come to that conclusion, using it for an explanation of how she'd known his bird wasn't quite what it appeared. They covered the remaining half kilometer in silence.

The sensation of malevolence intensified as they drew closer to the spot she'd identified. He stopped walking and thrust an arm in front of her to make certain she stopped too.

Sorcha waited, barely breathing. She would have forged ahead. Gotten near enough to determine what they faced. She angled her gaze his way and raised both brows.

Tavin shook his head, tilting it as if he were listening intently to something. She focused her hearing, but the only sounds that came her way were the cries of nighthawks on the hunt, owls, and the tide as it moved out. The moon rose, casting a vee of orange light across the sea, beautiful but brief. Within moments, it vanished behind Scotland's typical thick cloud cover, and the water turned dark once again.

A whirr of feathers presaged her raven's reappearance. After nudging her out of the cave, it had disappeared. It often left, but never for long, and she trusted it to return. Talons gripped her shoulders as her familiar settled into place.

"Follow me," Tavin whispered and led the way along a nearby dirt track that wound between two old buildings made of peat blocks and down a rickety staircase. Refuse littered a recessed place between the structures; the outraged squeaks of a hostile rodent population grew louder.

Adding its own squawking to the mix, the raven launched itself from her shoulder. When it reappeared, a fat mouse wriggled between the sharp halves of its beak.

"Why are we here?" Sorcha asked. She had a high tolerance for filth and mystery garbage, so the trash under her feet didn't bother her.

"To talk. Why else? We have enough earth around us, it should shield our words from prying ears. It scarcely seems possible, but I thought I sensed a portal. Don't know what else it could be. There's a definite liminal border. What lies beyond it is definitely not part of this world."

Sorcha frowned. "Gateway to where."

"I have no idea. It holds a wrongness, so it might be a fixed gateway, one through which evil enters our realm. If I'm correct, and I hope I'm not, Hell's creatures can come and go as they please. Once discovered—or once they've completed why they came here in the first place—they scurry for the exit." Tavin paused to take a measured breath. "There could be more than one of these things, whatever they are."

The thought chilled her. It was a very demon like thing to do, though. They fought dirty, and creating secret entrances meant they could race in, wreak havoc, and vanish before anyone discovered who was behind it. She blew out a thoughtful breath.

"I'm not trying to hide from the truth, but perhaps these portals—assuming you're right about there being more than one—are still in the construction phase. Granted, I've not lived anywhere near this era for a while, but if there are multiple portals, I'd have run across at least one of them when I did live in modern times. They're not all that subtle. And I never heard boo about them in Hell."

"One way to find out for sure." He cast an appraising glance her way.

"Indeed. That would answer the when of things," she agreed. "We go back in time. Not far, but a few years, and check to see if this location has the same rotten feel. It's better than the idea that was forming in my head."

"Which was?"

"Going through the portal to see where it comes out."

He whistled, long and low. "Christ, lass. Ye've steel balls. If the thing pumping out malevolent intent truly is an entrance to fell places, it has to be guarded. Otherwise, Hell or wherever it leads to would empty out damned fast."

She shrugged. Never one to retreat from a good scrap, she said, "What a grand excuse to exercise those blades in the back of your car."

"I like my plan better, but we're a team."

"Nothing says we can't do both," she pointed out. "Try to hit a spot maybe ten years in the past, first. Depending on what we find, we can play things by ear."

She was more of a "just do it" witch than a "sit around and talk about it" one. Neither half of her bloodlines conferred much in the way of patience.

"What do you think?" she asked her familiar.

It had finished the mouse and regarded her with its amber eyes. *"It is an entry point from...elsewhere, but I have no idea how long it's been here."*

"Another vote for time travel," Tavin muttered, having obviously heard her bird's comment. Magic jumped to his call, and she set the location vector, embedding it within his casting.

Bending time's veils was one of her métiers, but this trip was quick even by her standards. Almost before their spell launched, they rolled out of it. Sorcha glanced from one side to the other. The refuse-strewn hole hadn't changed much, but the trash beneath her feet wasn't quite as squishy—or odiferous.

"After you." Tavin followed her up stairs in slightly better repair than they'd been when she descended them.

She wanted to know precisely where they were, but she could tack that down easily enough. A newspaper stand would have the date. As if in response to her thought, a corner kiosk flashed past, and she snatched a flyer. "Not bad," she said, examining it. "Eight years."

Time travel was far from an exact undertaking. To hit a spot within two years of a goal required skill. She'd been off by as much as a century when she'd first learned the knack.

And then she focused her attention on the spot where Tavin had sensed a gateway. This time, rather than stopping, he led them right to the lip of the wrong place. Except it wasn't any different from everything else surrounding them. Centuries-old buildings, some in better repair than others, lined a cobblestone street.

"This is the spot, right?" she asked.

He nodded. "Aye, and 'tisn't here." He turned to her and dropped his hands onto her shoulders. 'This is verra good news. Means the gateways are on the newish side."

"Still under construction as I'd hoped." She screwed her face into a thoughtful expression. "But this is only part of the puzzle. We have to know where they go."

"I've been thinking about that," he said. "I'll take my bird form and fly inside a little way. Not far, just enough to see if I was right about it being guarded."

"Too dangerous. If it's demons, they'll know straight off you're not a falcon."

"Safer than walking through as a human."

"I'll go with him," her raven cawed.

A corner of Tavin's mouth twisted downward. "Thanks."

"Now, wait a minute—" Sorcha began.

"'Tis decided." He cut her off.

She curled a hand around his forearm. "What happened to being a team?"

"Part of you will be with me."

She wanted to punch him. "Yeah, like two birds, ones who don't normally hang out together, aren't a huge red flag."

"Maybe they are, but absent assembling more

Druids, I don't see a better path." He eyed her before going on. "What were you thinking? That you'd take a broadsword and race through the liminal space screeching like a banshee? No way can you sneak inside. If you drew an invisibility spell, another magic-wielder would see right through it. Plus, you escaped Hell. No one may have tried verra hard—or at all—to bring you back, but you can bet your last farthing if they stumble across you, they'll not bungle the opportunity to return you there."

The logic in his words was like a bucket of ice water dumped over her head. A shudder trailed down her spine.

He drew a key fob from his pocket.

"What are you doing?" she asked.

"As you know, time travel is a bit of a crapshoot. I'll be casting a seeking spell with my Renault as the object." He dusted a hand off on his slacks. "At least we won't waste time working our way back to the place we left."

Sorcha offered him points for thinking ahead and wondered what it would be like to have a home, somewhere she wanted to return to. She'd been rather like an escaped prisoner, running forward and back in time for as long as she could remember. So far, it was the only strategy that had kept her safe.

His spell snatched her up, and the battered old car

that had once been light blue but was now mottled with rust spots rose to greet her.

"This will go against the grain"—he skewered her with his green eyes, darker now, they resembled wet moss—"but you need to remain here. The Renault is warded, even when I'm not inside, so 'twill afford some level of protection for you."

"But I'll be too far away to help," she protested and caught the key fob he tossed her way.

His eyes pinched at the corners. "'Tis relative, lass. If things go badly, there won't be much you could do, even if you stood beneath the portal."

The raven bent and brushed its beak across her cheek. Its way of soothing her, but Sorcha wasn't buying it. The stiff set to Tavin's shoulders told her arguing would be useless, so she unlocked the car. Before she got inside, the raven moved to Tavin's shoulder.

She bit back hot words about it being a traitor. "See you soon," she said a shade too brightly, and jumped into the passenger seat, pulling the door shut behind her.

Concern etched into his features, but his high forehead, square jaw dotted with beard stubble, and sculpted cheekbones were still movie-star gorgeous. Damn. She fisted her hands where they lay in her lap. Why'd he have to be such a hunk?

He'd be a shit-ton easier to argue with if he were old and wizened and surrounded by a passel of bairns.

He tapped on the window, and she rolled it down a few inches. "Best get moving." Her tone was crisp.

"Ye'll be right here when I return?" he asked in Gaelic.

"Yup. Right here." A thought occurred to her, and she arched a brow. "Where will you be leaving your clothes?"

"Nearer the gateway."

"Why not in your car? Not like I haven't already seen you naked." The possibility of viewing his muscled torso excited her. Her suggestion had been tongue-in-cheek. She was still furious at being booted to the curb, but it didn't mean she was immune to wondering what his chiseled body would feel like pressed up against hers.

"Maybe next time," he blurted, clearly uncomfortable with her innuendo. Tavin turned and left at a lope with her raven flying beside him.

Sorcha didn't lose any time. She climbed over the divider and into the back of the car to take a closer look at the weaponry. After selecting her two favorites, she sent a pulse of magic to open the hatch and crawled out. A few experimental swipes, and she belted a slender longsword in place. Its hilt was carved of yew, and it fit her hand as if it were made for her.

She glanced to the east. Dawn wasn't terribly far off, which meant it was edging toward midmorning. The citizenry of John O'Groats would be out and about quite soon. A downward glance made her wince. Between her old-fashioned garb, poorly tanned leather clogs, and the blade strapped to her body, she looked like a movie extra, not someone who belonged in a rural hamlet.

Since it took less magic to make herself invisible than to craft a glamour, she swathed herself in spells, added a touch of "don't look here" for good measure, and hustled toward the liminal boundary marking the threshold to another world.

Sorcha didn't think too hard. If she had, her courage might have faltered. Hell was at the bottom of her list of preferred destinations. Demons might not be overly bright, but they had long memories, and they'd hurt her. Punishments in Hell lasted forever. Whatever you feared most happened again and again and again. Another favorite was making you relive your worst failures. So you had time to truly absorb just how badly you'd fucked up.

Worse, her jailors would make certain she was never near enough the exit to finesse a second escape. She wanted to reach for her familiar, interrogate it about how things were going, but a shot of telepathy might put both birds in even greater danger than they already were.

She had a plan, and by god, she'd see it through. Tavin had been right when he'd mentioned her standing beneath the gateway. It was precisely where she planned to be. If neither bird flew back out in a reasonable amount of time—ten minutes or so—she was going in to find them.

Tavin's scent made her nostrils twitch. She must have just run past where he'd left his garments. Not much farther. She paid out a slender twist of magic and moved to the right, correcting her trajectory. She was near enough, she felt the demarcation—Tavin had labelled it a liminal boundary—and it had demon written all over it.

Sorcha kicked herself hard. If she'd been half a kilometer nearer when she and Tavin approached this spot together, she'd have known the portal led to Hell— or maybe to a borderworld controlled by demons. Not much difference between the two. All the demons' worlds led straight to Hell. She'd visited a few over the years she'd resided there.

Fear gripped her, but she crept forward, checking her warding. It wasn't as if she hadn't understood Black Magic lay behind the gateway. She'd hoped witchcraft was responsible, but no such fortune played out.

Ha! Since when are the Roskellys and all the other Black Witches something to long for?

Sorcha didn't bother answering herself. Compared with demons, witches were pikers. They knew it, and it was the sole reason Rhea was so dogged in pursuing her.

Sorcha felt the tug of evil. It sang to her demon side, alluring, tantalizing.

Slowly, she lifted her head. A gateway formed before her third eye. Crafted of burning timbers that resurrected themselves as perpetual fuel, it screamed Hell-spawned workmanship. Once she saw it, the stench of ozone and scorched flesh surrounded her.

She tugged the blade free, holding it across her body like a shield. The metal smelled clean, pure. It made the Hell-scents more tolerable. Because she was rattled, she counted. When she'd reached 600, she figured more than enough time had passed.

The birds should be back.

They weren't.

Her throat was so dry, she couldn't swallow. For a fleeting moment, she considered retreat. She could summon the Druids, and her witchy kinswomen. Power lay in numbers. They'd be better off that way—

"Bullcrap," she said softly.

By the time reinforcements arrived, it would be too late. Tavin would be lost. She assumed her raven could escape any magical snare, but the falcon couldn't. It got by on stealth. She should have asked pointblank, but she was fairly certain Tavin commanded far more magic as a human than in his bird's body.

She took a step. And one more. The third step carried her through the liminal space. The feel of Earth vanished, replaced by the roar of fire and the stench of brimstone laced with decaying flesh. Rivers of liquid metal ran beneath her feet. She snorted. It was an old demon trick, one she'd discovered spying on Satan's princes. She barked a word, and the glistening metal formed a solid spot. Driven by instinct, she spun until she faced the gateway, except it wasn't there.

She skinned her lips back from her teeth. Another demon trick. Build a trap and bury the entrance so no one can find their way out. She'd always had solid intuitions, and she blessed the one that had urged her to turn around. Since she seemed to be alone, she walked fast, reversing her course. The solid spot beneath her feet traveled beneath her, simplifying her journey.

Three steps may have carried her inside. It took over twenty before she emerged through the gloomy liminal boundary. Her heart thudded hard, and she was panting.

Understanding punched her in the guts, almost doubling her over. No reason to waste demon power posting a guard anywhere near the gate. Not when illusion did as effective a job. She turned once again and faced the entrance. What could she use to mark it from the inside?

A beacon no one else would notice, but something to guide her to the exit. She had a feeling the portal would fade still more the farther inside she traveled. She still clutched the sword. It was sharp, and a drop of her blood fell to the ground, sizzling in the chill air.

"Of course," she muttered.

The solution was elegant, simplistic, and staring her in the face. She had enough demon in her, no one would notice a few drops of her blood. She'd leave a blood trail, like Ariadne's thread or Hansel and Gretel's breadcrumbs. Before she changed her mind and raised her mind voice to summon aid, she sliced an inch-long gash in the meaty part of her thumb.

After leaving a few drops next to her, she hurried beneath the portal, taking care to mark her path with her own blood.

All she had to do was locate Tavin and her familiar and reverse her trail.

It sounded so easy, but it wouldn't be. If Tavin and the raven had been able to find a way out, they would have. Sorcha hurried deeper into the tunnel. Just because the entry wasn't guarded didn't mean unpleasant surprises weren't lying in wait for her around the next corner.

She wanted to use magic to hunt for her bird but didn't dare do anything that might reveal her presence.

The sound of voices conversing in demonspeak—one of her many languages—brought her to a halt. Deepening her warding, she crouched low, intent on learning everything she could. The river of molten metal split and flowed around her. If her luck held, she'd escape notice.

If not…

She chased the thought away. No point cataloguing all the bad shit. The world was full of it, and no one ever got anywhere focusing on distasteful outcomes.

Yeah, plenty of time to wallow in might-have-beens if the fuckers catch me.

Sorcha smiled grimly. One benefit of her humble beginnings was she didn't waste time feeling sorry for herself. Or worrying overmuch about the consequences of her actions.

Tavin shucked his clothing for the second time that night in a secluded corner where two buildings formed an alcove. It was actually edging toward morning, but the telltale gray lining the eastern horizon was nowhere in sight.

Sorcha had been beyond furious at being banned from accompanying him, but the only way he saw a reconnaissance working was to get in—and out—as fast as possible. Two mages dripping magic would make them targets since their power would bleed through any warding.

Particularly hers. Blood called to blood. It didn't matter if the portal had been constructed by demons or witches. Both would recognize Sorcha.

He had no idea what he'd find beyond the boundary, but it was constructed and maintained by dark power, which meant some kind of early warning system had to be built into its weave.

"Can you hear me?" He tested telepathic communication with the raven.

It squawked. He took it as a yes. He already knew he could hear it. Sorcha's bird flew ahead as he summoned his falcon and shifted. Airborne, he winged after the raven. Two birds of prey on the hunt.

Except falcons and ravens didn't normally socialize.

Maybe demons didn't know that. They paid less than no attention to the natural world. If witches had constructed the gateway, though, they'd discern the oddity immediately. The raven crossed the liminal border and immediately vanished from sight, a clue if ever there was one that a different world lay on the far side.

He flew after it. The moment he cleared the threshold—constructed of burning logs with some magical way of renewing themselves—the air grew dense with the scents of brimstone and ozone—and rot. The raven was waiting for him, flying in circles. He didn't blame it for not wanting to land.

Beneath him, the ground ran with something that looked like molten copper, except it stank of evil. Heat rose from it in nauseating waves. No reason to stop here. Once they determined whether the passage linked to a borderworld, a witch's den, or Hell itself, they'd leave.

Did a way exist to obliterate the threshold—and this tunnel? Maybe if enough Druids gathered, and they threw the combined weight of their magic at the problem, they'd come up with a way to destroy the gateway.

That left the chore of finding other portals, assuming this wasn't the only one. It wouldn't make much of a dent in whoever had created them, but at least losing their entry points to Earth would slow them down.

The raven vanished around a bend but reappeared almost immediately. It flew high, its black plumage blending in with murky shadows. Tavin joined it and understood the familiar was hunting for a spot to land where it wouldn't be visible. Not many options. The floor was out of the question. The liquid metal—oily smoke rising from its smooth surface—would burn them to a cinder. Or at least him. He wasn't at all certain what impact fire would have on the raven. The smooth, glassy, rounded walls of the tunnel had been carved from the ether between worlds. That any air existed was unexpected, except everything living needed to breathe.

Wouldn't have made sense to construct a passageway no one could use.

He wanted to ask the raven what it had found, but maybe even the small amount of magic he'd have to summon for telepathy wasn't a good idea. The raven wouldn't have returned if it hadn't run into danger. Hoping it would intuit what he was about, Tavin stayed high, lost in the dim recesses at the top of the passageway. It was harder to breathe up here, but he didn't plan to stay long.

He flew slowly around the bend. His bright feathers were much harder to hide than the raven's, but usually no one spent a whole lot of time looking up. Two demons sprawled on planks jutting from the sides of the tunnel. A third floated above the ever-moving river that created the floor.

From horned heads to forked tails and reddish scales, they could have been poster boys for Demon Central.

"Damn your lazy hides." Demon three shook a fist at the other two.

"Take a load off, Iz," one of the other ones yelled. "No one's here. By Beelzebub's balls, use what few brains you have. No one could walk in here. We'd hear the fuckers screaming."

"Yeah," the other demon chimed in. "Besides, we're mainly here to make certain no one leaves. Humans may be a bunch of dumb asses, but they're not so stupid, they'd waltz through the portal. Pfft. This is a total shit assignment. Waste of time. We're done in a few turns of the glass. Do not make waves."

"Fine, be that way." Demon three floated to a third plank and sat heavily. "I don't like it here any better than you."

"If we sound an alarm," the first demon pointed out, "Satan and a few of the princes will be on us like stink on shit. We'll be lucky to ever see Hell again."

"You know how it goes." Demon two snickered. "You boys did such a great job, you get to stay."

Tavin had heard enough. He made the tightest circle he could and flew toward where he'd left the raven.

"Awk! There is something there," one of the demons, probably the third one, shouted.

"Stuff it," another yelled, followed by the sound of a closed fist hitting flesh.

Tavin scuttled around the ninety-degree bend that hid them from easy view. Breath puffed through his beak in little panting gasps. Part of it was the thick, hard-to-breathe air, but a bigger part was fear. The trio of demons hadn't spelled out what they'd do to intruders. They didn't have to. Anyone they caught was dead meat, best-case scenario. Worst case, they'd be passed up the line to one of Satan's princes, someone who'd made torture into a fine art.

The raven had located a spike sticking out of the

smooth walls and curved its talons around it. Tavin flew close and jerked his head toward the exit. The raven launched off its perch, and both birds headed for the gateway. They flew and flew and flew. He was certain they were headed the right way. The bend in the passageway lay behind them, and there weren't any side corridors.

Finally, he risked telepathy. *"We should be out."*

Instead of answering, the raven asked, *"Can you teleport in bird form?"*

"Nay."

The raven fanned its wings, slowing its forward momentum. Something was up. Tavin slowed and paced it. *"Keep moving,"* he urged. *"Whatever this is, we'll fly through it."*

"If we could have, we'd be back on Earth," the raven argued. With no warning, it turned and flew back the way they'd come, moving fast.

"Stop," Tavin called after its retreating form. *"Evil has you in its grip. Come back. Only death lies that way."*

Tavin treaded air, uncertain. Should he follow the raven? Had Sorcha's familiar fallen prey to an insidious message? One Tavin hadn't heard.

The raven winged back toward him. Thanks be to the goddess the bird had come to its senses—or broken free of the wicked enchantment that had snared it.

Tavin batted air with one wing so he'd be headed the proper direction, but the raven flew in front of him, blocking his path.

"What are you doing?" Tavin demanded, ready to engage in aerial combat if the raven had turned from friend to foe. He didn't know Sorcha well, or at all, really. She could be a spy as easily as anything else.

Aye, but a spy from where? She was telling the truth when she said she'd been on the run forever…

"Sorcha is below," the raven said, breaking into Tavin's troubled musings.

"What? It's not possible. I told her—"

The raven screeched laughter into Tavin's mind. *"She's her own person. Hurry. She's heading right toward the demons. I'll put her in danger if I employ telepathy."*

"You're using it with me."

"She's far nearer the demons. Come on."

Tavin pushed his misgivings aside, wheeled, and flew back the way they'd come. At least he thought it was the way they'd come. Something deucedly odd had happened since they'd crossed beyond the liminal space. Another Black Magic booby trap, no doubt. One of the demons had been clear their primary job was to ensure none of Hell's denizens used the gateway to exit Satan's realm.

He and the raven had obviously been snared by

illusion, except it was a hell of a powerful one since no matter how far they'd flown nothing changed, and they hadn't been any closer to leaving the tunnel.

Sorcha.

Damn the woman. Now all three of them would be lost in this infernal passageway. If he could locate a place to stand, he could shift. Once he was human, he could teleport. Maybe. He hadn't had any trouble hanging onto his bird form, but who knew how well the rest of his magic would work in here?

The raven flew lower, circling a blank place.

Tavin wanted to probe it with his magic, but it was a very bad idea. That one demon was certain he'd latched onto something that shouldn't be in here. Another might have slugged him, but it wouldn't make him less vigilant—or less surly.

The raven stopped flying, looking as if it were suspended midair, and then it vanished entirely. Tavin experimented. He extended his talons in the same spot the raven had been. Damn if he didn't connect with something solid. Sorcha swathed in warding and crouched in the hot metal river. How in the hell had she managed it? Her feet should have melted by now, leaving her screaming in agony.

When he looked closer, he noticed the molten copper river split a foot in front of her and flowed around where she knelt. Neat trick. He'd have to discover how she managed it.

They were too close to the demons to risk telepathy. The raven had been spot on about that assessment.

Sorcha stood, careful not to jostle him, and did a 180-degree about face. He wanted to tell her not to bother. That she only thought it was the way out. She kept up a good pace with him on her shoulder and the raven out of sight. Perhaps it had joined with her in whatever mysterious way witch familiars possessed.

Heat from the hot metal rose, surrounding them, but Sorcha didn't miss a beat. The island of solid material beneath her feet stuck with her. A brilliant red flare flashed to her left. Another to her right after a few steps. The lights were brief but easy to follow.

Tavin would have whistled if he'd been human. The damned woman had known about the illusion and created a trail to follow, one that would allow her to leave the passageway.

He felt cowed—and stupid. He'd flown through the liminal boundary big as you please without so much as a backward glance. If he'd stopped long enough to glance over one shoulder, he'd have understood.

Aye and taken pains to plant my own series of markers.

The trail she'd laid might defeat the illusion that the tunnel was endless. A big part of wielding magic was believing in results, and she'd had enough confidence in her strategy to venture deep into the passageway.

He wasn't too worried about demons following them. The one, maybe, but the other two were lazy bastards. All they wanted was to return home. Apparently, some wicked creatures actually liked Hell.

Why shouldn't they? 'Tis the only home they know.

Courtesy of Sorcha's trail, the exit was precisely where he thought it should be. They walked out into pouring rain and a gray, gloomy day. After the heat and stench of the tunnel, he welcomed water sluicing the reek from his feathers. He didn't know whether to rebuke Sorcha for not following instructions or thank her for a timely rescue.

He could have used telepathy but didn't. Maybe by the time he shifted and dressed, he'd come up with a middle-of-the-road path that accomplished both objectives.

She stopped next to where he'd left his garments and loosed her invisibility spell. "There you go," she said far too cheerfully. The raven was perched on her shoulder.

Sorcha held one of his favorite blades, its sharp edge coated with her blood. So that was how she'd managed to leave a track. It was brilliant. No one would notice demon blood in the middle of a demons' haven.

The raven cawed. It might have been agreement or something more complex. Like a warning not to take its mistress to task.

Tavin flew into the alcove where he'd left his clothes, his mind busy. He'd originally planned a leisurely journey through northern Scotland, but finding the portal put a whole new spin on things.

Added an urgency that hadn't existed before.

He had to let Arlen and the others know. Together, they'd have enough power to blow this particular gateway to bloody bits and pieces. With the additional manpower, they'd split up and search for more of these abysmal creations. It might put a crimp on Arlen's prioritizing of Rhea Roskelly, but it couldn't be helped. The old witch probably knew about the portals, given what he'd heard about her riding dragonspawn and loosing demons to terrorize the Druids.

She'd like as not forged an unholy alliance with demonkind to bring some of them across the psychic veil. Satan would buy into an idea like that whole hog since he rarely got juicy invitations to wreak havoc.

Tavin narrowed his eyes in thought as he zipped into his jacket, deploying the hood to keep from getting even wetter than he already was. If he were correct and

Rhea was using the demons' portal system, perhaps they'd run across her.

He rather liked the idea.

Chance meetings were every bit as useful as planned ones. No matter which, they'd be prepared to deal out maximum damage. He hesitated before stepping out of the protected nook between buildings. Should he pretend all was well—after he complimented Sorcha for having the foresight to leave a blood trail on the far side of the liminal border.

Tavin inhaled sharply; avoidance was the wrong approach. When too much bad water flowed under any bridge, trust dribbled away along with it. He and Sorcha would have to have words about what had happened. He felt like an ass because if she hadn't gone off on her own—ignoring his directive—he'd still be demon-meat. The raven could have left anytime. It's query about whether he could teleport suggested it wouldn't have had any difficulty casting a spell to draw it beyond harm's reach.

That it chose to remain with him when it didn't have to spoke to its character. He strode to where Sorcha waited with a fold from her tunic draped over her bright hair. She was wet, probably down to skin level.

"You look cold," he murmured.

"Yeah, but it's a good contrast to where we were. Ready?" Her usually forthright gaze scuttled away.

"Aye. We need to talk, but we can wait until we're inside the Renault. Where's your bird?"

"Within. It's not overly fond of getting drenched."

"Convenient." He started up a steeply canted cobblestone street for where he'd parked the car.

She made a snorting sound. "For the raven. Not for me."

"How'd you come by him—er, it?" Tavin was curious, and he knew less than nothing about witches and their familiars.

"It's the oddest thing." She lowered her voice. "Once I escaped Hell, it was just there, waiting. It told me it had waited for me for a long time. When I asked what it meant, it said it would explain, except it never did beyond a basic primer on witches and their familiars." She paused for a moment, maybe gathering her thoughts. "I never pressed it for exactly how it knew where to find me. The first few years were rough. I had bigger things to worry about."

Tavin had questions, lots of them, but they'd keep. He didn't want to divert their attention away from the gateway. It superseded his interest about witches and their familiars.

They passed several knots of passersby moving with purpose. He deployed a few experimental threads of magic, but the others were human through and through. He thought he'd aim for a positive note and asked, "Not that it wasn't a brilliant move, but how'd you know to leave a blood trail?"

"Purely accidental. It felt weird enough the first time I walked beneath the fire, I turned around to look at the entrance from the other side. It's an old trick I learned when I was on the run from...various things. Good to know what the route back looks like. It's usually quite different from what lies ahead."

He offered her points for intelligence. Before he hadn't looked much deeper than her thick, curly hair, enticing curves, lush lips, and aquamarine gaze. He rolled his mental eyes. What kind of an idiot judged a woman—or anyone—solely on their appearance?

Several excuses jumped to the fore, like he'd spent most of the past few decades with horses, but it didn't excuse him.

"So you turned around and—?" he prodded.

She licked rainwater off her lips. "As you've probably guessed, the portal had vanished. I couldn't have been more than a meter from it, but it wasn't there. I'll admit it scared me, so I hurried back the way I'd come. I couldn't go all that fast since I was stuck with the speed of the island I'd constructed to keep me out of the molten metal, but my three steps inside turned to more than twenty to leave."

"But you did escape?" At her nod, he went on. "I'm impressed by your bravery, lass. Not many would have had the will to go back inside."

"I didn't. Not right away." She rolled her eyes. "I waited like a good soldier. I suppose I was still nurturing the idea I could head for the car the minute you poked your beak out, and you wouldn't be the wiser I'd broken our pact."

"Except I never showed up. Did you try to reach your bird?"

Sorcha shook her head. "I had no idea what the two of you had gotten yourselves into, but I was afraid any magic might make things worse. Finally, I couldn't wait any longer. I'd been hanging onto the blade the entire time. It slipped, and I cut myself. Watching my blood turn to steam gave me the idea it would work to mark my way once I was back inside."

Sorcha withdrew his key fob and unlocked the car. She dropped the blade behind the front seat before sliding into the passenger side. He came around to the right and jumped in. Water sluiced from both of them, leaving puddles on the tattered floor mats.

"Doesn't come natural to me to apologize," she mumbled, "but I am sorry. I should never have agreed to remain here since I had no intention of doing so."

He waited for an "I told you so," one pointing out she'd saved him from his own stupidity. It never came.

The ground they'd covered was good enough. "Takes time to learn to work together," he said and offered her half a smile. "Mostly, I've spent my days with horses—or other birds."

She chuckled. "I have no excuses. I've been a barmaid. Plenty of human contact, but so long as I didn't pocket any of the money for myself, I got along well enough with the proprietor."

"How'd you learn Gaelic?"

"It's one of the few things Mother taught me, but even if she hadn't, something about my demon half allows me to understand—and speak—most languages with little difficulty."

"I'm jealous."

"Don't be. Not much is worth enough to sacrifice years growing up in Satan's realm."

He twisted, snapped up an old towel from the back of the car, and began wiping steam from the windows.

"Are you mad at me?" she asked.

Tavin shook his head. "I was. Fit to be tied, but I'm over it. 'Tisn't wise to stand on ceremony after someone saves your life."

"Awww. You'd have found a way out of there."

"Your bird wasn't convinced of that. It stuck with me, though. I needed something to stand on, so I could shift. I have to be human to teleport."

"Have you tried it while you're a falcon?"

"Aye. 'Tis how I know it doesn't work."

"Regardless, it all came together. We're both still here and none the worse for wear. What happens next?" She was turned to face him, her unusual gaze trained right on him. The wet tunic clung to the curves of her breasts, and water beaded through her hair and across her face.

He didn't realize he'd reached across, smoothed damp strands of hair off her face, until the touch of her skin beneath his fingertips sent jolts of desire racing through him.

"Aye, lassie. Did ye bewitch me?"

Sorcha shook her head right before turning her face up at just the proper angle for a kiss. He couldn't have resisted if he'd tried, but he didn't try very hard. It was awkward with the console between them, but he settled his mouth on hers. Soft, sweet, tentative.

She tasted of summers and every unfulfilled wish he'd ever had as she kissed him back, opening her mouth to his tongue. Leaning closer, she wove her fingers into his hair, threading them between his braids. The kiss deepened as they licked, bit, and sucked. He loved the way her mouth moved beneath his, all fire and heat and softness.

She pulled away, regarding him with an unreadable expression. "I am sorry. It wasn't respectful to agree and then welch. Even if it ended well, the way it happened wasn't right."

"Ye doona have to apologize." He'd switched to Gaelic. "We're square with one another."

Her mouth twitched into a grin, and she scooped the towel out of his lap and swiped it over the newly steamy windows. "Good because I liked kissing you, and I hope it happens again."

A laugh bubbled from him, followed by another. "I liked kissing you too. We need to get moving, but we should try one more sample before we leave."

Sorcha chuckled. "To make certain it wasn't a fluke?"

"Something like that." He pried the rag out of her hands, wrapped his arms around her, and closed his mouth over hers.

Nothing soft or tentative this time. Heat raced along his nerves. Years had passed since he'd held a woman close. Her scent, vanilla and herbs with musky undertones eddied around them. His long-neglected cock thickened, rising in a column against his belly. For once, he didn't ride herd on it.

They needed to let Arlen and the Druids know about the gateway, so they could be on the lookout for others like it, but a few minutes one way or the other wouldn't matter at all.

CHAPTER 7

Sorcha lost herself in Tavin's heady scent. The console pressed into her belly as she leaned over it, as close to him as she could manage. His mouth was firm and demanding this time. He kissed her like a man who knew what he wanted.

That he wanted her both thrilled and worried her.

She'd never thought beyond sex. No reason to develop anything deeper, not when her future in any particular place was so uncertain. Plus, she'd outlive any human, and the specter of falling in love only to sit vigil while the man died held zero appeal. Tavin would match her lifespan. Maybe they could tumble into sex and see what came afterward.

The more she considered it, the better she liked the idea.

Her nipples formed peaks where they pressed

against his chest, and she trailed her fingertips over his lushly muscled back and shoulders. Desire rose in waves, sweet and intoxicating. The car windows coated with steam.

Tavin lifted his mouth from hers and cupped her face in a hand. "If I kiss you more, we'll end up in the back of the car. 'Tisn't how I want things to be, and we have more pressing matters."

She moved back enough to gaze into his green eyes. They'd darkened to river-washed agates. She could lose herself in those eyes, swim to the bottom and never surface. Still mired in sexual heat, she reached to loosen the string closure on her tunic.

He placed a hand over hers to stop her. "Nay, lass. 'Tisn't the time."

"I don't understand." Her nub pounded like an extra heart between her legs. She hadn't come in forever, and here was a man who clearly wanted her. "Won't take long."

He shook his head. "That isn't how I do things. Not a quick grapple where ye lift your skirts and I unzip my breeks."

Heat rose from her chest and swept over her head. Quick grapples had been plenty good enough for her. She'd misjudged him. Or misread the situation. Maybe both. He might want her, but he didn't want her enough. Feeling like a slut—and an idiot—she straightened and sat in her seat, facing forward.

"You're right, of course," she muttered, not sure what else to say.

He was still facing her. His Gaelic washed over her, rich and musical. "I dinna mean to hurt ye, lassie. Ye're beautiful, and ever so hard to resist."

She wanted to demand why he was resisting her, if that were true, but she kept her mouth shut. He wasn't anything like other men who'd crossed her path. They'd been eager to bury themselves in her body if she encouraged such attention. Men were men, no matter if she found them in the sixteenth century or the twenty-first.

Except, apparently, this one.

Moments dribbled by. Finally, he turned his attention to the car and twisted the key. While the engine warmed, he retrieved the towel and cleared the windows sufficiently to drive. They'd been underway for a few minutes when he asked, "Did I hurt your feelings?" in English.

Her lust had abated, replaced by an antsy, uncomfortable sensation, but it too was fading. "Maybe," she ventured.

"If I did, I'm sorry," he went on. "This is more about me than you." His knuckles whitened where he gripped the wheel. "I'm old, which shouldn't come as a surprise. Many Druids are. I cavorted through a couple of centuries with a lot of women, mostly human, some not. I don't know why, any more than I know why the falcon bonded with me, but eventually I kept to myself more and more. Sex was enticing, pleasant, but in the end, it left me feeling empty."

Sorcha chewed on her lower lip. Should she ask questions? "If you don't want to answer me, I understand, but how long ago did you, um, decide being alone was preferable?"

He shrugged. "Maybe a hundred years before the falcon showed up. It wasn't so much a conscious choice as how things ended up. Before the bird, I was a musician, and I never had difficulty filling my days."

"You're so attractive, though. Surely women approached you."

"Not that much." He glanced her way and smiled. "Women are wise. They know when a man is interested—and available. As I moved into modern times, I assumed they thought I was gay. Never tried to dissuade them."

"But you kissed me. Why?" She sucked in a breath and held it, hoping hard he wouldn't say it was to thank her for leading him out of the abyss.

"A good question. Something about you calls to me. I fought it, probably still am."

"Because I'm half demon?" She exhaled, grimacing at her pointblank question, but she had to know.

"Why not focus on the half witch part?" he countered. "Druids and witches have never made particularly good companions. We don't trust one another."

"That may be so," she replied. "But my demon side is way more repellant than the witchy part in most circles."

"I bet you never told humans about either one."

She chuckled. "You'd be right about that. Same way you don't disclose you're a Druid, let alone a shapeshifting one."

"Hell, I even kept that last element secret from my Druid kin," he reminded her.

"So you did." She glanced at a passing road sign. "We're headed for Inverness, right?"

"We are, indeed. I don't want to trust what we found to telepathy. Too much danger of someone listening in. If demonkind—or Black Witches—know their portals have been discovered, they'll magic them up and make them a whole lot harder to locate."

"You're assuming there are more of them," she said.

"I am."

"You never exactly answered my question," she pressed, and then added, "The one about me being part demon," to make certain he understood.

He drew his brows together. "I admit it bothers me, but not a lot."

"So that wasn't why you didn't..." She'd been about to say fuck me, but it sounded crass.

"Nay, lassie." He retreated to Gaelic. "With everything we're facing, I wouldna have bedded any woman, even Aphrodite herself. Or one of the Sirens."

"You might not have had a choice with one of them," she pointed out.

"Maybe so." He angled a piercing glance her way. "Your turn."

"My turn for what?" she asked, genuinely confused.

"I admit I'm a wee bit rusty at this, lass, but people get to know one another by trading histories. I told you something about me, so..."

Anxiety tightened her stomach. She'd never gotten close enough to anyone to provide more than superficial details, and most of them had been lies. "'Fraid I don't have much to tell. Haven't led a particularly interesting life. Mostly I've been on the run from other Roskelly witches."

"Why didn't you join up with them? It would have been easier."

She gave him credit for cutting to the heart of things. Because it was tough to look at him and give voice to what lay in her heart, she stared at her hands, fingers twisted together in her lap.

"Mother was one and damned proud of it. She told me over and over about the Roskellys' long, checkered past. Things she crowed about made me want to throw up. Granted, she lost more and more of her mind, but she wasn't any of the things most mothers are. Even the demons were better caregivers than my mother."

Sorcha hesitated, searching for words. "Leaving Hell wasn't a snap decision. I planned for years. I knew if they caught me, I'd be punished, and punishments in Hell last forever. When Mother was ranting, she'd urge me to leave so I could locate Rhea. She told me Rhea would value me, love me, take care of me.

"Pfft. I never believed one word. From Mother's stories, Rhea was far worse than she'd ever dreamed of being, piling atrocities atop one another."

"So when ye walked out of Hell, or however you escaped, ye dinna search for your kinswomen."

"Ha!" She snapped off a bitter laugh. "Nope. Didn't take them long to find me, though. I came out in the 1960s with nothing, not even shoes. I hadn't expected my casting to work, so I hadn't brought anything with me. When the gates opened, I was afraid I wouldn't get a second chance, so I ran through them."

Tavin whistled. "Daring."

"Not really. I was more afraid of what the demons

would do if they caught me than of anything I'd find on the other side. There are far worse fates than being wet or cold."

"How long did ye remain in the 1960s, and where'd ye go from there?"

Sorcha smiled. "You're trying to keep me talking."

"I admit I like the sound of your voice, but I also want to know as much about you as you're willing to tell me."

"Fair enough." Over the next half hour, she chronicled all the spots she'd landed, from the early 1500s through her latest junket. She didn't know the current year, but Tavin provided it. Once she began talking, her hesitancy dropped away.

"So you can understand," she went on, "why I don't have a string of husbands or even boyfriends. I've never known how long I'd remain somewhere."

"Beyond that," Tavin supplied, "humans don't live long enough. I've watched many Druids pair up with them, and it never ends well. No one understands why the Druid isn't aging, and the human dies far too soon."

"Exactly." She unclasped her hands and flexed her stiff fingers. "I can't describe how amazing it is to have someone understand me."

"If that's an offhanded way of complimenting me, you're welcome."

She glanced down, suddenly shy again. "I've talked

more about myself in the past hour than in the whole rest of my life."

"How does it feel?"

"Good. Scary. I feel naked, but somehow you made it safe enough for it to be okay."

Tavin laughed. "A wee bit ago, ye were ready to lift your skirts for me. How is this different?"

"Sex is easy. It doesn't touch anything but my body, and only the surface of that."

"Which is exactly why we stopped." He pulled the car onto the shoulder. Once it rolled to a halt, he dropped a hand onto her shoulder. "Look at me, lass."

Something in his voice thrilled her, made her long for a different life, one where she wasn't perpetually starting over, a hostage of time and circumstances.

"If we make love," he went on, "'twill happen as part of something larger."

Understanding widened her eyes. "But I can't do anything 'larger.' What if I have to leave again? Scratch that. I will have to leave, probably in the dead of night with no notice. It precludes commitments I can't walk away from."

He nodded slowly. "That was when ye were alone."

"I'm still alone."

"Only if ye wish it." He still spoke Gaelic. "Ye've

three kinswomen and an untold number of Druids who will back you up if ye choose to fight."

She placed a hand over the one he still had on her shoulder. "Thank you for believing in me."

He narrowed his eyes thoughtfully. "I'm not a seer like Sean, but ye and I showed up at almost the exact same time—in the same place. It canna be sheer coincidence. There's meaning in how events fall together."

Letting go of her, he eased the Renault back into light traffic.

A sign flashed past announcing Inverness was twenty kilometers away. She considered what he'd said; hope flared bright and painful. She'd been alone forever. So long, it never occurred to her she might be able to stop running from Rhea. Before she got too comfortable, reality intruded, cuffing her briskly. Rhea wasn't just dangerous. She was vicious and spiteful. If Sorcha remained in close proximity to Gloria, Liliana, and Kat—and all the Druids—her presence would spell significant risk for them.

She blew out a tense breath. Nothing was ever simple, and this was no exception. She'd remain, help the others locate gateways and fight demons—and maybe witches—as long as she could. There'd come a time when she'd have to leave, though. Just like she'd always had to go. Until then, she'd do what she usually did. Be pleasant and cordial.

And unattached.

A part of her felt sad. No Tavin for her. No men beyond the ones she took to her bed, and since Tavin was who she wanted, there'd be no men at all this time around.

"Are we going to Sean's?" she asked, anxious to steer the conversation away from personal ground.

Tavin nodded and replied in English. "If we're fortunate, Arlen will be there too. It's logical. Sean's place is north of town, where Arlen's is a few clicks south." He followed it up with. "Are you all right?"

She looked away, hoping nothing in her expression would give her away. "Fine. Why would you ask?"

He frowned and cast a quick glance her way. "Something changed just now. At least I think it did. You can talk with me, lass. Not much I haven't heard in my long life."

"Thank you. I've done more talking in this car than in the last fifty years, though. I'm pretty talked-out."

They finished the last part of the drive in silence, but it felt more companionable than heavy. Thank the goddess she'd come to her senses. There were far worse things than being alone. Knowing someone she cared about was dead, their sole sin knowing her, would be a heavy load to bear. Far harder than jumping through time again.

Sean turned into a long, winding driveway, stopping in front of tall, cast iron gates covered with runic latticework. He rolled down his window and splayed an open palm across a reader plate. The gate creaked open.

"I wondered if I was still on the roster," Tavin said.

"What roster?"

"All the local Druids are programmed into Sean's gate system," Tavin explained. "When he created it, it predated electronics by a good, big bunch. Amazing what a determined Druid can fashion with magic."

Sorcha shook her head.

"What?" He rolled the window back up, probably because it was still raining like a hell-spawned bitch.

"The most disconcerting part of moving hither and thither in time is getting used to what's available in each era. There weren't even cars at my last stop. And if I'd told anyone about computers, they'd have locked me in an asylum."

"Many differences," Tavin agreed and drove slowly through manicured gardens. They had to be slathered with magic. Nothing grew this time of year, otherwise.

He turned a sharp corner, and an enormous castle rose before her. Four floors constructed of wood and stone complete with turrets and towers. Breath whistled through her teeth. "Christ! This is Sean's house?"

"More like his castle." Tavin laughed. "It was a falling down dump when he bought the place. He's responsible for all the renovations."

"But it must have taken enormous amounts of capital," she protested.

"Sean manages the Druids' money. One advantage of living a long time is many of us amassed rather significant fortunes. Sean makes certain we have access to our money, but that it remains invisible for tax purposes."

"Neat trick."

"It is. He's always been our magic man when it comes to funds. He says it's become easier to squirrel things away, what with Internet banking and offshore havens."

"But the Internet didn't exist when you left the group," she pointed out.

"I may have passed through on occasion," he admitted, looking sheepish. "Just to see how everyone was getting along."

"You missed them."

He nodded. "Mayhap. A wee bit. 'Tis our secret."

"I won't rat you out."

"I dinna think ye would, or I'd have held silent."

She patted his forearm. "You're a decent man, Tavin Shaw. And I love it when you speak Gaelic."

He pulled up at the far end of the monstrous building and killed the engine. "Why would that be, lass?"

"It's so musical, lyrical almost." She stopped there because the next words out of her mouth would have been it made her want to rip his clothes off. He'd made it clear sex with him came with commitment, and commitment wasn't in the cards. Not for her.

The castle's high wooden front door swung open. Arlen, Sean, Morgan, and the three White Witch Roskellys ran through it and down a set of flagstone steps. Tavin pushed his car door open. Sorcha let herself out before he could come around and open her side.

He was the type who would do things like that. Delightfully thoughtful and old-fashioned. Sorcha redirected herself. She liked Tavin. A lot. It wasn't smart. Her caring might spell his death. According to her mother, Rhea was famous for finding someone's weakest place and capitalizing on it. If she figured out Sorcha had an Achille's heel, she'd make the most of it.

And if Rhea got her claws into Tavin, Sorcha would be in deep waters. She'd do almost anything to buy his freedom, including indenturing herself to Black Magic. Protecting Tavin—and herself—from

Rhea's manipulations shot to the very top of her list. The best way to watch out for him was to clip their growing attraction off at its roots.

"We didn't expect you back for days." Gloria strode purposefully to her side.

"What happened?" Liliana asked.

"We'd all like to know," Arlen chimed in.

"A lot," Tavin replied. "I'd feel better talking inside, behind staunch wards."

"Of course." Sean nodded sharply. "And perhaps over a bottle of spirits and some fresh bread."

"We can do better than that." Liliana prodded her mate.

He kissed her cheek. "Henpeck away, *léannan*. I love it. And you."

Everybody broke out laughing. They trooped up the steps and inside, still chuckling. Sorcha tried not to stare as the castle's interior spread before her. She'd never been inside a home as grand as this one. Beyond being unbelievably huge, it was furnished with priceless antiques. From shiny, carved wooden furniture to crystal and silver artifacts and bronze sculptures. Oil paintings and tapestries lined whitewashed walls. Thick carpets graced hardwood floors.

"We can find you some clothes," Gloria told her.

"Maybe after we've talked," Sorcha replied.

Gloria furled one red brow. "That serious, eh? Makes sense since the two of you beat a path back here. We only arrived an hour ago ourselves."

They ended up in a formal dining room. Paintings of Druids engaged in battle covered the walls. She took a seat at a mahogany table that could have accommodated two dozen. Food materialized from somewhere. She was so busy keeping her mouth from gaping open, she wasn't paying attention to much of anything else.

She'd known wealth like this existed, but never seen it on display.

Magic rose. She wove hers in with everyone else's until they were enclosed in thick wards.

"All right." Arlen nodded at Tavin. "What happened?"

"We sensed a wrong spot from that vantage point above the wharf in John O'Groats and went to investigate..."

By the time he was done talking a quarter hour later, with a few additions from her, everyone wore worried expressions.

"You're damned lucky to be alive," Arlen sputtered. "Where's your bird?"

As if it had been an invitation to all of them, the familiars took shape and paraded up and down the long table cawing and cooing. Sorcha held out an arm, and her raven hopped on, using it as a ramp to her shoulder.

"There has to be a way to close the gateways," Tavin said.

"Aye, but if we shut one, they'll hurry to obscure the others," Arlen pointed out.

"Assuming this wasn't the only portal, we need to locate as many as we can find, first," Sean agreed. "Then we coordinate an attack. You're certain they didn't exist eight years in the past?"

"This one didn't," Sorcha replied.

"Good point." Tavin sent an approving glance her way. It warmed her and made her long for the impossible: a life where she wasn't perpetually on the run.

"These gateways, they're probably not only in Scotland and the remainder of the UK," Morgan said.

Arlen nodded. "Aye. I'll alert the Arch Druid in Europe. Predicated on what he finds, we may move our search farther out."

"Let's hope he finds nothing." Katerina's voice was lined with concern.

"Meanwhile, we'll create small teams—not more than two or three—and have them scour Scotland," Arlen said.

"I'll take care of that part." Sean nodded briskly. "I have encrypted ways of reaching most of us." He sent a pointed look in Tavin's direction. "So long as you've surfaced, do you have even the slightest interest in how your funds are doing?"

"None." Tavin grinned. "I've trusted you to take care of them for a long time. Naught about that has changed."

Sorcha was enjoying being part of a group of mages. The only other place she'd been where she wasn't the only magic-wielder was Hell, and it scarcely counted.

Don't enjoy any of this too much, she cautioned herself.

From long habit, she sent power in a full arc, searching for what shouldn't be there. Her first scan was benign, but the warding snagged most of its power. "Excuse me for a moment," she said and stood.

"Naught can get inside." Sean's words were reassuring, but she hadn't made it this far by trusting anything beyond her own magic.

"What about that demon?" Gloria speared him with her keen gaze.

"I got sloppy," he admitted. "Fixed the breach."

"You hope you did," Arlen muttered.

Sorcha had heard enough. She stepped through the warding, her raven in its customary spot on her shoulder, and deployed seeking magic one more time. Every direction but one pinged cleanly off her spell.

She returned to it again. Before she'd probed deeper, Gloria joined her. "Where?" she asked, her words tense.

Sorcha jerked her chin at the offending spot.

Gloria threaded magic in with Sorcha's, and they explored the place again. "What do you think?" she asked her sister.

Gloria shook a fisted hand at the air. "Several things. Sean did stymie prying ears, but that's Rhea as sure as I'm standing here, doing her damnedest to break through."

"From where?"

"Who the hell knows." Gloria's nostrils flared with disgust. "She could be elsewhere in time, or on a borderworld, or entertaining Satan's armies in Hell."

Sorcha turned to face her kinswoman. "Why'd she target us? Beyond the obvious shared blood, what's in it for her?"

"What else?" Gloria asked bitterly. "Making us miserable. It's what she lives for. You never got a chance to get to know her. Unfortunately, I can't say the same. Come on. Let's find you something to wear."

The other raven shimmered into visibility, talons curled around Gloria's shoulder.

Sorcha trooped after the other witch, her mind busy. "You make her sound like a demon. They're the same, feeding off fear and pain and desolation."

"Yes. Everything powered with Black Magic has that in common." Gloria stopped at the top of a flight of carpeted stairs. "You've never had any instruction in magic, have you?"

Sorcha shook her head.

"The goddess finally dropped you in the right spot. We'll begin to remedy that today. I have a feeling you'll be a quick study."

"Nothing wrong with my magic." Sorcha battled defensiveness.

"Nothing at all," Gloria agreed. "It just needs a spot of honing. Don't get your feathers ruffled, missy." A door to their right flew open, and Gloria marched through.

Sorcha joined her in front of several generous armoire cabinets. She pulled one open, and clothing all but spilled out. Woolens and silks and rayons in rich, vibrant colors. The raven cawed and flew to a low table, perching on it. Gloria's familiar joined it, and the birds proceeded to preen their glistening black feathers.

"But these are all too nice," Sorcha protested, running her fingers over the lush fabrics.

"Nonsense. You can't wander about in clothing from a bygone era. Dig in and find a few outfits. No one else is using them. I'll hunt down several pairs of shoes. Something is bound to fit." Turning aside, she began rooting through a nearby dresser.

Tentative at first, Sorcha pulled garments from several cabinets. The fabrics felt heavenly against her skin as she tried things on, adding her selections to a small pile of items she wanted to keep.

It would be tough—very tough—not to grow far too comfortable here, she warned herself. But somehow, she couldn't make herself worry enough to refuse the garments.

Or Gloria's brusque kindness.

Just this once, she told herself. *Just this once.*

It might be a mistake, but it was one she could recover from.

She hoped.

Sorcha cleared her mind. No point worrying about an uncertain future. She'd done a damned fine job of living for today, and she'd keep right on keeping on. Until it didn't work for her any longer.

Tavin was restless. He wasn't used to waiting for others or dealing with the intricacies of group decision-making. He'd done his part and provided as accurate a description of the gateway as he could. Sorcha had added a few details he'd missed since she was at ground level and he'd been flying.

She and Gloria had left. Shortly after their egress, Kat excused herself, saying she needed to tend to something to feed them tonight. Morgan teleported upstairs to Sean's library and lore books.

He looked from Arlen to Sean to Liliana. Should he apologize for deceiving the Druids? Before his thoughts ran too far down that track, Sean said, "I promised everyone I'd do my best to take a peek into the future."

"Not alone, you're not." Liliana trained green eyes on her husband.

"More magic is always welcome." He smiled warmly. "Particularly when 'tis yours."

"Remember what happened last time?" She arched a dark brow.

"How could I forget. You saved me, but that was a trip to the past. This time—"

"What makes you think Rhea's travels end in the 1700s?" Liliana inquired dryly. "Or the 1800s, for that matter. She's an all-season witch. And she knows where we are. I'd bet my familiar's goodwill"—the owl hooted from the center of the table—"Sorcha sensed Rhea. Mom either corroborated her find—or not. Regardless, neither thought it important enough to report back."

"I felt her." Sean made a face that looked as if he'd bitten into a piece of rotten fruit.

"Where?" Arlen narrowed his eyes at his second in command.

"Skulking about at the edges of the warding I reinforced around this castle." He traded the bitter fruit expression for a satisfied smile. "She can't get in. Not this time. I'm wise to her tricks."

"Don't underestimate her," Liliana broke in. "I did, and it cost me dearly. She hates to be foiled, and she's scheming to discover a way to break through."

"She won't find one." Sean stood and extended a hand, helping Liliana to her feet. The owl rose into the air and flew out the open door at the far end of the dining room.

"It remembers the way to your basement," Liliana said.

"Aye, or mayhap it recalls the mice down there." Sean grinned. The owl flew back into the room, hooting, before landing on Sean's shoulder.

"That too." Liliana walked briskly from the room with Sean by her side.

"Looks like it leaves the two of us," Arlen said, mildly.

"Convenient, eh? Except it doesn't appear accidental to me," Tavin observed. "I've known you far too long to believe this wasn't staged."

Arlen splayed his hands across the table's polished surface and skewered Tavin with his shrewd, dark gaze. He switched to Gaelic. "Don't dress this up with excuses. Why'd ye leave?"

"Why would ye have wanted me to remain?"

Breath hissed from between Arlen's teeth. "Since when do ye answer a query with one of your own?"

"It only sounded like a question. The answer ye seek lies within."

"Oberon's balls, mate. Answer me. I'm not in the

mood for a guessing game." Arlen slapped an open hand down on the table.

Tavin nodded. As Arch Druid, Arlen had an absolute right to the truth. "Ye recall the free-for-all in the cavern on South Ronaldsay?" At Arlen's nod, Tavin went on. "There's no easy way to explain my shapeshifting ability. I dinna understand the why nor how of it when it first occurred. In truth, I still don't, though I've grown used to carrying that brand of magic."

"Not understanding is one thing. Skulking off like a thief in the night quite another."

"True. Ye'll recall a few Druids engaged warding against evil through hooked fingers and suchlike. They'll never believe I havena been taken over by evil." He blew out a tense breath. "'Twould have placed you in an awkward position. If ye'd stood behind me, ye'd have split your community. Those who were convinced I'd fallen to wickedness would have left the fold.

"This way, ye lost only one: me. The other way, ye'd have lost better than two score judging by earlier today."

Arlen angled his head to one side. "Ye were protecting me from myself?"

A corner of Tavin's mouth twitched. "'Twasn't quite so altruistic as all that. I was guarding myself as well. I felt I'd been blessed by a miracle, and I dinna wish it sliced and diced nine ways from Beltane."

"Had we had the opportunity to 'slice and dice,'" Arlen observed, "perhaps we'd have discovered a way for more of us to shapeshift."

Tavin looked askance at him. "Is that a longstanding dream of yours?"

"Nay, but more magic is always welcome, particularly a variety that allows me to travel in secret."

"Pfft. Not so secret as all that. The moment Sean laid eyes on me and looked through a magical lens, he identified me. Sorcha knew right off the falcon was more than it appeared. And the demons in the passageway—one of them, anyway—recognized my presence too."

"Are ye back for good?" Arlen's question required an honest answer.

"I doona know." Tavin rolled his shoulders back, hearing the bones in his spine crack against each other. "I'd be lying if I said I've been miserable. I was a smith long before I was a musician. Returning to it felt right, natural. Something about the forge is soothing. The months I'm not smithing, I take my bird form and migrate south."

"I can see the appeal." Arlen's somber demeanor was broken by half a smile. "Did no one on the Isle of Lewis ever question your absences?"

"Nay. They grew used to me being gone through the winter months. Most of them wished they could do the same. Beastly weather, short days. Not much to hang about for."

Arlen stood. "We have a spot of time. Sean and Liliana are scrying. Morgan is buried in the scrolls she loves so much. Kat loves to cook, and Sorcha and Gloria are upstairs sorting through clothes."

"What'd ye have in mind?"

"I'd like to take a quick trip to 1870 Glasgow. If we get lucky, we'll hit the time Sorcha was there. I'd like to reassure myself she was truly a serving wench. Should be easy enough to locate the *Wild Pig Inn*."

"Beyond witch and demon, what do ye believe she might be?" Tavin bit back hot words in support of her. What he said, instead, was, "She saved me. She dinna have to. She could have departed with her bird, leaving me to the demons' mercies. For that fact, she dinna need to enter the tunnel at all."

"My point, precisely. Why'd she put herself at risk?" Before Tavin could answer, Arlen continued. "Either she was worried about you, or she was seeking an opportunity to parlay with the demons who raised her. I'd like to put that choice to bed once and for all."

"I'll accompany you"—Tavin pushed to his feet —"on one condition."

"Aye? What would that be?" Arlen's tone left little

doubt he was humoring Tavin. Not many Druids would saddle their leader with conditions.

"We tell Sorcha part of the truth. That we're interested in where she came from and planning a short trip back there. The advantage is we can use a piece of her clothing. It should lead us to the proper spot when we employ a seeking spell."

"And the disadvantage is she'll know we—er, I—doona trust her."

"Only if ye appear too guilty." Tavin furled both brows and extended a hand. After a short hesitation, Arlen clasped it.

"What if she wants to come with us?" Arlen asked.

"She won't. She was fond of the innkeeper and his family and felt bad about running away. No way to explain her sudden reappearance."

A knowing look scuttled across Arlen's austere features. "Ye got to know her rather well in a short time span."

"Maybe so."

"Care to say more about it?"

Tavin shook his head and made a sweeping half bow toward the door. "Shall we?"

"Aye. I'll just make a quick stop in the kitchen to let Kat know what we're about. We should be back in plenty of time for supper."

"Given we canna remain long in a spot where an

earlier version of ourselves resides, 'tis a safe bet. Which way did Gloria and Sorcha go? Or should I locate them with magic?"

Arlen loped from the room without answering.

Tavin followed more slowly. Deploying a slender thread of power, he sorted witch emanations and followed the ones coming from above him. Two flights up, he wandered down a hallway until he came to a partially open door and called, "Are ye decent?"

Peals of laughter met his question. "Depends." Gloria's deep contralto rippled with humor.

"How would you like us to be?" The door swung wider, and Sorcha walked toward him garbed in a long green skirt embroidered with golden lilies. Her hair fell to her waist, partially covering a cream-colored silky shirt and jade-green vest. Soft black leather boots graced her feet.

Tavin couldn't take his eyes off her. He whistled. "Beautiful. Ye're stunning."

"Clothes make the witch, I always say," Gloria cackled, and then added, "What's up?"

"Arlen and I are going to make a small trip into the past. We thought we'd scout out the *Wild Pig Inn*."

Sorcha's lovely expression faded. "Why?"

Tavin stuck to Gaelic and offered up his true reason for agreeing to the journey. "'Tis the last place

Rhea broke through that we know. Perhaps she'll have left a clue or two to make it easier to find her."

"Makes sense." Sorcha's tense facial lines relaxed. "I'd love to come along, but it's not a good idea. Karl and the others would recognize me and ask far too many questions."

Gloria closed her teeth over her lower lip. "I'd welcome the opportunity to square off against Rhea, but I need to help Sorcha with her magic. We'll move to the kitchens since Kat's ability is far less predictable —and not nearly as robust—as Sorcha's."

"Maybe I could teach her, and you could accompany Arlen and Tavin?" Sorcha suggested.

Gloria patted her shoulder. "Appreciate the offer, but Kat can barely manage simple witch spells. Arlen did a fine job polluting her witch power with Druid castings. I fear if we add demon magic to the mix, my granddaughter will never find her way."

"Back soon." Tavin offered an encouraging smile. "Might we borrow a small item from your discarded garments? 'Twill speed our endeavor since then we can employ a seeking spell rather than a time travel one."

"Good thinking, Druid." Gloria rooted through Sorcha's discard pile and handed him a sachet stitched into a square of homespun fabric.

"Are ye not used to Druids being capable of

independent thought?" Tavin asked in as deadpan a voice as he could manage.

"Take the sachet and begone." Gloria made shooing motions. "Or remain and spar with me. I've always appreciated a good debate."

"How about we save it for later?" He grinned. "Perhaps we could take up the gauntlet over supper. Druid versus witch."

Sorcha looked from one to the other of them. "I'm not used to anyone joking around. I like it."

"The most effective humor springs from truth," Gloria said.

It was tough to walk out of the room. He could have gazed at Sorcha for years and never grown weary of the sight. Arlen was waiting for him at the bottom of the stairs. "Did ye obtain aught for our seeking spell?"

"Aye." Tavin waggled the sachet in front of Arlen. It smelled like Sorcha, musky and feminine. The scent made him long for her.

"We'll leave from outside," Arlen said. "Tough to cast much of anything in the way of complicated spells from within Sean's warding. Unless, you're Sean, that is."

Tavin paced Arlen down long hallways to the front door. It had quit raining, but the skies were typical Highland gray. They trotted down the front steps until they stood in front of the castle.

"My casting." Arlen extended a hand, and Tavin dropped the sachet into it.

Magic rose, bubbling and boiling around them. Tavin remembered how strong Arlen's ability was and didn't add his own magic to the mix. It wasn't needed and might muck things up.

The neat courtyard, surrounded by trees and flowering plants, vanished, replaced by the blackness of a seeking spell. Dark, quiet cobblestone streets formed in short order, and Tavin cloaked himself with invisibility. Nothing like bouncing out of thin air and startling whoever happened to be close enough to have noticed.

Or have the bad luck to attract a cleric's attention.

Arlen drew them into an alleyway that reeked of stale urine and unwashed bodies. A quick glance reassured Tavin the people were dead to the world, no doubt drunk on cheap gin.

"We're in the right spot," Arlen murmured and pointed at a faded wooden sign at the end of the alley blazoned with *Wild Pig Inn*.

"Why wouldna we be?" Tavin countered. "Seeking spells rarely go sideways."

"This one did. It's nighttime, or did ye not notice?"

"'Tis mostly time-travel spells that maintain the same hour."

"Mayhap, 'tis true with yours." Arlen started

through the narrow byway, skirting sleeping bodies wrapped in everything from newsprint to patched cloaks.

"*Do we have a plan?*" Tavin switched to telepathy. They were already expending magic to remain unseen with no one the wiser. Adding a spot more shouldn't reveal their presence.

"*Aye. Look for the lass. See what she's about, and then return home.*"

Tavin hurried forward and wound a hand around Arlen's upper arm, forcing him to halt. "*Ye really do not trust her. Out of the witches in residence at Sean's, Gloria has magic to burn. It fairly gushes from her. When I left, she and Sorcha were thick as thieves. Do ye truly believe Gloria wouldna see through her if she harbored ill intent toward us?*"

"*I doona ken. Sorcha is her sister. Up until a day ago, Gloria had no idea she even had a sister. It may have altered her judgement.*" Arlen yanked his arm out of Tavin's grip and twisted to face him. "*I'm exercising reasonable prudence. Druids have remained safe under my care. Our order has flourished. I'd be worse than a fool to blindly accept a Roskelly witch— who's also a demon—without looking verra closely at her.*"

Tavin didn't answer, but he understood. If he stood in Arlen's shoes, he may have done the same thing.

"Come on." He gestured toward the *Wild Pig Inn* sign about twenty meters distant.

They reached the dilapidated alehouse. Three stories, constructed of planks with spaces between them, it had clearly seen better days. Many of the windows had boards instead of glass. The place was shut for the night, but the sounds of musicians practicing reached Tavin. Lutes, lyres, bagpipes, and a lone violin. Careful to be as silent as possible, he and Arlen worked their way around the inn.

A stable sat on the far side. Far cleaner than the alley, it was full of the odors of hay and horses and cows. Probably a goat or two and a bevy of chickens. Mingled with the rest of the smells, he scented Sorcha's enticing presence. She was here. Arlen's spell had run true. Tavin guessed she slept in the stable, probably in a loft of some type, originally constructed to keep hay dry and off the floor.

A door banged, and she walked out of the *Wild Pig*, heading for the stable, raven perched on her shoulder. Tavin longed to reach out to her, but this Sorcha wouldn't have met him yet. His presence would startle her—maybe propel her into fight mode. He locked gazes with Arlen, but the Arch Druid shook his head and held up a hand in the universal sign to wait.

Sorcha stopped walking with her hand on a side door into the stable. She tilted her head to one side, listening. Her nostrils flared as she scented the air. Between the length of two heartbeats, she sprang into action. A ward catapulted into being, surrounding her. Magic glistened and gleamed as she worked fast.

Tavin blinked, staring hard, but the thing he'd seen didn't go away. A spectral, glowing form that looked human was right behind Sorcha. Not touching her but pushing her to leave with such urgency even Tavin felt its resolve.

He recognized a time-travel spell, the witchy parts, anyway and leaned closer, concerned about the ghost—for want of a better descriptor—sticking to Sorcha like a second skin. He and Arlen seemed to have shown up at precisely the time she'd fled this era. Sure enough, a whirling vortex formed creating a gateway to other times. Running hard, tattered clogs slapping the rock-studded dirt path, she launched herself into the pulsing whirlwind with the spirit dead on her heels.

They were no sooner through than it vanished behind her as if it had never existed. Tavin was impressed by her speed and her command of magic—and worried about the thing linked to her at the hip.

"What the hell was that?" he asked Arlen.

"We can figure it out later. Look sharp." Arlen wasn't bothering with telepathy.

Tavin kicked himself for not having the foresight to bring a long blade. He tugged a dirk from a thigh sheath, and he and Arlen turned as a unit in time to see three dead witches blast through a hole in the ether. Red-rimmed eyes glowed with fury. Skin peeled away from bone. Dressed in frayed black robes, one witch had patchy red hair, the other black, except it only grew from the back portion of her skull. The one in the lead had long silver hair shot with black. Rhea looked far worse than his memory of her, but death was hard on a body.

Magic formed a glistening nimbus around Arlen. Tavin borrowed shamelessly from it. "Halt, witches." Power jetted from Arlen's palms. Where it connected with Rhea and the other witches, their garments caught fire, but they batted it out with bare hands, the stench of smoldering flesh acrid and cloying.

"Leave my witches alone," Rhea screeched.

"Nice try." Arlen sounded much too cheerful. "One of them is my wife, but then she never considered herself 'your witch.'"

Rhea's face contorted into a rictus, what was left of her lips skinned back from teeth showing most of their roots. With a bloodcurdling cry, she launched herself at Arlen, ran up against his magic, and bounced off. Her next attempt was preceded by a blast of dark, jagged lightning. It split Arlen's ward up the middle, and Rhea barreled through the gap.

The other two witches closed on Tavin, their

rotten-meat smell nauseating. He didn't bother with warding. Too hard to fight from behind it. Drawing his dirk back, he stabbed one of the witches in the eye. Gray goo spurted from her socket, and she shrieked outrage.

The other witch circled behind him, but he anticipated her and sidestepped, twisting so his back was against the stable. Having something solid behind him made things easier.

Arlen opened his mouth and uttered the long, eerie, ululating Druids' war cry. Tavin grinned. Every Druid who heard would come to their defense. Arlen closed his hands over Rhea's shoulders and shook her until her silver and black hair danced around her head. She swiped her filthy, broken nails down his face, leaving bloody gashes. They seemed to feed into her battle frenzy. Hissing, spitting, scratching, she kicked Arlen's legs.

Tavin plunged his dirk into dead witch flesh so many times he lost count. They were making an ungodly racket. Where the hell was everyone? But then no human in their right mind would get involved in a battle where magic pulsed red and black, and unnatural sparks lit up the night.

Anyone who looked at Rhea and the other witches would know right off they were dead. If that weren't enough to terrorize errant passersby, the eldritch battle unfolding would send the bravest soul scuttling behind closed doors.

"Leave my witches alone," Rhea repeated, coating Arlen's face with bloody spittle.

"If I doona comply?" He shook her again, lifted her off her feet, and heaved her a good ten feet into the air. She twirled and hit the dirt with a splatting noise. The crackle of breaking bones was followed by a pitiful moan.

She twisted at an unnatural angle. "If ye 'doona comply,' I shall hunt you through this time and all others until ye're sorry ye were ever born. I shall loose Hell's hordes to chivvy you. I'll not quit until every one of your Druids dies in agony."

Arlen shrugged. "Since when do demon spawn dance to your commands?"

She rolled to a sit, spitting broken teeth and blood. "Ye think ye know everything Druid. Hang onto your ignorance as long as ye can."

Arlen opened his mouth, but Tavin jumped in before he could spout off about the portals. "Leave now, while ye can. Druids are approaching. Many of us."

"Pah. Ye lie," one of the witches he'd poked chockful of knife wounds wheezed. Blood-soaked spit dribbled down her chin.

"Look for yourself," he countered.

"May ye rot in Hell," Rhea yowled, following it with words in a language he didn't know. Different from demonspeak. Perhaps the Black Witches had their own tongue.

An eerie fog, stinking of sulfur, rolled in, coating the three witches with streaming black ichor. Rhea kept up the cavalcade of words that were clearly a spell. The fog thickened. Where it touched Tavin, it burned, so he kept clear of it.

"They're leaving," he yelled.

"Aye, let them go," Arlen yelled back. "We made our point."

"But when the other Druids show up—"

"Some of them would end up dead. 'Tisn't worth the loss."

Tavin wasn't certain of that, but he held his tongue.

The fog was dissipating in long, greasy black strands when at least twenty Druids, many sporting swords and sabers, poured into the small space between the *Wild Pig Inn* and the stable. An earlier version of Arlen led the charge.

He planted himself in front of his doppelganger. "Too late, eh?"

"Aye," Arlen agreed. "Ye scared them off, though."

"And offered us opportunity to return to our own time," Tavin added.

"Is there aught more we can do?" the earlier Arlen asked.

"Spread enough magic about so no humans remember hearing or seeing what transpired."

"Easily done." The Druids gathered, chanting a familiar refrain.

Arlen withdrew a sliver of parchment from a pocket and walked to the far side of the stable. "What's that?" Tavin asked.

"A wee bit of a magical scroll from Sean's to guide us home."

Tavin nodded. "Do it." Home sounded welcome. Never mind it wasn't his home. Maybe his chosen separation from his kin had run its course. He bent and wiped his dirk clean on a convenient bush before sheathing it.

Magic boiled around them. Arlen's spell was close to full velocity when Tavin asked, "Now do ye believe Sorcha isna working the dark side of the street?"

Arlen nodded. "Aye. She's one of us whether she wishes or no."

Before Tavin could ask what Arlen meant, the spell caught them up in its maw. They stumbled out next to a peaceful lagoon behind the castle with swans gliding back and forth.

"Thanks!" Arlen slapped him on the back. "I've missed working with you."

Tavin snorted. "Nothing like a wee battle with an old comrade in arms. Any idea what that thing shadowing Sorcha was?"

"Nay. At first, I feared she had a demon escort, but naught about it carried the stink of Hell." He shrugged. "We could ask her, but I have other priorities just now."

"Ye do, indeed. Rhea got you good. Best see to your face before some godawful infection sets in."

"I've already sent healing magic to work on it, but Kat loves the hands-on parts." With a lascivious wink, he started for the castle door.

Tavin followed more slowly. Sorcha was inside. He sensed her presence. He couldn't wait to tell her about their fight with Rhea, but first he needed to clean up. He stank of Black Witchcraft and witch blood and the nineteenth century's general lack of sanitation.

Aye. He'd take a shower and find some clothes. By then, everyone should be gathered for dinner. After their meal, he'd see if she was interested in a moonlight stroll. Of course, she'd say yes.

Tavin dove headfirst into imagining what might happen after that. By the time he trotted downstairs, chasing the luscious scents of dinner, he had at least the evening, if not the rest of his life, more or less sketched out. Sorcha was meant for him. She must be his, or else why would the goddess have thrown them together? Whistling an old Irish folk tune, he entered the dining room. Arlen, Sean, Liliana, and Gloria sat near one end of the oversized table. Morgan slid past him and grabbed a seat for herself.

He blinked and looked again. Where was Sorcha? For that matter, where was Katerina?

The swinging door from the kitchen flew open, admitting both witches carrying trays laden with food. Tavin sprang into action and ran lightly to Sorcha. "Here. Let me help you with that."

"I've got it," she said. "If you want to help, there are more of these in the kitchen."

CHAPTER 9

*P*leasant conversation flowed among the seven of them. Sorcha enjoyed getting to know her kinswomen and the Druids better as they shared a chicken and barley casserole, assorted cheeses, and fragrant bread. After they'd first sat down, Sean began to relay what he'd found scrying the future, but Arlen had stopped him, saying, "Time enough for that. 'Tis been a difficult day. Shall we enjoy our meal?"

Every once in a while, she sensed Tavin's gaze on her, hot and intense. He had something up his sleeve, but she had no idea quite what. If he were any other man, she'd assume he was plotting how fast he could separate her from her underthings, but she'd offered herself. And he'd refused.

Doesn't matter. Her inner voice was brisk. *I'm not*

staying. At least not long enough for what he has in mind.

They'd moved to tea and a buttery confection, jam layered with sugary dough, when she decided dinner was done enough to talk about more important matters. "How'd you come by those scratches?" she asked Arlen.

"Guess they didn't heal fast enough to escape notice, eh?"

"No, but that's not much of an answer."

He chuckled. "Witches. Got to love them. We located the *Wild Pig Inn* about the time you bolted. Good thing you were quick. Rhea and two of her sisters showed up not two minutes after you left."

"That's terrible." Sorcha closed her teeth over her lower lip. "Did you kill her?"

"What a predatory question."

"Well, did you? She's already dead, but there are ways to make it permanent."

"Nay, we missed a solid opportunity," Tavin said. "Our magic isn't strong enough by itself to disable dead witches."

"And we didn't have a decent-sized blade to hand," Arlen added. "Quite the oversight, but I had no idea Rhea would show herself."

"Let alone engage us in a scrappy street brawl," Tavin muttered.

"Witches fight dirty," Gloria said.

"I'm sure they figured three of them would be more than a match for the two of you," Liliana cut in.

Tavin mock bowed from his seat. "Why thank you for the vote of confidence, Madame Witch."

"Don't mention it," she retorted coolly.

"I rustled up reinforcements," Arlen said.

"And I pointed out they were coming," Tavin added. "One witch told me I was full of shit, but Rhea chanted up a spell. Guess she didn't want to take a chance on dealing with more of us. What is that language, by the way?"

"Black Witchcraft has its own tongue," Liliana said.

"It's not a generally spoken language," Gloria chimed in. "Black Witches only use it for spells, but over time, a witch gets used to which words mean what."

"Will it work for any witch?" Tavin was curious.

Liliana shook her head. "Only those born to Black Magic carry sufficient power to kindle dark enchantments."

"We seem to have moved from polite dinner banter to serious topics." Sean cast a pointed glance Arlen's way.

"Aye. Tell us what you started to reveal earlier."

"Since we're not eating, I can get fancy. Back in a moment." Sean stood and strode from the room.

"What does that mean?" Arlen asked Liliana.

"He's off to get a laptop and projector. We mapped some of what we found, and a picture saves a whole lot of explaining."

Sorcha took advantage of the break to ferry plates to the kitchen and stack them next to the other dirty ones from their main course. She'd turned, intent on clearing the rest of the dinner debris from the dining room table, when the door swung inward admitting Tavin, his hands full of cups and bowls.

"Here you go." He placed them on the sideboard. "I'll help you with these later. Sean's ready to begin."

She felt flustered. Something about having Tavin standing right next to her did crazy things to her body. Her heart danced in funny little flip-flops, and keeping her distance was a challenge. Maybe because they'd kissed, and she yearned for more. Or maybe it ran deeper than that.

She gave herself a sharp mental slap. She didn't do deeper. Why the hell did she have to keep reminding herself?

He crossed the kitchen and held the door open for her.

"Thanks." She walked past, careful not to brush against him. She didn't trust herself, but she wasn't ready to blurt out her intentions to leave, either. They might have need of her magic. She'd been wrong to write off Gloria's offer of tutoring. The older witch had watched her cast a few simple spells and given her a whole new angle on leveraging the witch side of her power.

When Katerina had grumbled it wasn't fair things came so easily to Sorcha, her grandmother reminded her she'd only realized magic was real a few weeks earlier and that magic, like everything else, required time and study to truly master.

Sorcha made her way to the dining room, intensely aware of Tavin walking right behind her. To divert herself, she thought about Gloria and her instructions to incorporate more earth and water into her spells.

All magic required varying combinations of the four elements: earth, fire, air, and water. Her early lessons in Hell had been heavy on fire and air, lighter on earth, and water was never mentioned. Yanna had become progressively more unavailable as Sorcha grew older. Perhaps it was her long tenure in Hell, but she spent her days and nights locked in her own world. Much of the time, she had no idea Sorcha was even there. To learn to leverage any magic at all, Sorcha had relied on watching demons and reading. Hell contained two mostly unused libraries, and Yanna had taught her to read several languages before she checked out.

Still lost in memories, Sorcha took her seat. This time, Tavin slid into the chair next to hers. A computer whirred at the far end of the table, and a square of wall between two tall, leaded-glass windows lit up with the Microsoft logo.

"Here we go," Sean announced. "Lil and I employed location vector spells to unearth these." The logo flickered, replaced by a map of the U.K. Several red Xs were scattered across the map. Sorcha counted and came up with eight, mostly in Scotland, but one lay in Ireland and one along the coast west of Liverpool.

"I assume the Xs represent portals." Arlen's deep voice rumbled the length of the table.

"You'd be right," Sean said. "We copied the feel of the one we know about and used it as a pattern. I can't guarantee there aren't more of them, but we asked three times, and this is what we came up with. At least it's a manageable number."

"What else did you find?" Arlen pressed.

Sorcha blew out a breath, grateful someone else was asking the questions. Eight didn't feel very manageable to her. Not when each location held demons, but she didn't want to challenge Sean's assessment. Maybe they knew something she didn't.

"It's complicated," Liliana said. "And contradictory to some extent."

"Futures are never totally clear," Morgan leaned forward. "Tell us exactly what you saw. Not your interpretation, but what played out in your pool."

Sorcha filed the information away. Apparently, Sean used water for his future-seeing. Demons used fire and mirrors. And only Satan himself and his princes were capable of looking into the future.

"I can do that." Sean fastened his whiskey-colored gaze on Morgan. "You had a reason for asking. What is it?"

Morgan nodded, her silvery hair shimmering in light from a candelabra chandelier. Tonight, she wore a colorful dress that fell from shoulder to ankles in shades of teal, rose, and violet. Silver bracelets adorned both arms, and a matching necklace carried a generous chunk of fire opal.

"While you were in your workshop, I was in the library hunting down likely prophecies. I located a few that fit our circumstances, but I'll keep them to myself until I hear what you came up with."

"Fair enough," Sean replied.

Gloria angled her head toward Morgan. "Why didn't you include me?"

"I tried. You were so deep in mentoring Kat and

Sorcha, you never noticed when I opened the kitchen door."

"Too much to do, and all of it too important to skip over," Gloria mumbled. "Next time try harder. I'd prefer to make my own decisions about—" She held up a hand. "Sorry. I'm edgy."

"We all are," Morgan said. "No offense taken."

"In the spirit of honoring Morgan's request," Sean said, "I'll relay what I saw. The vision was complex enough, I didn't cast another future-seeking spell. This will sound like a story, but those are what play out in my scrying pool." He wrapped an arm around Liliana who sat next to him. "Jump in if I miss something."

She smiled softly and leaned against her husband. "I would have anyway, but it's nice to have permission."

Jealousy jabbed Sorcha in the vicinity of her breastbone. Liliana and Katerina had mates, Druids who loved them. She saw yearning and affection whenever Arlen or Sean focused on the women they loved, and she wanted the same.

I'm half demon, she reminded herself. It changed the parameters, made her less desirable mate material— except maybe for another demon. The thought was so depressing, she forced her mind to blankness as she listened to Sean.

"Close your eyes and picture a circle of standing

stones," he began in a hypnotic cadence. Untangling his arm from Liliana, he folded his hands in front of him. "The stones are gray and weathered with age, and they sit on a hill overlooking a restless body of water. Ocean rather than lake because the tide was rolling in. I watched the stones for a long time. Water almost reached them before it receded.

"Sea birds wheeled overhead, cawing and screeching. Sometimes one landed on a stone but never remained long. The tide had shifted to going out when a golden peregrine falcon winged its way to the tallest stone. It perched atop it, beak opening and closing, wings extended as if it weren't certain it was going to remain. A shadow formed behind it, ghostly, spectral. I had no idea what it might mean at the time, but the bird didn't pay it any heed. It may not have known it was even there."

Perhaps it was all the bird talk, but her raven swooped from where it lived within her and circled the room. The other familiars joined it, but the birds were quiet. None of their usual raucous hooting and screeching. Both ravens, the owl, and the eagle perched on a sideboard, lined up like crows on a fence. Sorcha was certain they were listening to Sean's tale.

"I assumed the falcon was Tavin," Sean went on, "but I kept my mind completely open so as not to influence what showed itself in my pool. A drop of blood ran down the stone. And then one more. The falcon hopped to the sandy earth and shifted. It seemed to take him a long time, but eventually Tavin stood next to the stone, steadying himself with one hand.

"A long gash ran down one side along his ribs. Blood welled. He brushed a hand down the wound. Magic flared, and the gash began to knit together." He eyed Tavin. "Do you recognize that time?"

"Aye, 'twas just afore I left Isle of Lewis on my way south, except the lot of you were pumping out so much magic, I changed my plans. I'd been in a fight with another falcon who thought to rob me of my kill." He arched his coppery brows. "I won, but not without a wee bit of damage."

"Were you aware of whatever was shadowing you?"

"Nay." Tavin frowned.

Sean narrowed his eyes. "Something lies behind that nay."

"Mayhap. Not sure. Something about your description struck a chord, but I can't locate the connection. Give me a few minutes to toss things around."

Sean took a long drink from his wine goblet. "The scene scrambled then. The stones disappeared, replaced by a village. I'm guessing 1800s, but Liliana thought earlier than that."

"The architecture wasn't modern enough," she spoke up.

"You're probably right," he murmured before going on. "It must have been market day, but it was early. Horses and wagons were still hauling items into the town square. An old church made of bleached flagstones sat in the center of town, and its bell tower marked the hour with carillon."

Sorcha squelched a rapid intake of breath. His description had been general enough it could have depicted a lot of places, but she'd lived in a hamlet very like that a few leagues north of Edinburgh. It was where she'd been before the *Wild Pig Inn.*

Sean had begun talking again. "A commotion, lots of yelling and screaming, grew louder still. Sorcha ran out from between two buildings." Sean turned to her. "Does this sound familiar?"

She nodded. "My employer, a cobbler, accused me of stealing food. I hadn't, and I was running to avoid being whipped."

Tavin placed a hand over one of hers. It felt good, supportive, but she couldn't let her guard down, and so she tugged out from beneath his touch. The place his palm had laid across her hand felt empty, but she told herself she was being ridiculous—and dramatic.

Sean nodded. "I saw you running and two men behind you. One was fully corporeal with matted blond hair. The other more ghostlike, not dissimilar to the projection I saw behind Tavin within the circle of standing stones."

"Not possible. There was only one," Sorcha insisted.

Tavin sat straighter. "Arlen."

"Aye?" The Arch Druid quirked a dark brow.

"The thing shadowing Sorcha near the *Wild Pig* looked a whole lot like what Sean just described. But I'm confused. How could the same otherworldly being stalk me as well?"

"Let's keep listening, shall we?" Arlen suggested smoothly.

"What do you mean about something tracking me next to the Wild Pig? I sensed no such being, and I swear only the cobbler was after me," Sorcha spoke up. The information had rattled her, badly. Her magic was plenty strong enough for her to pick up emanations from anything stupid enough to get close to her.

"The cobbler's energy was obvious, which made you believe he was alone," Sean stated before going on. "You escaped by sleight of hand. You'll know this next part, but the others don't."

He swept the small group with his gaze before continuing. "Sorcha dove beneath a low wagon, and I felt a jolt of discharged magic. By the time the man after her bellied beneath the wagon, she was gone. Here's where it gets interesting. The man was back on his feet, mud running down the front of his shirt and screeching at the top of his lungs someone had stolen his property when the ghostlike projection reappeared. It doubled up a fist and slammed it right into the cobbler's windpipe. He dropped like a stone, and the ghost frittered to nothing but vapor.

"I hope Rede died," Sorcha muttered. "He was a bastard."

"The next scene in my pool," Sean continued, "was a recreation of our gathering on South Ronaldsay. Tavin and Sorcha dropped out of nowhere, but the ghost was there all along—before either of them showed up."

Morgan was nodding, a satisfied expression on her face.

"Don't just nod," Arlen told her. "How does this fit with whatever you unearthed in the lore?"

The librarian got to her feet and paced around the table stopping to fluff the birds' feathery heads as she passed them. "Sometimes the spirit world has plans, things that have to happen in a certain order. It's difficult for them because we're not aware of their presence much of the time. They can't talk directly with us. All they can do is—"

Arlen made a chopping motion. "Tell me what you think this means. I don't care how the spirit managed to flatten someone. I assume he dragged psychic energy out of a handy human who probably felt like burnt parritch for the next month."

"All right," Morgan said, tightlipped. "My interpretation is Tavin and Sorcha have critical roles to play in either finding Rhea, disabling her, or both. They're also linked in some way to the portals. Regardless, someone worked their tush off to make certain they ended up together. Right place. Right time. I'm assuming their magic is additive in some way and that we need the combination to prevail over whatever Dame Fortune throws in our path."

"Sean?" Arlen nailed his second with a penetrating look.

"About what I came up with," Sean said. "Except Lil and I weren't clear about the ghost—or spirit or whatever it is."

Arlen's gaze settled first on Tavin and then on Sorcha. "Have the two of you combined your magic to work on anything significant?"

"Not sure about significant," Tavin replied, "but we joined our ability to scan John O'Groats."

"And?" Arlen pressed.

"We work well together," Sorcha answered. "I was surprised how effortless it was to join our magics, but then I'm not used to working with anyone, and I assumed it was always that easy."

"'Tisn't." Tavin said and then turned to Arlen. "Does that answer your question?"

Arlen nodded. "It's growing late. Do we attempt to shut the portals first? Or do we go after Rhea?"

"Shut the portals," Gloria said. Her raven squawked agreement. The birds rose and flew to their respective witches.

Sorcha held an arm out for her familiar. Its talons were sharp, but she'd grown used to their bite long since. The spirit, or projection, or whatever had been riding shotgun. Was it here in the room? The idea of an invisible shadow herding her toward a particular destiny made her squirm.

"Sorcha!" Arlen's voice held an edge.

"Yes. Sorry."

"Sometime between now and tomorrow midday, you and Tavin will put your combined ability to the test. I want a full report on what you can—and cannot—accomplish. Once we've established that, we'll plan how to take down the portals."

Tavin leaned closer and asked her, "Would you like to do a wee bit tonight? Or are you too tired?"

Still feeling disconcerted about her future being laid out behind her back, she sniped, *"Demons"*—she stressed the word—"don't need much sleep. I'm good if you are."

His expression, which had been solicitous, pleasant, turned unreadable. He stood and said, "You pick our practice arena."

"Better if you do." She got to her feet. "I don't know this castle nearly as well as you. But we should be somewhere we can't damage if anything goes awry." She addressed her next words to Arlen. "Are we excused for the night? I'll take care of the dishes once Tavin and I are done."

"I'll do them," Gloria said. "Your task is far more important."

"Thank you." Sorcha considered around the table and giving her sister a hug, except neither of them were the hugging type.

Tavin had moved to the arched entry. She joined him, and they walked to a staircase leading down. "Where are we going?" she asked.

"Sean's workshop. It's shielded and warded. Worst we might do is knock the castle off its foundation."

She stopped mid step and balanced between two risers. "You're joking, right?"

"Aye, lass. What's wrong?"

She opened her mouth to counter, "What's right?" but shut it with a *clack* before anything snarky escaped. Her inner turmoil wasn't his fault. They continued down more stairs. Recessed lighting flickered to life as they passed, illuminating the way. A hallway at the bottom of the last flight led to an underground room with no windows. A stone fireplace took up most of one wall, and Tavin sent magic to kindle a blaze.

More magic pushed the door shut behind them. She took in a rounded room with thick area rugs scribed with runes. The walls were rock-studded dirt. More of the same magical lights reflected off one another.

"Take a seat." Tavin pointed to a low sofa near the fire.

"But we have to work," she protested.

"Magic is finicky," he said. "Something changed in you when Morgan was talking. Once we lay it to rest, we'll work on combining our magic."

Sorcha shook her head. Rather than sitting, she clasped her hands behind her and paced from one side of the chamber to the other and back again. "I've been on my own practically since I was born. The idea of being manipulated behind the scenes infuriates me—and gives me the creeps. If something magical is skulking about, why can't I feel it? Why isn't it talking to me directly?"

"Because spirits can't communicate in that fashion. I could ask the same questions as you about the ghost—

or whatever it is." He'd stood still while she circled him like an overactive satellite.

Sorcha came to a stop in front of him. "Why aren't you?"

"Because it doesn't matter to me."

"It should."

He shrugged. "I like to think I'm my own man, but apparently I'm needed here. Does it matter how I arrived? If Arlen had taken the trouble to hunt me down—and he could have if he'd chosen—and asked me to return, I might have refused. This way, I assessed the situation for myself and determined greater needs than mine were in play."

"Mmph." She turned his words over, considering them.

He stepped close enough to circle her upper arm with a hand. Warmth from him seared her, made her long for things she'd never have. "You said it all, lass, when you said you'd always been alone." He switched to Gaelic. "Afore, ye were alone because ye had no choice. Ye're no longer alone—if ye wish to alter your situation—but it entails trusting those around you. Learning to work in conjunction with others."

She took a chance and gazed into his green eyes. Golden flecks mingled with the deep green irises. "I don't know if I can."

A hint of a smile curved his mouth. "'Twas honest. 'Tis a good start. There's only one way to find out."

She set her mouth in a determined line. "If I run screaming from the room, you'll know I couldn't do it."

"I'll keep it in mind, lass, but I have faith in you."

Emotion rocked her, loosened her moorings. Before she did something stupid, like throw her arms around him again, she twisted away from his grip. "How do you want to begin?"

"With magic we've already used. Where else? Start with the known and work outward from there."

The raven had stuck with her through her frenzied pacing. It shimmered into a ball of light and dove within. Sorcha understood. It was offering its magic to augment hers. It wanted her partnership with Tavin to be successful.

"Your bird disappearing takes some getting used to." He turned until he was facing her.

"It's here." She tapped her chest. "When it's within me, our magics are additive."

"Thank it for me. I want us to succeed too. There's a lot at stake, and if we're the crucible that makes a difference, I'm all for it." He positioned himself to face the fire, hands extended in front of him.

Sorcha did the same. When power crackled from his extended fingertips, she threaded her magic with his, letting it build. The same sense of rightness that had filled her in John O'Groats was back in spades. Their magic was synergistic, born to be joined.

Excitement thrummed a tattoo up and down her spine, and her reservations fell to the wayside. She could always leave.

Beyond taking his falcon form and working over his forge, Tavin hadn't used much magic since his self-imposed exile. He marveled at Sorcha's power; it slammed into his, scouting out deficiencies and filling them. Combined magics were always strongest, and between the two of them, they covered witch, Druid, and demon power.

He'd only meant for tonight to be experimental, a bare beginning, but once they began, he was caught up in her enthusiasm—and his own.

"Let's try that borderworld transit once more," she said, pushing hair back from her sweaty forehead.

"Aye, 'twas a wee bit on the rocky side," he agreed.

"Only on account of you were worried we'd end up on one of the demon-controlled worlds by accident."

He nodded. "'Twas a fifty-fifty proposition, lass. What do ye say we bring blades this time?"

She grinned. It lightened her features and made her look young and carefree. She might still be on the youngish side as magic-wielders went, but she'd never been carefree. His heart had gone out to her when she'd told him bits and pieces of her past, but he knew better than to cluck over her or offer sympathy. She was proud, and she'd reject anything that looked like him feeling sorry for her.

"So long as I can bring the one I used in John O'Groats," she replied.

"Ye liked that one, eh?"

"It fit my hand perfectly, and it had enough heft to create a good swing."

"Done. It's in the car. I can run up and get that one plus another for me."

Sorcha tossed her discarded vest over her shoulders. "Waste of time. Let's teleport outside, grab the weapons, and we can leave from there."

The words were no sooner out of her mouth than he felt the bite of her power snatching him. One moment, they were in Sean's workshop. The next, they stood next to his ancient Renault. He opened the hatch and moved aside while she rooted through the pile of craft-honed steel. Once she'd extracted the longsword and its belt and sheath, he hunted for a heavier blade.

"Why not bring one like mine?" she asked, casting her gaze over the one he'd selected.

"This way, we'll have a choice." A corner of his mouth twitched downward. "I can cut off two heads in a single swipe with this one."

"Are you truly thinking we'll have to fight our way out of something?" She raised a blonde brow. "I've ended up on a few borderworlds. Most have been empty."

"And the others?"

"Demons, but at that point they recognized me as one of them."

"Maybe they still would," he ventured.

"Not a chance. The word's gone out long since that I defected. Hell doesn't tolerate traitors. Or much of anyone else, truth be told. Are you ready?"

He slammed the hatch to make sure the latch engaged. He was more than ready, but it was because combining their magic was heady, intoxicating. He'd started to talk with her about how unusual everything about their joined power was but had held back.

At first, he'd thought it might be a fluke, but as their magics warmed to one another, enchantments became easier and stronger. They'd built spells from all the elements, varying the amounts to check how it impacted the results. A quick teleport into Inverness had provided humans to doublecheck invisibility spells and telekinesis and the effects of mind control.

Sorcha had stopped a fight between four drunken band members. By the time she was done, they were slapping one another on the back and exchanging apologies.

He'd moved groceries from a storage shed behind a supermarket to a homeless shelter. The grocery chain would never miss the few crates, and the shelter would make good use of the unexpected bounty when they located it the following morning.

"Tavin?" She tapped his arm.

"Sorry. Got distracted. Some of my magic may be a wee bit on the rusty side from disuse, but I've never seen the like of what you and I create together. Not only that, 'tis effortless. I don't have to reach for results. They just happen, exactly as we visualize them."

She crossed her arms beneath her breasts. "While I agree it's easier when we work together, I'm not used to my spells failing." She smirked. "Of course, I mostly call on magic when I'm running away from someone who wants to hurt me. Means I'm motivated to make things happen right on the first try."

"Why not stand and fight? Your ability outshines almost everything I've come across."

She looked away, perhaps uncomfortable with his compliment. "If something were truly important, I would have. But I've never been attached to anywhere I've lived. Probably because I've come to expect I'd be leaving sooner or later."

"You went back through the liminal boundary hunting for me."

Her expression turned solemn. "That was truly important. I couldn't walk away and leave you there. My bird would have found its own way out. That it remained absent told me you had to be in trouble, and it was watching over you."

He was touched beyond words by her concern. He started to thank her, but he already had several times over. The temptation to draw her into his arms was close to overwhelming, but she'd scuttled away from him every time he'd touched her. Something had altered from when she'd snuggled into his arms in the car.

Had his refusal angered her? Made her determined to maintain distance between them?

"We should go." His tone was brusque to mask his attraction and his need.

She turned her penetrating aquamarine gaze on him, her features shuttered and unreadable. "I'll start the spell."

"Less fire than last time."

"You sound like Gloria, though I'll admit an hour with her was worthwhile."

The air developed the incandescent glow typical of Sorcha's enchantments. Burnished copper flowed into lighter shades, and the scent of her power permeated everything. Vanilla. Wildflowers. Herbs. Each time, the mix was a little different, but he'd know that smell waking from a dead-to-the-world sleep.

"Planning on helping?"

Her question broke through, and he understood he'd been lost in staring at her and breathing in the scent of her power. He slid the sword belt beneath his jacket and buckled it into place. Enchantment flowed from the earth beneath his feet, and he fed it into her casting.

Sean's courtyard faded, and they floated in the dark, airless void between worlds. This part was a lot like time travel.

"How far should we go?" she asked, using telepathy because it was damned difficult to converse when you couldn't breathe.

"Your choice."

She threaded her fingers with his to strengthen their connection. Regardless of her rationale, he loved the touch of her skin against his. Maybe he'd been a fool to turn her loose earlier, but he meant what he'd said. She was different, special. He didn't want just a tumble in the hay. He craved far more than that.

Power surged through him, linking him with

Sorcha. It formed an infinite loop, glowing brighter every revolution until he was surprised he didn't burst into motes of brilliance scattered through the universe.

Worlds flashed by, giving him a peek at their contents. It was how he'd selected the last one. He'd waited for one without a trace of life on it—to be certain they wouldn't roll out into a band of hostile demons. Not that they were the only evil scattered about. Trolls, giants, Furies, Sirens, Harpies, Medusa, the Minotaur, and odd combinations like griffons, kelpies, and hydras could all be found on various borderworlds.

Long ago he'd picked what he thought was a deserted world to get away from his Druid kin for a while. The Minotaur had come out of nowhere, intent on his destruction. Tavin had barely made it out of there. Nowhere to hide, and the Minotaur was unbelievably fast for its bulk. Smart too and skilled in strategy.

"Here," Sorcha announced.

Their spell dissipated, and a mysterious world came into focus, stretching around them. Three moons were transiting a deep-violet sky, providing plenty of light to see by. A pale, icy ocean licked glowing reddish sand. Mountains ringed their side of the beach. Trees with white bark and orange foliage grew in groves, their leaves rustling in a brisk breeze.

Sorcha turned in a full circle, taking it all in. "This is surreal."

"It is, indeed. And cold." He still had hold of her hand while he paid out a thin thread of magic, hunting for anything alive.

"I scanned before I picked this world," she said. "I'm fairly certain it's deserted."

Tavin almost withdrew his magic, but he wanted to verify her assessment.

Sorcha laughed and drew a circle in the wet sand with the toe of her boot. "What? After all that hype about how powerful my magic is, you don't trust me?"

"Don't take it personally, lass. I scarcely trust myself. Humor me. Take a look in that stand of trees. The one to our left."

"I tell you, there's nothing there. I'll prove it." Sorcha took off running toward the grove, the saber rattling against her legs.

Tavin raced after her. "Sorcha! Don't be stupid."

She was quick, but he was faster, courtesy of his long legs and being a man. He caught up to her a few feet from the first tree. The leaves were rattling far harder than they had been, though the wind hadn't changed. He didn't try for elegant. He jumped on her and drove her to the ground.

She writhed beneath him, hissing in annoyance. "Christ! What is this? A soccer match?"

"Use your head, wench. We've never been here before."

He lay full length on top of her, and the motion of her body as she tried to free herself was doing wicked things to him. His cock sprang to a full-blown erection and pressed into her bottom. She must have felt it because the sounds coming from her changed from annoyance to soft moans.

Embarrassment sparred with arousal. He loosened his grip, intent on rolling off her and apologizing, but she twisted beneath him until she lay next to him. Her mouth was full and soft and enticing, and she twined her arms around his neck just before she kissed him.

The sabers jangled against each other but weren't in the way. For the same reasons she shouldn't have run off half-cocked, they shouldn't do anything that diverted their attention from the borderworld. With warnings tolling deep in his mind, he kissed her back anyway.

The luxury of feeling all of her against him overpowered common sense. He wrapped his arms around her, holding her close as he plunged his tongue into her mouth. She tasted of magic, sweet and heady. The kiss began at 110 percent and took off from there. The points of her nipples jammed into his chest, and she captured one of his legs between hers, pressing the heat of her core against him.

His hips settled into a rhythm, thrusting against her belly. He was so hard, his cock ached, and his breath came in harsh gasps against her mouth. If he didn't watch it, he'd orgasm in his pants. He had to slow things down. Get them home, back to Sean's where they'd have a bed.

The borderworld had been cold when they arrived, but frost had gathered on them while they grappled with one another. The trees were making an absolute cacophony of noise, like nothing he'd ever run across before.

Tavin ripped his mouth from hers, arousal fading fast.

She gazed at him, heat lust warm in her eyes. "What? We need to take some clothes off, yes?"

"Sorcha. Something's not right here."

"Silly. They couldn't be righter." She tried to draw him into another kiss.

"Look." He shook bullets of frost off his sleeve. "We'll freeze if we stay much longer."

The desire in her eyes turned to confusion. He untangled his arms from around her and sat up. Thick, gray clouds had rolled in, and it was so cold he began to shiver. Orange leaves had blown off the trees and formed an unbroken circle around them. He didn't understand exactly what it was, but he recognized evil intent.

"Get up carefully," he instructed. "Do not step on those leaves."

Sorcha nodded and flowed to her feet. He joined her. The leaves intuited their intent, and the circle moved inward. "What happens if they touch us?" Sorcha asked.

"I doona wish to find out." He started toward the rustling orange boundary, intent on jumping over it, but it changed shape, became an undulating orange viper with hundreds of eyes peppered across multiple heads.

Tavin drew his blade. He heard the swish of metal against leather as Sorcha drew hers. "Whatever this is, if it can change shape, it can regenerate itself," he said, looking for a break in the thing's body. Anywhere his blade would buy their freedom.

"If it can, then it's driven by something else. Maybe someone's hidden in the trees, or maybe something a long way from here has hold of the puppet strings."

He didn't question her assessment. He swiped the blade downward in a lethal arc. Three of the viper's heads rolled off, spewing gray-and-green ichor that smoked when it contacted the layer of thick frost coating the ground. The wound sealed over fast; new heads began to form.

"Didn't faze it," Sorcha muttered. She leapt in place. The viper rose to match her height. "Mmph.

Didn't think it would be as simple as jumping over it."

Tavin looked at his blade. Where it had connected with the viper, the metal was bubbling, melting before his eyes. He wiped the sword against the ground, but it didn't slow things down.

"Either sheathe it or leave it here," Sorcha said.

Tavin didn't want to risk sheathing it. If the viper's blood was enough to make a steel blade decompose, his leather sheath had no chance at all. He laid the blade on the ground and extended his hands. Sorcha grasped them.

"Our best way out is teleporting, but it won't be easy," he cautioned. "Borderworlds have a hell of a pull when they don't want you to leave."

"Got it," she said, sounding calmer than she probably was. "We run wide open and don't stop until we're free."

"That's my lass." He didn't have to add that if they didn't leave this place, and damned soon, they'd be dead.

There was nothing graceful or elegant about what came next. Sorcha slammed her magic into him, and he herded it into the strongest spell he could muster. He didn't bother visualizing Sean's. That part could come later. His only target was away from this borderworld.

"Hurry," Sorcha urged, sounding far less sanguine than she had a moment before.

The totality of his attention was on their spell. He couldn't spare any to look at the orange monstrosity or ask Sorcha why she'd urged him to move faster. The viper could have turned into a dragon for all he knew. Fire would be a welcome addition to this bizarre world. Anything to cut the infernal cold. It was sapping him, but he ignored it.

Heat from Sorcha's hands seeped into him, almost as if she intuited what he needed. He waited, letting the spell build. The moment it peaked, he ignited it. The borderworld shimmered but didn't vanish.

"More," Sorcha shrieked.

Energy pulsed into him. He latched onto it and gave the spell one more huge boot in the ass. This time, an outraged howl scored his eardrums. The viper closed around them. Wherever it touched him, it burned with an icy heat that tried to cleave flesh from bone even through his clothes.

He pushed harder than he ever had. Dug deeper. Opened magical channels he had no idea he even possessed. Finally, the borderworld exploded, leaving them floating in the airless void between worlds.

He and Sorcha were locked in each other's arms, their bodies still alight from the magic they'd summoned to escape. Both of them were panting in short, harsh gasps.

"We did it." She tilted her head and looked at him, her expression feral and defiant.

"By the skin of our teeth, lass." He panted harder. *"No air here. I'll get us to Sean's."* he finished in telepathy.

He summoned a visual of Sean's castle, but had a tough time hanging onto it. Sorcha helped. When his mental image wavered, she overlaid her own. It took far longer than their outward journey, but they finally fell out of the ether between worlds.

He had no magic left to cushion their fall, so he shielded her with his body. They landed with a heavy thud between the castle and the carriage house. "Are ye all right, lassie."

"Of course. You're who fell on your back in the dirt," she retorted. "I should be asking if you're hurt."

"I'm not. Aside from the spots where that horror touched me. The wounds are deep, but they'll heal. On the plus side, we have material aplenty for that report Arlen requested." He let go of her and rolled to a sit. Standing would come once he got his wind back.

She rose to a crouch. "I'm sorry. Running off like that was stupid. You called it. I was showing off, and it was a really bad place for me to do that." She shook her head. "I don't understand what got into me, but I nearly got both of us killed."

He started to tell her it was all right, but it wasn't. Not really. Instead, he angled his head until he captured her gaze with his own. "'Tis a good thing ye realize it," he said in Gaelic. "We've all used our magic for ill-advised stunts. 'Tis how we learn wisdom."

She rolled her eyes. "What did you ever do to rival that?"

He snorted laughter. "Landed on the borderworld where the Minotaur lives. 'Twas just as close a call, but the Minotaur is smarter than that orange thing. Faster too."

"Pfft. You're just saying that to make me feel better."

He shook his head. "Truth. Cast a spell if ye doona believe me."

The tight set of her shoulders relaxed. "I guess you're right. We learn by making mistakes." She stumbled upright and extended a hand. He grasped it and joined her.

"We can leave your blade in the Renault."

Nodding, she let go of him and unbuckled the belt holding it in place. "Too bad about yours."

"I can make another. I'll vary the magic for the next one. Perhaps 'twill be stronger." He detoured past the car and dropped both belts and her longsword across the folded-down rear seat.

Somehow, her fingers ended up laced with his. Together, they walked slowly inside.

He should let go of her, bid her a good evening. What was left of it anyway, but he couldn't get the words out. He didn't want to leave her side. They were at the bottom of the main staircase when he let go of her hand and turned her to face him, hands atop her shoulders.

"I—" His throat wouldn't cooperate, so he started over, feeling like he was fifteen and asking a girl out for the first time. Except this was ever so much more than that. "Lass, I—"

She threw her arms around him. "After all the magic that's passed between us, we don't need words," she murmured just before she rose on tiptoe and crushed her mouth over his.

CHAPTER 11

Sorcha reveled in the feel of his lips against hers. They were firm and demanding and delightful. A distant part of her screamed to stop this nonsense immediately. She wasn't planning to stay. This was a complication she scarcely needed. One which would make it far more difficult to walk away.

The arousal that had ignited earlier burned with a steady flame. She was intensely aware of every square centimeter of her body pressed against Tavin's richly muscled frame. She could let go, mumble some lame excuse, and bolt for the upstairs room where the clothing chests were. A small bed had been tucked into a corner, and she was certain no one would care if she claimed it.

Sean hadn't been exaggerating when he said the

castle had an unprecedented amount of unused real estate.

But she didn't want to leave. The magic she and Tavin had woven together linked them in ways she didn't understand, but she didn't question the knowledge.

He teased her back with his fingertips, inscribing small circles that flowed into bigger ones and then tightened again. His cock swelled, pressing into her belly. She ached to strip him naked, examine that magnificent body at her leisure. Her breasts felt heavy, the nipples hard as marbles where they were crushed against his chest. Liquid dribbled from her swollen labia, wetting her thighs.

Their scents—rain-wet greenery and herbs and musk—simmered around them. He ran one hand down her back and cupped her ass, snugging her against his erection. A decidedly male sound, like a big cat purring, rumbled from his throat, vibrating against her lips.

He rocked his hips against her. The rhythmic motion sent sparks shooting outward from her center. Her raven rose in her mind's eye, wings spread, cawing its approval. Not that she needed an extra push, but she couldn't live one more moment without touching him.

She moved a hand, insinuating it between their

bodies until her fingers curved around his girth. He was long and thick, and the heat from him rolled through her like an aphrodisiac, crafted just for her. His cock jumped in her hand, and she squeezed it.

He groaned. The hand that cupped her ass dragged her skirts upward until he cupped her vulva skin-to-skin. Undergarments weren't part of her nineteenth-century wardrobe, so she hadn't bothered with them here, either. He rubbed her slick, hypersensitive nub, teasing it by sliding a calloused finger up one side and down the other.

Their kiss had deepened to infinity, their tongues tangling together as they sucked and bit one another's lips. Her heart hammered against her chest, and breath rasped in and out until she felt dizzy, drunk with wanting him. She'd moved from squeezing to stroking.

He jammed two fingers deep into her, withdrawing and probing. Her hips writhed against him. She'd never been in quite this place before, where she felt she'd die if she didn't come. Her legs shook, not willing to bear her weight any longer.

Tavin broke their kiss. Her mouth felt odd, naked without his slashed across it. Reaching between them, he pried her fingers from around his cock. "If ye do that much longer, I'll spend, and I doona wish to. Not yet." His green eyes bored into her, alight with desire.

She stroked the side of his face, loving the feel of

stubble over skin stretched across bone. "Where can we—?"

Magic shimmered, turning the air around them liquid and glistening. She welcomed the touch of his power, almost as familiar as her own. The downstairs hall disappeared, replaced by a bedchamber tucked beneath the castle's eaves, judging from the steeply slanted walls. A double bed adorned with a colorful wool blanket and piles of pillows sat beneath dormer windows. Another corner of the space held a small desk and chair. Empty shelves suggested the room was unused most of the time. Wooden beams crisscrossed the ceiling with whitewashed plaster between them.

"This is where I've stayed when I was here before," Tavin said. "I believe it was part of the servants' quarters back in the day, but 'tis quiet."

She started toward him, intent on separating him from his clothing as expeditiously as possible, but he shook his head. "Sit." He sank to the bed and patted the place next to him.

Confused and still hot enough to burst into flames with zero provocation, she joined him. Twisting so she faced him, she drew her legs onto the bed and crossed them beneath her.

He offered a lopsided smile. "Most men would call me a fool, tell me I should bed you and sort out the pieces later, but I stopped doing that a while back." He hesitated long enough to take a measured breath. "I've not had time to totally dissect this, but the magical beings on the borderworld took advantage of what they considered our weakness."

Sorcha frowned. "How is being drawn to one another a weakness?"

"Normally, it wouldn't be, but in this case, something we're not aware of—suggestion or outright magic—was in play. I'm attracted to you. Anyone with a child's grasp of enchantments could pick that out of my mind. The orange monster needed our attention elsewhere. If we'd not been so engrossed with one another, we'd have noticed long afore the thing encircled us."

"And taken measures not to end up trapped." She closed her teeth over her lower lip. "Where are you going with this?"

He switched to Gaelic. "Ye mean why are we talking instead of loving?"

She looked down, embarrassed he'd seen right through her question. "Something like that."

"A greater magic, elements beyond us both, made certain we found one another for obvious reasons. Our magic is a perfect match and incredibly powerful. 'Tis a wee bit of a reach, but if there are divine beings in play who want us to be together, it follows other elements would be just as invested in us being dead."

"But the borderworld was an arbitrary pick." Sorcha wrapped her arms around herself, chilled by the implication. At least the sexual haze that had clouded her mind was clearing.

"Was it?"

"I don't know." The words came hard.

"Nor do I, but it dinna feel accidental we were targeted."

"It was because the trees misinterpreted my actions, thought I meant them ill," she insisted.

"That might be true. Or not. 'Tis just as possible they looked within you and found impatience and hubris and took advantage of both." The corners of his eyes crinkled. "None of us are perfect, and our faults were nearly the death of us. The lesson, hard-won as it was, is we canna afford to let our guard down."

Tavin placed a hand on her thigh and went on. "I've learned to trust my instincts over the years. And now, I'm asking you to trust them as well. I doona know what ye have in mind for your future. Ye've been on the run your whole life. If we make love, and I've never wanted anything more than I want to take you to my bed, I suspect 'twill reinforce our magical bonding."

"Hard to see how we could be solider than we are." She was making light of his statement because she saw what lay behind it, and it frightened her, meant a commitment she'd never faced before.

He tightened his grip on her leg. "I've chosen to be alone. You're the first woman who's ever made me question that choice."

"It might be why you understand me. Alone was easier than leaving a piece of my heart every place I ended up. None of them were planned beyond jumping far enough ahead in time—or backward—to stymie Rhea for another few months." She took a ragged breath. "I wasn't under any particular illusions about how important I was to her. I'm sure she had other priorities—lots of them. But when things slowed down, or she got bored, she remembered the half demon who had Roskelly blood."

"Aye, 'twould have been a simple enough matter for her to locate you."

Sorcha nodded agreement. "It's why I figured she was toying with me, using me as a diversion. She could have tracked me every single time I ran, but she didn't."

"Mmph. Mayhap your demon blood made it harder than ye think." He scooted closer to her. "I doona wish to talk of your Black Witch grandmother."

"Great-grandmother."

"Aye, same difference. I came within a hairsbreadth of taking you standing up in the downstairs hall. I want you that much, lass."

The same breathless desire roared back. "We can make love. Sort the fine points out afterward."

He moved his hand from her thigh to cupping the side of her face. "The first part of what ye said is accurate. I'm not sure how much latitude we'd have sorting anything once we've consecrated our magical bond with our bodies."

"It's kind of who I am, though." Sorcha leaned into his touch. "Might be the demon part, but I jump first and figure it out later."

"Kind of like ye did today when ye'd have run into the corrupt arbor?"

"Exactly like that."

"Ye'd love me even if doing so cuts off your usual escape hatch? Because it will." His expression had turned solemn. Her answer meant everything to him.

Sorcha swallowed hard. Now was a time for absolute truth, even if it cost her the man sitting so close his sheer masculinity was tantalizing—and overwhelming. She craved him with an intensity that stole her wits.

But did she yearn for him enough to sacrifice her freedom?

"You can't know what will happen if we make love." Sorcha was grasping at straws, but she wanted Tavin's arms around her again, the press of his mouth on hers, and the weight of his cock in her hand and buried in her body.

"Not in any normal way, yet I do. Will ye join your

life with mine, lassie? 'Twould mean significant changes—for us both. The first few months, or even years, might be rocky."

"We could keep working together, deploying our combined magic, without that extra step."

Tavin nodded. "We could—and we will—but the longing that throws us into one another's arms willna go away. 'Twill be a fine torture to have ye so close and yet not. Worse still to know ye're plotting your exit. This time, ye'll not be forced to flee. When ye go 'twill be because ye wish it. Rhea canna stand against Druid and witch power combined. 'Tis why she comes with reinforcements and runs when the going gets dicey."

"Rhea is precisely why I can't stay. If I do, I'll place everyone in danger. So far, no one has died on account of her perverse fascination with me. I'd like to keep things that way. Looking at that side of the coin, it almost doesn't matter I may not be good lifetime partner material." She glanced away from his direct gaze.

"I may not be capable of a long-term commitment, either." He turned a hand up pragmatically. "Some choices requires a leap of faith. Speaking of choices, ye can make them for yourself, but ye must allow others to decide their own futures. I canna see anyone chasing you away for fear your presence will draw the wrath of your Roskelly kin. From the sound of it, this group dealt with plenty of that long before you showed up."

"Why does everything have to be so convoluted?" Sorcha jumped from the bed. She couldn't stand being so close to him. It did crazy things to her mind. Made it next to impossible to think.

"The important things are never simple, lass. We both could use a spot of rest."

She folded her arms beneath her breasts. "Why aren't you trying to talk me into..." Her tongue stumbled over the word marriage, so she tacked, "this," onto the end of her sentence.

"Would ye really want me to?"

She shook her head. "I guess not. I have to think about what you said. About what I want, and about what I can offer you." Sorcha walked closer. "And you need to think long and hard about me. My father was a demon, the horn-and-forked-tail version. I have no idea what that would mean if we had children. Beyond genetics, I have a temper, and not a whole lot of patience."

"I've noticed. I'll take my chances." He smiled softly. "'Tisn't about me. I made my choice when I held you in the car and told you I wanted all of you. Naught has changed about that."

She opened her mouth to tell him she didn't deserve anyone as decent as him, that she'd done some pretty horrific things in her life, but everyone had baggage. He saw something in her that she didn't see in herself. If she could latch onto how he viewed her, she might be less critical.

Not just of herself, but of others too.

Sorcha studied her feet, unsure and conflicted about how to finesse such a major alteration in the way she understood the world and her place in it.

She had no more words, so she drew magic about herself and teleported to the manicured gardens behind the castle. Dawn was breaking, a thin, gray line across the eastern horizon. She walked along gravel paths, her mind a jumble. The raven swooshed from her, flying ahead. For want of a better plan, she followed it.

A lagoon with swans came into view. She crouched on its bank watching the graceful birds paddle to and fro. They pair bonded for life. It was touching, tender, and felt totally unrealistic. The raven settled on her shoulder, fluffing its feathers. "What should I do?" she asked her familiar.

"*What do you want to do?*" it countered.

"I don't know."

Footsteps crunched not far behind her. Sorcha sprang to her feet, hands extended, magic at the ready.

"Stand down," Gloria called. She came into view

wrapped in a black woolen cape. Unbound red hair cascaded past her waist.

Sorcha slowly lowered her hands and faced her sister. "You being out here can't be accidental."

"It's not. Walk with me. Movement loosens the tongue."

Sorcha snorted. "What if I don't want my tongue loosened?"

Gloria rolled her blue-green eyes and repeated, "Walk with me." Compulsion accompanied the words, enough that Sorcha fell into step next to her kinswoman. "Better." Gloria angled a glance her way. "What happened tonight?"

"That's a fairly general question," Sorcha began, hedging as she sorted which parts she wanted to share.

"Let me put a finer point on it." Gloria's words were brusque. "You and Tavin were gone for hours. Where'd you go? Once we've got that part nailed down, what just went on between the two of you?"

"I'm not seeing where it's any of your business."

The raven pecked the side of her head hard enough to hurt.

"Your familiar doesn't agree with you," Gloria said. "Christ, woman. I'm offering you an opportunity to talk. It would be easier for me to drag what I'm hunting out of your mind."

Sorcha drew back. "You wouldn't."

"Oh, but I would if I deem it important, and this is."

"I like Mother's approach better."

"The one where she ignored you?" Gloria's tone hacked at Sorcha like a dull knife.

"Yeah." Sorcha stopped walking.

Gloria rounded on her and thumped her in the chest with an index finger. "I care about you. She didn't. Why the hell would I have taken the trouble to chase you down out here if I didn't give a crap?"

"But you barely know me," Sorcha protested.

"You're blood. And my sister. It's good enough for me. Now talk." Gloria started walking again.

The anger bled out of Sorcha. She started with the magical practice session, the joy and allure of sharing power with Tavin. From there, she relayed the borderworld that had nearly been the death of them.

"What do you think?" she demanded. "Is there some malevolent force out there hell-bent on making certain Tavin and I never get a chance to release the full brunt of our combined magic?"

Gloria slowed her pace from a half jog to a fast walk. "I don't believe in coincidences, so something on that borderworld had it in for you."

"Something as in?" Sorcha pressed.

"Demons pissed you gave them the slip is the most likely. Or maybe Rhea in conjunction with demons.

You and Tavin will have to be damned careful, particularly when you leave Sean's warded estate."

Sorcha inhaled sharply, blew it out, and did it once more. Should she confide in Gloria? Or had she said enough? The raven nuzzled her with its feathered head.

"What happened after you and Tavin returned?" Gloria's words were tinged with more coercion, almost as if she knew Sorcha would be loath to answer.

"Easier to tell you what didn't happen. He didn't bed me, but we came close."

"Why'd you stop?"

"It wasn't me, but him."

"And? Don't make me drag this out of you ten words at a crack."

"He says if we make love it will consecrate our magical bonding, and we'll be married or mated or something."

"I agree. So, is that why he chased you away?"

Sorcha stopped walking. "He was the willing one. I'm who left."

"Oho. I suppose you were out here hunting answers."

"I was. Do you have any?"

Gloria's harsh expression softened. "No, but let me tell you a story." She walked ahead, and Sorcha hurried to catch up with her.

"A long time ago when Liliana was quite young, I'd moved to the States to avoid my Roskelly kin and make certain they never identified Liliana's very human father. I was out walking in the Nevada desert one summer evening. It was warm and pleasant, and I walked farther than I normally did.

"Liliana was in a carrier on my back. She started making cooing noises, and I hunted for what had wakened her. I didn't have to look far. Fae danced around a magical fire. Humans would never have seen them. It required magic to see beyond the veil they'd crafted.

"A beautiful man greeted me, welcomed my daughter and me. We remained for the night, and then the next day." Gloria's tone had softened, become wistful. "Days stretched into weeks, and weeks to more than two months. I knew I had to leave."

"Why?"

Gloria stopped and extended one finger. "Liliana needed humans and maybe witches, but not Fae. The faerie folk weren't constant. They might be here now, but they could vanish in an instant." She extended another finger. "I worried what my Roskelly kin would do to Severin if they found out about him. At the very least, they'd make his life miserable. I loved him. I couldn't do that to him. Or so I told myself."

"Were you scared of making a promise you might not be able to keep?" Sorcha cut to the chase.

Gloria nodded. "It was the real reason, and I've had well over thirty years to regret it. I left, amid Severin's protests. After a week away from him, I missed him so much, I returned to the desert to tell him I was willing to be his mate, but the Fae had left. I tried for years, cast every seeking spell I knew, but I never found him again."

"Some doors only open once," Sorcha murmured.

"Aye, sister. Ye're a quick study," Gloria said in Gaelic.

"Does Liliana remember your time with the Fae?"

Gloria shook her head. "And I'd just as soon things remained so."

"You've no worries on that front from me." Sorcha glanced at the sky. Night had departed, so it must be midmorning. "Thank you."

"You're welcome. If you turn Tavin down, make damned good and sure it's for the right reasons, and not just because you're scared to your bones."

"Sorcha!" Tavin's voice blasted into her mind.

"I'm outside with Gloria."

"Get back to the house. Now."

Gloria exchanged glances with her. "Crap. Sounds serious. I'll get us back there. Teleporting is faster than walking."

"Should I ask him what's wrong?"

"And risk having someone overhear?"

"Sorry. Stupid question."

"I'll do the teleport part. You ward us. No telling what we'll find. Last time a demon had broken through."

"Got it." Sorcha summoned power.

By the time Gloria's spell swept them up, Sorcha had built what she hoped was a robust barrier around them both. Gloria's story had touched her soul and cast the Tavin problem in a whole new light. She'd been so scared of anything that smacked of commitment, she'd totally overlooked how she might feel if he went away.

She'd always been the one who left. Never the other way around. She'd talk with him, tell him she was ready to take a chance on them. Right after they dealt with whatever the current problem was.

CHAPTER 12

Tavin lay awake for a long while after Sorcha left. She'd asked why he hadn't spun arguments—or rained compliments on her—to change her mind. He understood all about "getting to yes," but he'd be damned if he'd employ stealth or pressure or manipulation where affairs of the heart were concerned.

She had to want him with the same singlemindedness that burned through him, shining with a steadfast flame. For her to capitulate because he pushed the right buttons, said the right combination of words for her to lay her reservations aside, would only provide a short-term fix.

It wouldn't last.

In the end, she'd resent him for not offering her space to come to her own conclusions.

His cock throbbed hotly, and he cradled it in one hand. He'd never be able to sleep without bringing himself off. He was too aroused. He'd nearly come twice. That he hadn't spoke to riding a ragged edge of control, a battle he'd won by the slimmest of margins. His balls ached with unslaked lust. Her scent—and residual magic—clung to his skin and his clothing, adding to desire scraping through him.

A quick flick with the other hand released both buttons and zipper, and his cock all but dove out. He didn't blame it. He'd ignored his sexual side for so long, it had turned into an art form. He ran his fingers from base to tip, shivering as sensation spilled through him.

Thinking about coming would probably be enough, but he curved his fingers around himself, stroking gently. An image of Sorcha plastered itself across his closed lids. In his fantasy, she held a breast in one hand and jammed the other between her legs. She kept her unusual eyes glued to him as she rolled her nipple and rubbed her nub, hips moving faster and faster as her arousal spiraled out of control.

The gentle touch he'd started with vanished, replaced by hard, fast strokes as he fucked his hand. Moans rose from his throat, feral, guttural, but he was far enough away from the rest of the castle's occupants, no one would hear him. His balls tightened, semen pooling, gathering momentum.

He wasn't so far gone he couldn't time his release with Sorcha's. She was fingering herself now, plumbing herself with her fingers while the breast hand had moved to rubbing her clit. Shudders racked her, and she cried out.

It was all the encouragement he needed. He came hard. Semen juddered from him in hot little blasts of white-hot need. He came for a long time, gasping and panting and grunting with long-repressed lust.

He opened his eyes, intent on cleaning up the mess on his belly and getting his breathing under control. Maybe then, he'd coax his overactive brain into an hour or two of rest. The room had a washbasin, and he lurched his way to it. He'd no sooner swiped a warm cloth across his stomach when a blast of wicked power so potent it doubled him over plowed into him. Tavin battled shock and outrage. What the hell was it? He sent magic in an arc, hunting the source, but nothing felt out of place.

Impossible.

He dropped the washcloth into the basin, set his clothes to rights, and hunkered into a crouch, every magical antenna fully extended. Moments ticked past. He hadn't imagined the one-two punch from evil. His gut still burned from its onslaught.

Had anyone else felt it? Or was this something personal, meant just for him?

He didn't care for the direction of his thoughts. He'd never undressed. Made his life easier as he rose and bolted from his room on the castle's top story. Either everyone else would be awake, or he had to warn them, make certain no one was caught unaware.

As he raced down flights of stairs, he raised his mind voice. *"Sorcha!"*

"I'm outside with Gloria."

Relief pummeled him. Thanks be to all the gods she was safe. *"Get back to the house. Now."*

Sean and Liliana met him in the downstairs hall. From the looks of things, they'd dressed in a hurry and skipped shoes. "So you felt it too," Tavin said, not bothering to elaborate on what "it" might be.

"We did," Liliana muttered.

"Unsettling since it breached my defenses, the perimeter I just reinforced. Sean nailed Tavin with his gaze. Ideas?"

"None."

Morgan clattered down the stairs, silver hair flowing around her slight frame. "The lore never suggested an outright attack. Not this soon." Her keen dark eyes flitted from one to the other of them. "Where's everyone else?"

"Sorcha and Gloria are outside," Tavin offered.

"I can't believe Arlen and Kat slept through the evil that rolled through this house." Sean dragged the heels of his hands down his face. "For that matter, I don't see how anything could have gotten close enough to bother us. I shored up my warding, made it strong enough to withstand a dozen Roskelly witches."

The far end of the hall turned liquid with witch power. Sorcha stepped through a gateway right after Gloria. A wave of her hand and a few words of Gaelic, and the portal winked out.

"What happened?" Gloria strode toward them, moving fast.

"We don't know," Sean said.

"Where are Arlen and Kat?" Sorcha stopped a few feet from Tavin.

Sean started up the stairs, but then must have changed his mind. "Arlen!" he shouted, adding a shot of telepathy for good measure.

Tavin expected the Arch Druid to either come running or tell his second to shut up. Neither happened. He sent seeking magic outward, hunting Arlen's distinctive magical signature. When nothing pinged back from close quarters, he extended the reach of his spell. Somewhere along the way, Sorcha's magic joined his.

"He's not here," she said in a flat voice.

"Did he tell any of you he was leaving?" Morgan asked.

"Nay, not me," Sean murmured.

"Would he have?" Tavin asked.

"Depends." Sean drew the word out as if he were considering Tavin's question. "Given all the problems we've had lately, probably."

Gloria pushed around Sean. "We won't solve this standing here."

Liliana joined her. "Goddammit, Mother. You don't suppose this is some twisted end run to kidnap Kat?"

"It's precisely what I'm thinking. Of course, Arlen would have gone after her immediately without bothering to let any of us know."

"He wouldn't have wanted to lose a moment," Sean said. "Trails go cold fast when they lead through time or between worlds."

Gloria didn't hang around to toss words back and forth. She and Liliana vanished up the stairs. Tavin and Sorcha followed them with Sean and Morgan bringing up the rear. "Third door from the end of the hall on this floor," Sean called.

"As if Gloria couldn't locate her own blood," Sorcha mumbled.

"I was trying to be helpful," Sean said stiffly.

"Sorry. Of course you were."

Tavin stopped behind Gloria and Liliana, both of whom stood in the doorway of a spacious bedroom. The covers were piled in a jumble, sliding half off the king-sized bed. The owl and raven flew around the room, probably seeking clues. A jolt of magic from beside him told him Sorcha's raven was joining the hunt.

She gripped his hand. He understood and loosed power to marry with hers. This was a different spell from any they'd done before, one that recreated past events, except it only worked on things that had happened very recently. Different from a scrying spell, this one latched onto energy remaining in a particular spot and used the clues to reconstruct history.

Sorcha hummed, the sound growing as images formed in the air. At first, they looked promising, but frittered away before they showed anything useful. He experimented with musical notes to complement her efforts. The familiars perched on various pieces of furniture, remaining still so as not to disturb what crumbs of psychic energy remained.

Tavin reminded himself to breathe. He needed air to work magic. Gloria took up a spot next to Sorcha. The weave of their casting brightened as she fed magic into it. His hands were busy keeping their mixed magics from going off the rails, so he jerked his chin to invite Liliana to help.

She shook her head. "Thanks, but my magic isn't up to snuff."

"Mine is." Sean's words were grim, and he stepped into line amid the flash of Druid power.

Tavin's job grew far harder. The disparate magics each had a will of their own. Sorcha mumbled, "Fuck," and turned up the demon part of her ability. It did the trick. The images they'd been playing cat and mouse with took off like an old movie, flickering and in black and white but easily visible.

Tavin almost expected to hear the hiss and crackle of celluloid and the whirr of an old-fashioned projector. Arlen and Katerina lay in bed, arms twined around one another as they made love. Their bodies strained together, the tempo of their sexual dance increasing as they moved toward a crescendo. Kat laughed, low and throaty, and Arlen flipped them over so she straddled him. Hair like living fire streamed down her milky skin as she balanced herself with hands splayed across his chest.

Arlen called out in Gaelic, part entreaty part prayer, for the goddess to bless them with a child. Pressure built around Tavin. Whatever he'd felt when he was upstairs was closing, heading full speed toward Arlen and Kat. Lost in each other, they weren't paying the slightest heed to anything beyond their joined bodies and the passion splashing through them.

Sorcha's grip on him tightened until it hurt. She felt it too, the malevolence rushing forward. This wasn't a scary movie on late night television, though, where you had the option to look away. Her humming changed to words, first Gaelic and then demonspeak as she ran wide open.

A long gash opened near the window. Blood red, it ripped the fabric of the weave between worlds asunder so fast, Tavin felt the same gut-wrenching reaction he'd had upstairs in his chamber. Except this time, he couldn't fall to his knees. Power seared him. Guiding the casting was his job. The others provided the magic, but it was up to him to ensure it yielded information.

A chill wind blew through the gash.

Kat jerked away from Arlen. Naked, she scrambled to her feet facing the gaping hole that had no place in her bedroom. Both she and Arlen were sunk so deep in passion, neither reacted quickly. Kat swayed on her feet, staring at the breach, a dumbstruck look on her face. Arlen leapt into position behind her. Magic shot from his hands, and he chanted harsh and low, intent on suturing the rip before anything could get through.

Goddamn it, Tavin cursed. Arlen's spell was a decent choice, but it was like sending a bow and arrow to deal with a full battalion of warriors.

Sure enough, the gash pulsed, glowing red. A black horse galloped through, hooves churning through air but still gaining purchase. Its mane was long, lush, and extended partway down its thick chest. Not a horse, he realized, with a sinking feeling. A Kelpie. Shape-shifting water spirits, they inhabited the lochs and pools of Scotland. They could take human form, but never shed their hooves. While human, they mesmerized children and young women, raping, killing, and then eating them before turning back into horses.

"Tavin." Sorcha's voice was low, urgent.

"Aye. I'm still in the game." He wrenched his attention back to ensuring the integrity of their casting.

The first Kelpie was followed by a second with Rhea riding it. Arlen screamed in outrage and changed up his spell, but it was too little and far too late. Rhea swooped in, grabbed Kat, and plopped her on the riderless black horse. As quickly as they'd arrived, they galloped through the gash, which zippered shut behind them as if it had never existed.

Kat had struggled, tried to throw herself off the horse, but to no avail.

Anguish poured from Arlen as he roared his torment. He dragged on clothes, boots, a long cape, and snatched up gemstones to augment his power. Once he'd buckled a longsword in place, magic bubbled around him, and he was gone.

Tavin let the threads of everyone's magic unravel. "Sheathe your power for now," he ordered.

"But we have to hunt for them," Sean protested.

"Different spell," Sorcha said. She was panting with effort, her forehead damp from sweat.

A low moan rose from Liliana. She stuffed a fist into her mouth to get herself under control.

"We'll get her back," Sean said.

"Aye, we'll get them both back." Tavin barely recognized the harsh words falling from his mouth as belonging to him.

"Kelpies." Sorcha spat the word. "They're Hell-spawned."

"Nay. They're fell creatures from the lochs," Sean corrected her.

"It's what they want you to think." Sorcha pushed hair out of her face. "When they vanish into the water, they return to Hell and have a good laugh with Satan and his princes over their latest victims. Satan adores them. They're kind of like his pets."

Gloria clapped her hands together smartly. "We need a plan, people. Arlen was wise to follow immediately. We should do the same."

"Aye, but where?" Tavin asked. The universe was a big place. They could spend years searching and never locate Arlen or Katerina.

"Let's catalog what we know," Gloria said. "Rhea wants Kat to perpetuate the Roskelly line. Means she won't kill her. At least not right away." She pressed her lips together. "Arlen is not only expendable, but a liability. He's why we need to hurry. Rhea and her associates will focus on ridding themselves of him as soon as they can."

"Never thought I'd say this," Sorcha muttered through clenched teeth, "but I need to return to Hell. I was always very good at skulking about unseen. I bet this attack will be a prime topic of conversation."

Tavin opened his mouth to tell her it was a terrible idea, but he had no rights where she was concerned. They were magical partners, nothing more, nothing less. Besides, it was a decent idea, altruistic as hell, and the fastest way for them to glean needed information.

"Would Yanna help?" Gloria asked.

"Ha!" Sorcha spat grim laughter. "If I happened to catch her on a good day, she might—emphasis on might —not turn me in to the demon patrol."

"How will you get in?" Tavin asked.

She turned the full force of a very determined look on him. "We just found an entry point. Or did you forget?"

He hadn't, but the tunnel running with molten metal on the far side of the liminal boundary had been so unsettling, he hadn't considered it.

"I can enter that way and leave by the same path I took last time," Sorcha continued.

"Which was?" Gloria crooked two fingers in the air.

"The gates open to a particular combination of demonspeak and a light spell."

"What makes you think they didn't change the combination after you escaped?" Gloria asked.

"They may have. If they did, I'll figure something else out."

"I don't like it. It's too dangerous," Sean said.

Sorcha shrugged. "Too bad. Not your choice. I don't answer to you, Druid."

"I say we search the nearer borderworlds first," Gloria spoke up. "We can always take you up on your offer if we come up empty-handed."

"By then Arlen will be either locked in a cell suffering unimaginable torture, or he'll be dead. And Rhea will have secured Kat somewhere we'll never find her," Sorcha argued.

"We're so few." Dark hair streamed down Liliana's back, swishing around her as she twisted to face Sorcha.

"True enough." Sorcha lifted her hands and hastily braided her hair, tucking the ends beneath her clothing. "I'm used to working alone. Nothing about that has changed. And I'm leaving. I'd appreciate being able to take a blade with me." She glanced at Tavin.

"Of course." He squared his shoulders. "But here's the deal, lass. Ye get the blade, and me as well."

A horrified look rippled over her features, turning

them harsh and forbidding. "No! Risking myself is one thing. I'll not put your life in jeopardy."

"Not your choice."

She swallowed hard. "Nothing like having my own words stuffed back down my throat."

The raven winged across to Sorcha and perched on her shoulder, cawing loudly.

"See. Your bird agrees with me," Tavin said smoothly.

"If you see Mother," Gloria's words were soft, "tell her there's a place for her back on Earth if she wants it. Not to practice Black Magic, but as a White Witch."

"She must have been a better mother to you than me," Sorcha muttered. Turning to Tavin, she asked, "Ready?"

"Nay, but it's never stopped me before. First stop is the Renault. We'll find likely blades and then teleport back to John O'Groats."

Her familiar squawked again and vanished in a flash of light.

"Good hunting," Sean said. "Bring us back a solid lead, goddammit. 'Tis self-serving as fuck of me, but I don't fancy taking Arlen's place."

"We'll launch our own search," Liliana said. "If we find anything, we'll try to reach you."

Sorcha shook her head. "Don't. Any magic hunting

us might give us away. We'll return—assuming we can —hopefully with news."

She latched a hand beneath Tavin's arm. Magic, harsh and primitive, snatched him up and dropped him two meters from his car. He tugged the hatch up and handed her the sword she'd used earlier.

"Sorry," Sorcha said, buckling the weapon's waist belt into place. "Didn't mean to be so rough. I have to do this. You don't. Plus, it's far simpler for me to sneak around in Hell alone. My magic blends in, more or less. Yours will stick out like a sore thumb."

"Are ye certain of that?"

She cast a startled glance his way. A jolt of what could only be dark magic followed. It burned where it bored into him, but the pain vanished immediately. "What was that?" he demanded.

"You asked a question. I got us an answer." She furrowed her forehead into thoughtful lines. "Your magic is far from pure Druid, but I couldn't sort out the pieces with such a quick scan. Probably why I knew right off your falcon wasn't only a bird, though."

"We can determine what I am later." He hefted a blade before latching its belt into place. This one rode low on his hips, which made it an easier draw.

"But I'm telling you to remain here."

He closed the back of the car and grabbed one of her hands, weaving his magic with hers. Colors rose around them, gleaming with possibilities. "This," he said, "is why I'm coming with you. We're strong together, lass. Strong enough to defeat most any enemy. 'Tis why the goddess made certain we found one another."

"But I couldn't stand it if anything happened to you," she blurted.

Her words jolted him. She did care. He was certain of it. He wrapped his other arm around her, holding her close. "What if I feel the same way? Let's be gone, shall we?"

She didn't answer with words, but the colors around them formed a spinning vortex. They dove through it. Next stop would be the liminal boundary in John O'Groats.

After that, things would get interesting. He considered entering the passage to Hell in bird form but discarded it as impractical. For one thing, his magic wasn't nearly as strong. For another, he'd have to leave the blade behind.

"Good call." Her words in his mind told him she'd helped herself to his thoughts. *"Not that I don't love your falcon, but it has no place in this undertaking."*

Tavin wasn't so certain of that, but he was sure of something else. He loved Sorcha. She was courageous and gutsy and intelligent. It was more than magic. More than sex. More than her undeniable beauty.

Once they were done with Hell, assuming they came through unscathed, he'd tell her. Bare his soul, and hope she'd take a chance on him.

Before, his arguments held a philosophical bent. What he had to say next would be personal, deeply so.

CHAPTER 13

Sorcha had been nonplussed when Tavin announced he was going with her. She hadn't anticipated it, and it put her in an untenable spot. She wanted him by her side, but she also wanted him safe. The two didn't match up.

But here they were.

He can take care of himself. She turned her attention to the task ahead. If anyone had suggested she'd volunteer to head back into Hell, she'd have told them they'd lost their mind.

It's the only way.

Maybe not the only one, she corrected herself, *but surely the quickest approach.*

They came out in a deeply shadowed alcove not far from the liminal boundary. She'd picked this spot because it partially hid them from view, and she didn't want to waste any magic she didn't have to on things like invisibility spells.

Once the teleport magic quit vibrating around them, Tavin gripped her upper arm. "Talk to me, lass."

She nodded brusquely. "We enter through the tunnel. I'll extend my platform so you have something to walk on."

"I can build my own. Couldn't have done it as a bird, but it will be easy enough when I have access to my full power. Probably better that way. We can separate our presences behind individual warding."

She frowned, considering it. "All right. Might work since I wasn't planning to ward myself."

His hand tightened to the point of pain. "What do ye mean, not ward yourself? What? Are ye planning to waltz in there and offer yourself up like a plucked goose ripe for the table?" He'd switched to Gaelic, which was a clue how upset he was.

Sorcha leveled her gaze at him. "You're hurting me."

"Sorry." He loosened his hold but didn't let go.

"I know where the demons are. There are only three of them. I can take them out easily, but not if I'm wasting magic on a ward. Meanwhile, it will provide a diversion, and you'll waltz through. I'll meet you on the far side of the guards' station."

"I'm not in the habit of scuttling to safety while someone else fights my battles."

She wrenched out of his grasp and planted herself squarely in front of him. "This is my plan. My mission. You said you were coming, but I'll be damned if I'll fight you every step of the way. I know Hell. You don't." Sorcha glared at him, determined to win the upper hand. She hadn't been kidding when she said she couldn't argue with him at every turn.

If she had to, this project was doomed from the gate.

Tavin nodded tersely. "All right. But if ye run into problems, I'll not stand on the sidelines and let you be captured—or killed."

She raised a brow. "Captured. Satan will want to make an example of me. Suffering is kind of his gig, and the dead don't suffer. Not much, anyway. Besides, it's fucking hard to kill me between the demon and witch blood."

She didn't want to waste any more time, so she started for the liminal boundary with Tavin right behind her. The same malevolence that had tipped her off to its existence hadn't abated. If anything, the stench of rot and brimstone was stronger to her demon-enhanced senses.

Humans were damned lucky to be immune to smelling shit like this.

They ducked inside, and she crafted a small float to keep her above the molten metal. This time it smelled more like bronze than copper, but at least it was a clean smell. Not that it did much to counter Hell's reek, but she welcomed any assistance.

Next to her, Tavin created his own platform. He worked fast. Maybe because he was scared, but more likely because he was still furious with her. Men didn't like ballsy women, and she'd jerked the reins out of his hand.

Couldn't be helped.

Her sense of his presence vanished. *"Perfect. Nice work."*

He grunted something unintelligible in telepathy, but it reinforced her theory he was less than pleased with her.

Sorcha started through the tunnel. Her familiar's magic pulsed brightly within her, and she blessed its unwavering presence. She started to search for Tavin but chided herself for splitting her attention. It wasn't a good idea. Plus, if she sent magic in any direction, it was like waving a flag in front of a bull.

The passage stretched before her. She passed the spot where she'd hidden last time as she eavesdropped on the demons. Sorcha stopped long enough to listen, but the sound of voices was absent. Did it mean they weren't there? Or only that they weren't in a chatty mood. Demons didn't sleep much. Nor did they read. It made chores like guard duty onerous.

She slowed down after she went around the ninety-degree bend in the passage and readied destructive power. Assuming there was more than a single guard, the first one would go down easy, but once he fell on his face, it would alert whoever else was there.

She wouldn't even try to kill them. Talk about a power drain. But she could immobilize them for several hours. If she was careful, they'd never know what had hit them once they woke. Sorcha aimed for caution. Last thing she needed were a couple of gossipy demons running to Satan with tales they'd seen her.

Something like that could make escaping Hell much harder since the Dark Lord would turn his domain inside out hunting her. If he hadn't bothered to change the gate passcode, he'd remedy that little oversight now.

She balanced power between her hands, watching it arc back and forth. The closer she got to where the guards had been, the surer she was there weren't any. She wasn't warded, and magic flaring around her would have alerted them. Running wide open, she punched forward.

Two demons lay on their backs, obviously unconscious.

What the fucking hell had happened? No one took on demons unless they had to. Never one to kick a gift horse in the teeth, she raced across the clearing. The molten metal was gone. It only extended from the guards' post to the liminal boundary. Made things easier, and she withdrew the magic powering her float.

As he'd promised, Tavin was waiting on the other side. *"Hurry,"* he urged. *"We're doing well so far."*

Understanding walloped her between the eyes. *"You flattened them."*

"Who else?" He sounded insufferably smug.

"It wasn't the plan—" she began, but ended with, *"Never mind."*

"Stealth and magic go a long way."

"Not the point. We had a plan."

"Nay, ye had a plan. I tried something afore ye arrived. It worked. Now can we get moving?"

Sorcha recognized wisdom when she heard it. She reeled in her temper. Never her longest suit, it conceded ground slowly.

"The tunnel branches just ahead," Tavin went on.

"We'll want the one heading down." Derision lined her words. Guilt followed on its heels. Tavin was just being Tavin. She should value him, not pick every little thing to pieces.

"They both do," he pointed out in a neutral tone.

She hurried ahead to look for herself. Sure enough,

two downward canting trails came into view. She walked a little way along each, sniffing. One was far better used than the other. Had to be the right way.

Tavin joined her. *"Aren't you going to ward yourself?"*

"I hadn't forgotten." She dragged magic around her to mask the witchy parts. The demon segment would blend right in.

"How far?"

"Not very. Look, Tavin. No heroics. Stay behind me. As you pointed out, I know where I'm going, and we'll be shadowing Satan and his princes in hopes we'll hear something."

"I'll be good. Promise." Understated humor ran beneath his words.

"We can't talk from here on in. No telepathy. Nothing."

"I understand."

Sorcha could have hugged him. Instead, she moved forward at a brisk pace. Her favorite hiding spot had been in a small system of interlocking byways that paralleled Hell's main streets. She'd tried to imagine who would have had the balls to build them and finally decided Satan himself was the only logical choice. He ruled with an iron hand and a zero tolerance policy for anything that smacked of disloyalty.

Spying stations were how he kept an eye on his subjects.

Except he'd grown lazy and rarely used them anymore. She'd never run into him on her forays to gather information. Hell, its totality, weighed on her soul. She'd hated it here. The only bright spot had been her endless plotting to find a way out.

And now I'm back.

She swallowed hard. This wasn't a place to think too long or too hard about anything. If she did, fear would creep in. Before, she'd been one of many dissatisfied conscripts filling Hell's halls. No one paid her much heed. Her escape changed all that. If anyone spotted her, she'd become an example of what happened to anyone who had the temerity to thwart Satan.

Only if I get caught. Her mind voice was thin and shaky. Sorcha gave herself a sharp mental slap. She'd never been apprehended before. No reason for today to be any different.

She couldn't feel Tavin but assumed he was still right behind her. If anything bad had happened, it would have created a commotion. Years had passed, but she still knew the way, and she guided them first into Hell proper and then up a flight of crumbling stairs to a boardwalk laid between brimstone posts.

They were close now. Satan's wickedness

surrounded her, making her skin prickle and her blood run cold. She'd adapted to always being afraid when she lived here, but she'd lost her competitive edge.

No reason she couldn't tap into it again.

Sorcha closed her heart and soul to everything but getting into position to spy on Satan. Voices reached her. Demonspeak interspersed with diabolical laughter. She edged near enough to see Satan's favorite chamber. Perpetual fires burned at both ends of the oblong space and raced up and down the walls. Like all of Hell, the floor was dirt. What a difference from Sean's castle. No art objects here. No finely crafted rugs. Barely any furniture. Satan sat in the only chair in the room, a battered wooden affair that looked as if it had come from a junkyard. Everyone else stood.

Something had obviously happened, and Satan was pleased. He rarely laughed that long or hard about anything. Sorcha moved a little closer. Not nearly as close as she used to, but near enough.

"Brilliant," Satan crowed.

"It was inspired, sir," someone agreed.

"When the Kelpies return, make certain to reward them," Satan went on.

Sorcha wanted to fist pump the air. She'd guessed right, but then all Kelpies lived in Hell. When they weren't out doing Satan's bidding. The thought stopped her dead. Was Rhea in cahoots with Satan? It was a possibility since she'd been gifted two Kelpies to help her.

"I'll do that, sir. They might be back now."

Come on, Sorcha urged silently. *Back from where?*

"Probably not," Satan said smoothly. "I told that pesky witch to pick a distant borderworld. I'm sick of her bothering me, and this way, her captives will stay put."

"Erm, I'm fairly certain she didn't heed your instructions, master," another voice cut in.

"Why not?" Satan thundered.

Sorcha rolled her eyes. His good moods never lasted long.

"Because I heard from Xera that the Kelpies are already back."

Satan's roar of displeasure was followed by hordes of minions running toward him, all of them inquiring how they could help. Sorcha bit back a smile. At least one thing about Hell hadn't changed one whit. It was still chockful of ass-kissers.

"Bring a Kelpie here. Now," Satan bellowed.

It must have been close because one galloped into Satan's meeting room a few moments later.

"What are you planning on doing?" Satan sneered. "Neighing in my face?"

Amid the noise of tearing skin and breaking bones, the black horse shifted to human. She'd never seen the transformation before. Hooves were just plain perverse in place of feet. How did Kelpies ever lure women looking like that?

"Apologies, sir." The Kelpie bowed low. Long black hair fell to his knees, shielding most of his nakedness. He straightened but kept his dark eyes downcast.

"Where did you leave the witch and her captives?"

"Gamma Four, sir."

"Fuck all of you! Why does no one follow my instructions?" Satan was still screaming with enough decibels Sorcha covered her ears.

The Kelpie stood taller. "With all due respect, sir, all you told me was—"

"Get out. Now!"

"As you wish." The Kelpie turned and trotted from the room, its hooves making a clopping sound against the dirt.

Sorcha slithered backward, intent on leaving. The passageway wasn't tall enough to stand, so she remained on her belly. They had what they needed. Now all they had to do was see if Hell's gates would still yield to her. Skidding and sliding, she hurried away from Satan, who was still ranting at the top of his lungs. His tempers were legendary for a reason, and she didn't need to hear any more.

She put some distance between them and Satan's group of lackeys, hopefully enough. If anyone had noticed her or Tavin, they'd have come after them by now. After a few twists and turns she emerged into a hallway. Standing was a luxury after being bent into a pretzel for so long.

Sorcha took a chance. Telepathy was the smallest magic she knew, the least likely to be detected. *"Tavin?"*

"Aye?"

She didn't need to say anything else. He was still next to her. She hurried to where the exit used to be and found a blank wall of crooked gray stones. What the fuck had happened? Sorcha stood and stared at the wall for long moments.

"What?" Tavin breathed the word into her mind.

She started for the stones, intent on seeing if they were illusion but changed her mind at the last moment. It would be very like Satan to set a trap, create something that looked different to everyone who gazed at it. The gates may well lie behind the wall, but she'd be worse than a fool to test it. She bet her last farthing the thing was booby trapped.

Apparently, her impromptu exit from Hell hadn't escaped notice. Satan might be a lazy bastard, but he didn't appreciate being duped.

Yeah. You can dish it out, but you can't take it.

Two possibilities remained. They could retreat the way they'd come in. It was probably smartest, but not especially quick. Or they could teleport. Maybe. An idea blasted into her mind. Best of both worlds.

"Change of plans," she said and scurried toward the tunnel leading to John O'Groats.

They were perhaps halfway there when Tavin's terse, *"Hold up,"* stopped her. She backtracked until she saw what had alerted him. A side channel that looked a whole lot like the one they'd traversed earlier. Made sense. According to Sean's map, many portals crisscrossed Scotland.

She didn't believe in coincidences. Tavin had unearthed this trail for a reason. Question was what? It could be a good thing for them, or another of Satan's infernal tricks. Quite the jokester, Satan.

She ducked beneath the low lintel. After twenty meters, she risked a small shot of seeking magic. The corridor wound upward and appeared promising. Regardless, she stopped to caucus with Tavin.

"I think this goes," she said, keeping her voice low. Telepathy was far less of a risk with tons of stone around them than within Satan's halls, but no one could hear her spoken voice, either.

"What happened to the main gate?"

"No idea," she whispered back. "Either moved or gone or hidden behind illusion. Felt sketchy."

"This should take us out of here. I checked as best I could."

"The safest course is to retrace our steps."

"Aye," he replied. "But this is faster, and now that we know where Arlen and Kat are..."

He didn't have to say any more.

She checked her warding and bolted up the increasingly steep incline. If the other passage was guarded, like as not this one would be too, but she'd deal with whatever stood in their way. Once they located the demon guards, they'd be almost back on Earth.

Voices reached her. As she'd expected, this contingent of sentries were very much alive. From the sound of it, they were engaged in a game of either cards or dice. She listened long enough to decide only two demons guarded this portal. The next part would have to happen fast. Before, she'd started unwarded, so nothing changed in the warp or weft of power to alert the guards.

Not that it mattered. Tavin had taken care of them. She wanted to push him aside, tell him it was her turn for a spot of fun, but she had no idea where he was.

Sorcha crept closer to the voices. One more bend in the passageway and she'd be able to see them. Because she had to know what she faced, she risked moving nearer still. Her eyes widened. Not two demons, but four. The other two were lashed to boulders with lengths of iron chain.

What the fucking hell?

Had Satan authorized this punishment? Or were these rogue demons who'd taken matters into their own hands—or claws. It happened. Someone didn't care for one of Satan's edicts, so they meted out punishment in His stead.

Doesn't matter. The other two won't be a problem.

She let power build between her hands. One of the demons slapped the dice cup down in the dirt and whipped his head around. "Who's that?" he demanded.

"Bugger off, El," the other demon said. "You're having girl dreams."

"I felt something," El insisted.

Sorcha tossed her warding aside and ran forward, magic blazing from her outstretched hands. Recognition flickered in El's red-rimmed eyes, but her spell would take care of that.

Dark, jagged lightning flared from El and his buddy, but she sidestepped it neatly. These were minor demons with minimal power at best. She blasted first one and then the other, leaping nimbly over their puny blows.

Both demons fell onto their sides. Tavin flashed into view next to her. No reason for him to remain warded, either. "What do ye want to do about those two?" He jerked a thumb at the bound demons.

"Free us," one demanded.

"Aye," the other chimed in. "We'll keep your dirty little secret. We'll be far too busy giving our friends a taste of their own medicine."

"No friends in Hell," Sorcha taunted.

"Say." One narrowed his beady red eyes. "You look familiar. Aren't you—?"

Tavin blasted him with magic before he finished his sentence.

Sorcha took out the other one. They wouldn't remember jack when they woke up. As an added bonus, she broke their chains. At least it would be a fair fight this time—if they woke first.

"Come on." Tavin was on the far side of the guards' post.

She ran lightly after him. This passage didn't feature a molten floor, so they made good time. The unused saber rattled against her leg. It had been inconvenient crawling around in her vantage point above Satan's chamber, making sure the length of steel didn't clang against anything and give them away. Regardless, carting it along provided a psychological boost. Nothing like knowing you had the perfect weapon if your magic wasn't enough.

"Focus on the exit actually being there, lass," Tavin instructed.

She understood. No blood trail to lead them out of

Wonderland this time around. He fed magic ahead of them, lighting the way. She threaded hers in with it, visualizing freedom. Maybe it was their combined skills, but one moment they were in the passageway, the next it vanished, and the clean, sweet air of Earth hit her square in the face.

Reaching the far side of the liminal border was a relief even though she'd known they were safe once they dispatched the guards. She sucked air into her lungs and laughed. It was pretty bad when the polluted air of modern times was a welcome change from where she'd been.

"We did it!" She threw her arms around Tavin. Her saber clattered against his.

"We did half of it," he corrected her. Tavin hugged her back for an instant, but then let her go. Magic built as he crafted a teleport casting.

"Are we headed for Gamma Four?" she asked, intuiting his intent.

"Aye, but first we're stopping at Sean's. If anyone's there, we'll tell them where Arlen is. We'll also raise the alarm with every Druid within telepathy range."

"And then we're going to Gamma Four," she pressed, eager for a showdown with Rhea. The old bitch had dogged her forever, and she was done running.

"Aye, darling. Ye'll get your war."

"Who said I wanted a war?"

"Ye dinna have to say aught. I understand you. Sharing power as intimately as we do has...side benefits."

"Good." She was smiling when his teleport spell spirited them back to Inverness.

Tavin's brief sojourn in hell gave him a whole new appreciation for Sorcha. He'd known she was resilient, determined, gutsy, but now he knew why. The place drained hope and everything associated with it. Negativity was stenciled into every aspect of the netherworld from its drab, depressing surroundings to its inhabitants to the constant fires burning everywhere. No daylight. No sunshine. No fresh air.

The place made his skin crawl, yet she'd survived there long enough to grow up. Survived by her wits since neither father nor mother had anything to do with her. Goddess's tits. Had she been the only child in Hell's galleries? It seemed likely. He hadn't seen any evidence of anyone young. Nothing he'd ever associated with children lay scattered about. It wasn't as if demons needed to reproduce. They lived virtually forever unless someone went to a lot of trouble to kill them.

Sean's great room formed around him and Sorcha. His spell wasn't done shimmering to nothingness when he employed magic of another sort to see if anyone was here.

Sean ran into the room. "What'd you find?"

"Yes. Tell us." Gloria and Liliana said nearly in unison from behind him.

"Gamma Four," Sorcha said.

Sean whistled. "Something went right. Nice work, you two."

"At least it's close," Gloria muttered. "Won't take much magic to get there."

"Any idea who's on G4 with Arlen and Kat?" Morgan asked from the doorway. She wore her usual disheveled look, part academician, part dreamer.

"The Kelpies were back in Hell," Tavin replied. "It's how we found out where they'd taken them—just before Satan cussed them out. Apparently, he's heartily sick of Rhea and wanted her much farther away."

"To avoid her bouncing in and out of Hell asking for more favors, no doubt." Gloria scrunched her face into a sour expression. "We have to assume Rhea isn't by herself on the borderworld. Her magic is strong, but no match for Kat and Arlen 24/7."

"She probably conscripted a few more dead Roskellys," Liliana said followed by, "Does it matter? We need to get going. Before Kat or Arlen engages in some stupid, ill-thought-out heroics and ends up dead."

"Arlen would never do anything like that," Sean said stiffly.

"He went after Kat, didn't he?" Gloria asked, barely avoiding an I-told-you-so tone.

"Aye, but he dinna place anyone else in danger by doing so, only himself," Sean argued in Gaelic.

Tavin sensed Sorcha's impatience. He wanted to get moving as well. The sooner they returned the Arch Druid to his rightful spot, the sooner he could have a heart to heart with Sorcha. Lay all his cards face up on the table and tell her how much he loved her.

Before, he'd walked around the topic. No more.

Sean held up both hands. "Absent Arlen, I'm Arch Druid. This is how we will proceed. I shall summon as many Druids as answer my call. Since G4 is close, we'll teleport in a few small groups, so we all arrive at close to the same time. We will bring blades."

He stood tall. "I'm heartily sick of Rhea Roskelly. She will not leave G4, no matter what it costs us. We will behead and burn her and every other Black Roskelly Witch we find."

Sean wasn't asking for discussion or agreement. He raised his mind voice and uttered the Druids' war cry.

Eerie, haunting, it rolled through Tavin's mind and bounced off the walls of Sean's great room.

Sorcha edged closer to Tavin and placed her mouth near his ear. "We don't have to wait for them to get organized. We could go on ahead, scout things out."

His mouth formed a crooked grin. "Rather like an away team?"

"More like a forward guard. I've watched TV and old movies too."

Tavin gripped her hand. It made sense. He waited until Sean was done rustling up his troops to say, "Sorcha and I will meet you there."

"We should all go together," Sean replied. "Too dangerous."

"Christ, mate. We just braved Hell. Gamma Four will look like a paradise by comparison."

"Ever been there?" Sean furled both brows.

"Nay, but after Hell, it canna be that bad."

"Please." Sorcha tossed a single word into the mix.

It was so unlike her, Tavin stared. Was she really groveling? Or simply playing Sean to get him to acquiesce?

"We'll do this," Gloria announced. "I'll accompany Tavin and Sorcha. The rest of you come as soon as you can."

Tavin waited for Sean to tell his mother-in-law no. It never happened. He might be Arch Druid for now, but it didn't mean he wanted to get into a spat with Gloria. Between her magic and kickass attitude, she'd probably have handed him his balls on a platter, and Sean knew it.

Gloria sidled to him and Sorcha. "Chop, chop, children. I'm as anxious to kick sand in Rhea's face as you are. Remember, I actually knew her. Broke bread with her. Had to put up with her horrible lectures about what a loser I was for walking away from Black Witchcraft."

"Were there a lot of them?" Sorcha asked.

"You have no idea. Now let's go." Gloria summoned magic.

As it built around her, Tavin added to it. Sorcha blended her particular elements into the weave last of all. The walls of Sean's castle fell away, replaced by the familiar dark void that lay between worlds. Originally, the borderworlds had long, convoluted Celtic names. Sometime after the birth of the twentieth century, a Druid with an astrological bent had renamed them using the Greek alphabet and numbers. Tavin never understood why the worlds nearest Earth weren't labeled Alpha X, but he'd never run into the Druid in question to ask about it.

Regardless, the current labeling system was a vast improvement.

"*Ward yourselves,*" he cautioned.

"Do you think I need a reminder?" Gloria's reply was caustic even in telepathy. Tavin didn't blame Sean for not challenging her.

Borderworlds came in as many iterations as there were worlds. Some were as strange as the one hosting jagged peaks and orange trees. Others looked a whole lot like Earth. Not much point in second-guessing this one. He'd find out soon enough. It had to have a breathable atmosphere, though, or Rhea wouldn't have chosen it. Beyond that, anything was possible.

"Be prepared for Hell's denizens," Gloria said.

"Unless G4 has turned into a demon-specific borderworld, how would they leave Hell in the first place?" Sorcha retorted. *"Satan isn't particularly generous with His resources."*

"We've dealt with a demon who nearly broke through Sean's warding and into the castle. Beyond that, Sean and Liliana saw Rhea and a few other Roskellys astride dragons back in the 1700s."

"What in the nine Hells did the old bitch do to ingratiate herself with Satan? Fuck him while swinging from a chandelier?" Sorcha's smirk was obvious.

"It's not wise to underestimate her," Gloria answered. *"She and Satan are old chums. It's how Mother ended up mesmerized by demonkind and ensorcelled in Hell."*

"Pay attention. We're nearly there," Tavin warned.

He shored up his warding and made certain it circled the women as well. Black shaded to gray as the emptiness between worlds ceded to a jungle overgrown with tangles of vines hanging from trees. Garbed for a Scottish winter, Tavin began to sweat immediately in the heat and humidity.

Gloria rolled her eyes. "The old biddy always favored the tropics. Makes sense she'd choose a world like this. Do not use magic. Not for telepathy or anything else. I don't want to offer anything for her to latch onto."

"What do you want to bet she hasn't even posted a guard?" Sorcha raised one blonde brow.

"Like I said before. It's not wise to underestimate her. She's well over a thousand years old, and she—"

"But she's dead, right?" Tavin cut in.

"Yeah, but it hasn't slowed her down much."

Something that sounded a lot like a flock of monkeys chittered overhead. Tavin glanced up but couldn't see through the thick canopy blocking out the sky. "Watch out for snakes," he cautioned.

"How do we choose which way to go absent magic?" Sorcha asked Gloria.

The other witch sent a pointed glance her way and tugged a dirk with a nasty-looking six-inch blade from a sheath hanging off her belt. She jabbed her index finger and turned it over to let blood drip. Tavin expected it to fall straight down, but a crimson globule floated parallel to the ground before moving forward a few meters.

Gloria snatched up the wandering blood and licked her finger. The wound sealed immediately, and the bubble of blood vanished. She tucked her dirk back inside its leather covering.

"Looked like magic to me," Sorcha mumbled.

"Blood-fueled seeking spell." Tavin was impressed. "'Tis the type of thing we're taught when we first come into our magic and forget almost immediately because it's not very powerful. The flip side of not very powerful is it's also not accompanied by the flare of energy announcing your presence."

"Exactly." Gloria had started in the direction indicated by her blood. "Only reason it had any chance of working at all was because Rhea and I are related."

Sorcha yanked her foot free of something in the lush undergrowth and stalked after Gloria. "Damn it."

Heat was an oppressive constant companion as they chopped their way through jungle that made navigating the Amazon rainforest look like child's play. He swiped the back of his hand across his forehead for the millionth time, but sweat dripped into his eyes anyway, making them sting.

Not being able to see more than a few meters ahead was annoying. Everything looked the same except for the beaten track behind them where they'd forced their way through. Vines. Trees. Brush. After half an hour, he said. "Hold up. I have a better idea."

Gloria and Sorcha turned to face him. "I already thought of loosing my familiar," Gloria said, "except Rhea would recognize it. Witchy familiars have a particular magical feel to them."

"Aye, but my falcon doesn't have that liability." He hesitated for a beat. "Shifting will create a blast of magic, but it will be short-lived. It's possible the two of you could ward me while I shift."

"Let's do it." Sorcha blotted sweat from her face with her vest. "Any desire I ever had to go to the Caribbean vanished five hundred steps back."

A distinctive pair of boulders lay ahead of them. Tavin beat his way through brush until he stood on a circle of bare ground flanked by their bulk. By the time he'd stripped out of his clothes, witch magic pressed in on him from all sides. He didn't tarry but summoned his bird form. Unlike his earliest shifts that had been painful, they happened quickly now.

Beating powerful wings, he rode updrafts until he cleared the forest canopy. While still hot, he no longer felt he was suffocating. He scribed widening circles. They were near the edge of the worst of the jungle. It looked more travelable half a kilometer to the east of where the women were. His falcon's eyes were very sharp, designed to pick out small prey from hundreds of meters in the air, but no matter which direction he flew, he didn't see any evidence of Rhea or her captives.

So long as he was airborne, he flew a grid. Like many borderworlds, this one was on the small side, which made it manageable. Unlike Earth, it was flat, suspended in the void between worlds where it floated much like a ship bobbing on an endless sea.

A quarter of an hour later, he landed between the boulders and shifted to human. He hated to put his thick clothing back on but scrambled into it anyway. As he dressed, he said, "The good news is 'tis easier going a wee bit to our east. The bad news is I couldn't find them."

"Not possible," Gloria said. "If other Roskellys weren't here, my blood spell wouldn't have worked."

"Could it have been reacting to me?" Sorcha asked.

"Sure, but it didn't track toward you."

A deep, rolling boom crashed against something a long way from them. Another followed it, but somewhat closer. The ground quivered beneath Tavin's feet before it bucked and groaned.

"Sean and the others should be here by now," he said.

"We were just talking about that," Sorcha agreed. "It's worrisome."

"We could see one group going astray," Gloria added, "but not everyone."

Tavin shuffled through possibilities. There had to be some reason other than liking hot, sticky weather Rhea had chosen this location. He was certain the Kelpie wouldn't have lied to Satan. There was no reason for it to, plus Hell's overlord probably had ways of sniffing out untruths.

"Have you heard any more monkeys?"

"Nope." Sorcha said. "No animals at all."

Tavin leveled his gaze at Gloria. "We need magic to solve this, plus I have a feeling—" His words were cut off by the same crashing noise, except far nearer this time. He braced himself in time to ride out the earthquake that followed.

"I believe the monkeys were illusion, meant to reinforce whatever other deceptions are in play here," Tavin said. "Rhea's borrowed the equivalent of a "don't look here" spell and swathed the borderworld in it. Given the results of your tracking spell, she seeded the place with her blood. Regardless, there's nothing here of interest. No reason to stay."

"So where are they?" Sorcha demanded.

"They'd have to be underground," Gloria said.

"Which suggests entrances somewhere, but we'll never find them without magic," Sorcha mumbled.

The dirt shuddered beneath their feet; Tavin's skin

crawled with premonitions of evil on the loose hunting them. "We can't remain here," he said and herded them back into the jungle.

The next detonation nearly deafened him. It started beneath his feet but ended with the boulders crashing into each other as the dirt beneath them fell away. The air filled with dust and grit, whipped by a strange wind that blew up out of nowhere. In defiance of the principles of physics, the wind was cold.

"She must know we're here," Sorcha said.

"Nay," Tavin replied. "She knows someone is here and is applying countermeasures since her tropical jungle cover didn't chase us off."

"Us or some of the Druids who were heading this way." Sorcha shook herself from head to toe. "Sorry, sister, but I'm using my power. I'll be quick about it—and I'll lead with my demon side—but we need information before this whole borderworld implodes around us."

"Not that you need my permission but go ahead. I was about to do the same, absent demon magic," Gloria muttered.

Tavin staggered back a few meters and looked at the place they'd stood beneath the boulders. Rather than standing upright, they'd fallen against one another forming a granite vee. Beneath it, a yawning chasm still spit dirt and pebbles. It might be a path to whatever lay beneath the borderworld's surface, but it also wasn't very stable.

He hustled back to the women. Sorcha was reeling in her magic. Fury twisted her beauty into a grim mask. "This whole thing is a false front. Gamma Four is a short jump over."

"I don't understand how we were tricked," Tavin said.

"Easily," Gloria growled. "Think about how you delineate a location when you teleport."

"It's a lock-and-key match. So Rhea perverted the combination and linked it here?"

"Not that difficult to do." Gloria shrugged. "Kind of a lot of trouble, but she's devious enough to not want to be disturbed. Not without a whole lot of warning."

"She booby trapped this place." Sorcha snarled low in her throat. "Fuck her."

"Might explain where the other Druids went," Gloria continued. "This might not be the only 'extra' spot Rhea earmarked to subvert teleport spells."

Magic bubbled around Sorcha, tinged red from her anger. "I don't care if the others show up. I'm done letting that conniving bitch run me around in circles."

"She couldn't have done all this by herself," Gloria cautioned.

"Fine. We'll figure it out as we go." Tavin sided with Sorcha. He'd only known about Rhea's meddling for a week or so, and he was already sick of her.

"Sorcha will control the teleport," Gloria said. "No wards this time. Full power from the moment we emerge."

The spell simmering around Sorcha circled him and Gloria. Before he could take a deep breath, it dropped them on a sunbaked plain. Cracked dirt spread in every direction. Two suns sat directly overhead, suspended in a mud-colored sky. Boulders littered the plain. Mountains rose in the distance, capped with puke-green snow.

A strident cry split the still air just before a black dragon winged into view, clearly heading right toward them. Fire spewed from its mouth, and its front talons were extended, gleaming red in the sunlight.

"Goes against the grain," Tavin cried, "but we have to bring it down."

The full force of Sorcha's magic slammed into him. Gloria dove into their linked power. Tavin spread his arms. Lighting bolts shot from his fingers. Ivory tinged with red, they chased the dragon as it tried to evade them.

"Oberon's balls," he muttered. "Since when did Druid power turn into a heat-seeking missile?"

"Not Druid. Demon. Complaints?" Sorcha was breathing hard.

"None, lass." He altered his aim, loosing a second volley of lightning to chase the dragon. It bugled its contempt and annoyance but didn't fly closer. Another dragon, a red one, popped into view on the horizon, screeching merrily. The first dragon's attention flagged as it glanced over a shoulder at its companion.

Tavin took advantage of the split second and sent a blast of magic straight into its open mouth. It shrieked just before it exploded in a fiery eruption. Scales and bone and wet, pink tissue gushed in every direction. The second dragon wheeled, flying back the way it came. It wasn't bugling anymore.

"Coward!" Sorcha shook a fist at it.

Tavin balanced power between his hands, waiting for the next onslaught. He felt sad about the fallen dragon. They were noble creatures. Once upon a time, they'd chosen to aid those with pure magic. When had they switched sides? He hoped it wasn't all of them.

Gloria turned in a circle, power deployed as she hunted for Arlen and Katerina. Before she was finished, Druid magic filled the air. Tavin blew out a tight breath. Finally. Given all the unknowns, having a spot of assistance would be welcome.

A phalanx of Druids ran through a gateway that formed in the dry, still air of the borderworld. Liliana and Morgan were with Sean, one on each side. Sean looked as if he'd chewed through a box of nails for breakfast. Water dripped from him, forming puddles in the dirt.

"Goddess damn that witch to Hell and beyond," he exclaimed. "We ended up in a frozen ocean inhabited by sea serpents."

"At least it's warm here." Liliana bent to wring water from her skirt.

"None of that matters," Tavin said. "We can compare notes later."

"Arlen and Kat are that way." Gloria pointed. "Same direction the dragon vanished."

"It looks dead to me." Morgan gazed at the still-twitching carcass and winced.

"There were two," Sorcha explained.

"I see. No friends on battle days, eh?" Morgan laughed coldly at her own joke.

"Come on." Sean started across the plain at a lope. Everyone fell in behind him. Portals opened on both sides; more Druids hurried through.

Tavin stopped long enough to scoop up a dragon horn from where it had fallen. Still warm, it pulsed with magic. Maybe it would come in handy. One thing he'd learned from his years bending over a forge was to never throw anything away.

Sorcha materialized by his side. "If we find Arlen and Kat, Sean will want to leave."

"Not what he said back in Inverness," Tavin reminded her.

"Yeah, but this has become so much harder than any of us anticipated, and wise men pick their battles."

He laced his fingers with hers. "If it's a backhanded way of asking if I'm still determined to rid us of Rhea, the answer is yes."

Gratitude flared through their linked hands. "Thank you. I want her gone, but I can't do it alone."

"Ye're coming to trust me, lass," he said in Gaelic.

"Yeah, but how can you tell?"

"I bet ye can count the times ye've asked for help on the fingers of one hand."

Sorcha didn't answer, so he knew he'd guessed right. This might be the first time she'd ever curried assistance from any quarter, and he was grateful she'd chosen him.

It meant the trust between them was a two-way street.

CHAPTER 15

Bugling dragons dragged Sorcha's gaze skyward. She expected to see dragons, but flying between them were Harpies. Three of them. Half bird, half woman, they were soul stealers.

Tavin tightened his hold on her hand. "Watch out for them, lass. If they get close enough, they'll suck out your soul through your mouth."

"I know. They visited Hell often enough. Goddamn it. What kind of influence does Rhea have? I've never known Harpies to do anything but what they wanted. They even told Satan to fuck off."

"Doesna matter. When this is over, they'll return to the Strophades Islands in the Aegean. Until something else crops up that interests them."

"Battle lines," Sean shouted.

Sorcha took a good, hard look and counted fifty-three Druids. A respectable number if all they faced were half a dozen dragons. The addition of three Harpies shifted the equation. The way they got close enough to steal your soul was their breath immobilized you. She'd only seen it happen once, and it hadn't been pretty.

She ran lightly to the front line with Tavin and Gloria. They flanked Sean.

"Wait until they're closer," he instructed. "We'll blow through too much magic striking from fifty meters away."

The dragons held back, though. No doubt, they all knew about their fallen companion. Dragons were old and canny. They'd been part of the original making, their bones part of Earth's beginnings. Sorcha pushed an image of the one they'd killed to a distant place, one where it wouldn't haunt her.

The Harpies winged toward them screeching like a pack of vultures.

"Ward yourselves," Sorcha called, augmenting her voice with magic to make certain everyone heard her. Huge white wings surrounded milk white breasts, and multihued hair that tangled with the feathers. The creatures straight out of legend would have been beautiful if she didn't know how deadly they were.

Laughing and squealing, they divebombed out of

the skies, pulling upward at the last minute. "They're playing with us. Not attacking. Why?" Sorcha yelled.

"To demoralize us, why else?" Gloria yelled back, her gaze glued to the skies.

"'Tis rather like a game of cat and mouse," Tavin muttered, "and I don't fancy being the mouse."

With a final cacophony of screeches, the Harpies flew back toward the dragons. The aerial host parted, and a griffon winged its way toward them with Rhea astride its back.

"Quite a show of power," Sean said.

"We'll find out why very soon," Gloria growled. "Rhea always had a taste for the dramatic. So far, we've had the Greek chorus, but she's the main attraction."

"Only in her own mind." Liliana's words were bitter.

The griffon floated to the dirt a few meters from them. Rhea sprang from its back looking damned sprightly for a corpse. Dark robes swathed her skeletal form, and her black-and-silver hair fell to knee level. She rubbed her hands together.

"Well, well, well. I have all of you now. All my pretties. Ready to finally embrace what you were born for? Especially you." She extended a bony index finger in Sorcha's direction. "You've led me on quite the merry chase. Satan promised you to me, but you left before He could deliver."

"How inconvenient," Sorcha sneered.

"It was, a bit, but I've enjoyed chasing after you."

"Terrorizing me, more like. Thanks to you, I've been on the run forever."

"It can all stop right now." Rhea spread her arms. "Come to me." Compulsion hurtled from her, so strong Sorcha actually took a step forward.

Tavin grabbed her arm. "Hell no, lassie."

She pulled demon power as fast as she could and threw it at Rhea. It bounced off, but at least the inexorable desire to walk forward right into Rhea's outstretched arms abated. A Harpy flew near, hovering above her.

Tavin directed a flow of bright magic right at it. One of its wings began to smolder. It hissed at him but flew a few feet higher.

"What have you done with Arlen and Katerina?" Sean demanded.

Rhea narrowed her aquamarine eyes. "Wouldn't you like to know? The deal is this, *Druid*." The way she said Druid made it sound like an obscenity. "If you leave without additional fanfare, I shall release your pet Arch Druid. He can accompany you wherever you wish."

"I'm not leaving without my daughter." Liliana detached herself from the battle line, squaring off in front of Rhea.

"Oh you're not, are you? You're scarcely in a bargaining position, Liliana. Not after that shit you pulled impersonating Katerina."

"You killed my husband."

Rhea shrugged. "Still beating that tired old drum? I see you found another one. They come cheap. Druids are somewhat of an improvement over humans. But you're a Roskelly Witch." Rhea's voice shrilled. "You bound yourself first to human scum and now to pathetic White Magic. Grow a set, granddaughter. Be who you were born to be. Claim the power that courses through your blood."

Sorcha tensed. Rhea's compulsion spell was back in play. She kept a close eye on Liliana, ready to launch countermeasures if necessary.

Liliana spat in the dirt. "I'd rather die."

Rhea raised a hand. "You said it. Happy to accommodate a traitor."

Sorcha's power was primed and ready. She launched a volley at Rhea's feet, hoping the witch hadn't bothered to ward herself that low. Rhea screamed like a banshee. Her robes caught fire, and she hopped from foot to foot.

Magic flew from her in uncoordinated volleys until she got herself and her burning garment under control. Most of her insidious dark enchantments bounced off warding, but a few moans from behind Sorcha told her some had found targets. More witches poured into the fray. They could have come through a portal or emerged from the earth. It didn't matter. Not all of them were dead, and anger pulsed from their ranks. Somehow, Rhea had managed to amass an army.

The Harpies—all three of them—flew overhead screaming encouragement.

"Charge!" Sean ordered.

Druids ran headlong toward the ragtag witch throng, magic arcing from extended hands. The griffon paced behind Rhea, wings extended, lion's tail swishing back and forth. Rhea barked a command, and the creature wheeled, ready to strike. Sorcha focused the power she shared with Tavin and shot it between the eyes. Its head blew apart, and a piece of the skull hit Rhea in the back.

Fury pumped from the old witch, and she raced forward, clearly intent on retribution. Sorcha yanked her blade free from its scabbard. She'd only get one chance. Rhea was sunk in bloodlust, but she had to get closer.

Out of the corner of her eyes, Sorcha saw Tavin draw his blade as well. He'd been a warrior in another time. She hadn't. That he was backing her meant everything. Sorcha dropped her warding to lure Rhea nearer.

She skinned her lips back from what was left of her

teeth and attacked. Dark power rained from her hands. It burned where it touched Sorcha, but she could take it. Her demon side was tough. She raised her blade. "You want to fight, Rhea? Come on. I'll stand you a good scrap."

"You're a fool, Sorcha. I could have offered you the world. Instead you chose poverty, men pawing at you."

"Freedom has quite the allure."

"No one is as free as a Roskelly witch."

Rhea stood before her, clearly not cowed by the raised length of steel. Why? Behind them, the sounds of battle rang out. Shouts, cries, the sizzle of white magic hitting dark.

Sorcha swung the blade. When it connected with Rhea's neck, it stopped. Black Witchcraft surged up the blade heading straight for her heart, but she was powerless to stop it. Too late, she understood her kinswoman had lured her right into a trap.

"Drop the blade, Sorcha!" Tavin screeched just before he raced behind Rhea and swung his broadsword from the top of her head all the way through her body. It cleaved her in two. The insidious darkness that had already reached Sorcha's hand stopped there.

She shook her arm, trying to get feeling back into her fingers. The blade that would have been her death fell into the dirt, but the blackness didn't leach out of its edge.

Tavin stood over Rhea's twitching remains and barked a few words in Gaelic. Mage fire sprang to his command, and Rhea's body turned into a smoking pyre. A Harpy flew far too near, but it was behind Tavin. He was so intent on feeding magic into his fire, he didn't seem aware of it.

Sorcha reached deep. Power jetted from her hands. The one that had been numb felt as it someone had soaked it in liquid ammonia, but she didn't let up. This time, the Harpy was warded, and Sorcha's magic sloughed off its feathers.

"Tavin. Behind you."

He spun. The Harpy was close. He staggered, but before she could immobilize him with her breath, he tugged the dragon's horn out. It blazed blue-white as he threw it at the Harpy. When the birdwoman, her attention diverted by the shiny object, reached for it, he swung the broadsword one more time. The Harpy's head rolled from her shoulders, still screeching.

Sorcha ran forward and gave the head a good kick. It soared through the air and bounced a few times. The Harpy flew to its head, picked it up, and set it back in place. The wound began to knit together while fury poured from her whirling silvery eyes.

Tavin stared. "What the bloody fuck?"

"They're truly immortal," Sorcha said, breathing hard, "but I bet what you did will be enough of a deterrent they'll leave. They enjoy the game, but not when they're losing."

Sure enough, the Harpy wheeled and flew away from them. The other two joined her, and they vanished in a blast of golden light. The dragons had left as well. Without Rhea as ring mistress, nothing was driving them to remain.

Sorcha turned and gazed at fallen Druids and witches littering the field. Greasy smoke still stained the sky from Rhea's pyre. Gloria and Liliana ran to her. "We still have no idea where Kat and Arlen are," Gloria said. "I checked where I thought they were, but it was a false lead."

"Are you suggesting I should have stood still and let Rhea kill me, so she'd still be around to question?" Sorcha asked.

Gloria wrapped an arm around her shoulders and squeezed hard before letting go. "Not at all. Just stating facts." She twisted her head from side to side, scanning the field. "Aha. I know that one."

"Which one?" Tavin asked, but Gloria had already taken off at a run to where Sean grappled in the dirt with a witch with matted black hair.

"Sean!" Gloria's tone was sharp. "Don't kill her. Not yet anyway."

He glanced her way, and the witch took a swipe at his face, aiming for his eyes.

"Esmeralda," Gloria cooed in dulcet tones. "You don't want to hurt that nice Druid."

"I don't?" the witch sounded confused, and Sorcha understood Gloria was employing some sort of hypnosis. She hurried closer, hoping to pick up the mechanics of Gloria's casting.

Sean rocked back on his heels. "If you can get anything out of her, more power to you. I've interrogated every single witch I've gotten my hands on. None of them told me shit."

"You didn't go about it the right way," Gloria said and turned her attention back to Esmeralda, hunkering next to her.

The witch stared at her through unfocused eyes. "Gloria."

"Yes, dear. It's me. Rhea's gone. Really gone."

Esmeralda's blue eyes filled with tears. "So I can finally be dead? Truly dead? No more being dragged from my crypt?"

Gloria nodded. "Yes. Truly dead. Where are the captive Druid and his Roskelly witch mate?"

Esmeralda struggled to a sit, rheumy eyes darting from side to side until they fastened on the smoky pyre. She pointed with a bony finger. "Rhea?"

Gloria nodded. "Like I said, truly gone. Not something I'd lie about."

"The Druid and his mate are locked behind an enchantment."

"I assumed as much. Where?" Gloria persisted.

Esmeralda drew in the dirt with a broken fingernail. "A lake lies about a kilometer from here. To the northeast. Their prison is on its far side."

"How are they bound?"

"Black Witchcraft." Esmeralda cackled. "How else?" Her voice developed a singsongy aspect. "One strand widdershins one strand not. Coiled at midnight with oil of rattlesnake and a bit of spider's blood."

Gloria smiled resolutely. "I know that binding. And its antidote." She sat back. "Thank you. You're free to go to your eternal rest, Esmeralda Roskelly."

The space where the witch had lain developed black edges. Smoke rose, followed by black flame. When it cleared, Esmeralda was gone.

Gloria pushed to her feet.

Sean had moved away and was pacing through the field. The fighting was over. The only witches who remained lay motionless.

"Should we cut their heads off and burn them?" Sorcha asked.

Gloria shook her head. "Rhea was the ringleader.

Many of them are a lot like Esmeralda. All they want is peace."

Sorcha snorted. "After a long life of sowing mayhem and discontent."

"True enough, but I'm more invested in freeing Arlen and Kat. These witches won't bother us."

"What makes you think Esmeralda told you the truth?" Tavin spoke up.

"I set a truth spell between us and added compulsion. She had no choice."

Sean ran to them. "I've instructed everyone to return home."

"Losses?" The skin around the corners of Tavin's eyes pinched with concern.

"Three Druids fell today. The others will see they're taken away from this place. Once we're all back in Scotland, they'll receive heroes' burials. You found out where Arlen and Kat are, right?" he asked Gloria.

"Yes. We'll teleport. It's faster."

Liliana joined them. Morgan too. "I still can't believe Rhea's really dead. As in permanently," Liliana said. "I've hated her for as long as I can remember."

"You'll hate her even more before we're done," Gloria retorted. "We have to cast Black Magic to free Arlen and Katerina."

"A small price. Let's go."

"Maybe if you tell me the spell," Sorcha said, "I can do it and spare you. My power has dark roots."

Tavin draped a hand around her shoulders. "Our conjoined magic should do the trick. It was enough to run the Harpies and dragons off."

"And enough to kill Rhea, once and for all," Morgan said in a satisfied voice.

"We'll see if anything except Black Witchcraft will work to reverse the binding." Gloria didn't sound hopeful. "I'll send you an image of where we're going."

Sorcha saw a lake, intuited where it was, and summoned magic to take her and Tavin. Sean, Liliana, Gloria, and Morgan shimmered into being next to them. The lake was an oddity in the borderworld's barren landscape. Judging from the white residue rimming it, the water was either alkaline or outright poison.

She deployed a reveal spell, scanning back and forth until a cage made of what looked like bamboo staves came into view. Roughly three meters square and two high, Arlen and Kat were indeed within it. Sprawled on the ground, they appeared to be sleeping.

Or dead.

Sorcha switched up spells fast, seeking heartbeats. Breath whooshed from her. "They're alive."

"The coma is part of the spell Rhea bound them

with," Gloria said crisply. "Ensures they don't manage to escape when she's not here to prevent it."

"Do you know the casting well enough to reverse it?" Liliana asked.

Gloria didn't answer. She paced around the prison, probing here and there with magic.

Sorcha and Tavin joined her. "I don't understand why the enchantment hasn't collapsed," Tavin said. "If Rhea's magic was what powered it, the cage should have fallen along with her."

"Doesn't work that way," Gloria said. "Not with Black Witchcraft. Things crafted with it last forever."

Sorcha probed with her own magic, examining what held the enclosure together. Strands, red, black, and violet came into view. They wrapped around Arlen and Kat many times before winding around the pieces of bamboo in an intricate pattern.

"Why can't we just cut the strands?" she asked.

"If we do, we'll kill Arlen and Kat," Gloria replied.

"What's the matter?" Liliana joined her mother. "Why aren't you doing something?"

"Because if I get this wrong, the whole thing will go up like a torch. Damn Rhea to her scorched bones. She added a few things to this casting that I've never seen before."

"If Arlen and Kat were awake," Sean said slowly,

"they could work from within to neutralize their bindings."

Tavin finished his sixth transit of the cage. "Not sure this will work," he said, "but I could fly inside. Once I'm there, Sorcha can add to my magic. Maybe it would be enough to wake them."

Gloria nodded tersely. "While you're about it, I'll begin unraveling the magic wound around the pen. It will take a long time because there's a lot of it, and I have to be careful not to let the different colored strands touch each other."

"What happens if they do?" Sorcha asked.

"Not sure, except it won't be anything good," Gloria muttered.

"I'll help you," Sean said.

"What can I do?" Liliana stretched her hands toward her comatose daughter but stopped shy of grasping the bamboo staves.

"You and I will begin unwinding from the opposite end Sean and Gloria are working with," Morgan said. "'Twill go faster that way."

"Be very careful to keep the strands taut," Gloria cautioned.

"We will," Liliana said, adding, "I'm as invested as you in this working, Mother."

For once, Gloria didn't snipe back.

Tavin had stripped out of his clothes. His falcon

formed fast and flew around the cage. Sorcha bit hard on her lower lip. He'd have to cant sideways to make it inside without touching anything. Her raven broke free, wheeling overhead as it, too, assessed the problem.

With a determined cry, the falcon twisted and flew into the pen, fanning its wings almost immediately to avoid hitting the other side. Tavin fluttered to the ground, staying clear of the binding threads.

Sorcha walked as close to the cage as she could get without touching it and fed magic to Tavin. The air around the falcon brightened and pulsed. He pecked lightly at Arlen's ankles.

The Arch Druid groaned.

"Arlen." Sean's voice was sharp. "Do not move."

"Got it." Arlen's voice sounded rusty as if he hadn't used it in centuries.

"You're bound in Black Witchcraft," Sorcha told him. "We're working on freeing you."

"Kat?" Arlen asked, desperation lining his question.

"Right next to you," Sean answered.

Tavin moved to Katerina next. It took a lot of pecking up and down one leg until her eyes fluttered open. "Don't move," Sorcha cautioned.

"Where's Arlen?" Kat slurred her words.

"Next to you," Sorcha replied. "Tavin, I need you back out here."

The falcon flapped, but there wasn't enough room for him to become airborne. He fluttered back to the dirt and waddled to where Morgan and Liliana were working.

"Hang on," Morgan said.

Liliana clipped a black strand. It fell away, and she kicked it aside while Morgan held the rest of the weave taut, so the strands didn't touch. Three more cuts, and the opening was big enough for the falcon to push through. A feather sizzled where it brushed a red bit, but Tavin was through and shifting before any damage occurred.

He hurried to Sorcha's side, not bothering with his stack of clothing. "I'm not familiar with this casting. What happens next?"

"I'm not either," Sorcha said, "but once you begin dismantling anything, speed is critical. In case the whole mess is programmed to explode."

"If it were going to do that, it would have already," Gloria said, not looking up from the place she and Sean worked.

"Arlen," Sorcha said. "Join your magic with Kat's and see if you can address the binding around your bodies. If we can sever your connection with the cage, it will make things easier."

She grabbed Tavin's hand to more readily access Druid magic and funneled an additional boost to Arlen.

The air around him and Kat brightened and pulsed. One by one, the threads of Black Witchcraft surrounding them fell away, writhing in the dirt as if they were alive.

"Did I get them all?" Arlen asked tersely.

"Looks like it," Sorcha said.

"Does that mean we can sit?" Kat asked.

"Maybe. Hang on." Sorcha let go of Tavin and walked around the cage, surveying its occupants from every angle. "Yes. You can sit."

"How are things going?" Tavin asked Sean.

"Not particularly well. This thing's like a Gordian knot."

Sorcha had already tested her magic on a few of the strands. Dark magic had boomeranged back at her, which told her pushing harder wasn't the answer.

"Fuck!" Gloria cursed. "Sean, hang onto your end."

"I am," he protested.

Fire snapped and crackled between two of the strands, spreading fast.

"Teleport," Sorcha shrieked at Arlen. "Do it now."

His expression grim as death, Arlen wrapped his arms around Kat. Druid power glistened silver around them, but it exacerbated the fire problem. Sorcha looked through her third eye. Dark power did battle with Arlen's, effectively subverting his teleport spell.

Tavin recognized the problem. His power slammed

into her, and she sent a whopping load of magic winging to Arlen. All of it. Druid. Witch. Demon. No time to be elegant. Or careful. Arlen's magic took off. The spot where he and Kat had been was empty, but the surfeit of power ignited the strands, and the cage turned into a raging inferno.

Sorcha hustled backward, along with everyone else.

"Where are they?" Tavin shielded his eyes with a hand and scanned in a full arc.

"There!" Sorcha pointed to where Arlen and Kat had just come into view.

Liliana ran toward her daughter, scooping her into a hug. Sorcha reached them in time to hear her say, "Thank all the goddesses you're all right. I've never been so scared."

"You and me both." Kat clung to her mother for another minute before she let go and fell into Arlen's arms.

Arlen reached around his wife and shook Sean's hand. "Thank you."

Sean grinned. "Och, I had ulterior motives up the ass, mate."

"Why do ye think I appointed you as my second?" Arlen returned Sean's smile.

Tavin was getting back into the armload of clothes

he'd scooped up before putting distance between himself and the fire.

"Is there any way to put that out?" Sorcha asked Gloria.

"No. But it will only burn until the power imbued in it is consumed. Not much longer." A breathy sigh pushed between her clenched teeth. "Touching Black Witchcraft makes me feel dirty."

"Hopefully, you'll never have to do it again. Besides, we won. Nothing else matters." Tavin draped an arm around Sorcha.

"Won as in, Rhea's gone?" Arlen locked gazes with Tavin.

"Aye, beheaded and burned to a cinder."

"Wahoo!" Katerina whooped and left the shelter of Arlen's arms to do a victory dance.

"You're right then," Arlen concurred. "Nothing else matters. Let's go home."

Sean laid a hand on his arm. "We sustained losses. Three Druids."

"We'll honor their memory." Arlen's tone turned somber. "Who fell today?"

"Gregor, Luke, and Moira," Sean replied.

Kat joined them. "We shall, indeed, honor their courage. I'm ready to leave this place."

Sorcha circled Tavin's waist with an arm. "Home

sounds good. Not that I actually have one, but Sean's castle will do for now. We need to talk."

"Aye, that we do, lass."

Sorcha tried to smile. He sounded serious. Was this where he told her she was a nice girl, but not quite who he had in mind?

She stood tall and summoned the power to return them to Inverness. She'd say what she had to, tell him how important he was to her. If he didn't share her feelings, she'd find a way to live without him. Somehow.

She'd been on the move forever. She'd done her part here, and now she could settle anywhere. Actually make a home for herself. She wanted that home to be with Tavin, though. Not knowing if he felt the same was a huge stumbling block to making future plans.

I'll figure it out. I always do.

Big words, but this was one place where hubris wouldn't carry her through.

Tavin wove his magic in with hers, and the teleport spell snapped them up.

"Next stop, Inverness," Tavin joked.

She gripped his hand, and he squeezed back. She took it as a positive sign, but maybe she was deluding herself.

CHAPTER 16

Tavin inserted his own vector into the spell so they came out in the gravel driveway near his car. He unbuckled his sword belt and dropped it into the back of the car. Sorcha handed over her belt. "Sorry about the blade."

He shrugged. "Och, lass. I can make more. They get a wee bit better every time. Would ye like to walk a bit?" He closed the Renault's hatch.

"You're back to speaking Gaelic." A smile teased the corners of her mouth.

"'Tis a more natural tongue for me. About that walk?"

Sorcha laughed. "Sure, but did you even notice it's pouring rain?"

He'd been so focused on what he wanted to say to her, he hadn't. Drops cascaded from the skies, running down his head and wetting his clothing. "Come on then," he urged and gripped one of her hands. "We'll find a cozy corner within."

He led her through a side door that came out on a landing midway between the basement and ground floors. She was quiet, but she hadn't withdrawn her fingers from his grasp. They walked up a flight and along one of the castle's many branching hallways until he stopped and twisted a knob.

Years had passed since he'd been in the aviary, but it was just as he remembered it. A solid glass wall looked out over gardens. Wooden stands of differing heights were scattered about, most containing water and food dishes. Birds perched everywhere, chirping and singing. Small swinging mesh panels allowed them to come and go as they pleased. Sorcha's raven emerged with a swoosh, cawing merrily. For some reason, the songbirds didn't flee. Perhaps they recognized this raven meant them no harm.

Sorcha clasped her hands in front of her, eyes wide with wonder. "It's delightful. I had no idea the castle had an aviary. You've made my familiar deliriously happy."

He tugged gently on their joined hands and guided her to a low-slung sofa in front of the glass wall. "Sit, please."

She let go of him and sank onto the creased leather,

tucking her legs beneath her. She was smiling, but a layer of unease ran very close to the surface. Maybe he should put this off. They'd both had a hell of a couple of days. What he had to say might go easier after food, rest...

I'm a right, bloody coward.

He sat next to her but turned at right angles so he could look at her. Where to begin? "You were amazing today."

"No. We were amazing. Our magic was born to be used in tandem." She tipped her chin at a defiant angle almost as if she were challenging him to contradict her.

Regardless, it was as good an opening as he was likely to get. "Not just our magic, lassie. I'm in love with you. Ye'd make me a verra happy man if ye'd agree to share your life with me."

Sorcha's blue-green eyes widened and sheened with moisture.

Remorse smote Tavin. He'd startled her, upset her. "I'm so sorry. 'Tis far too soon. Ye need time to recover from—"

She threw herself at him and wound her arms around his neck. "Shut up, Tavin Shaw. Don't ruin it apologizing. I love you too. I was shocked because I've almost never gotten anything I've wanted, and I was expecting you to tell me, oh I don't know, but anything except what you just did."

He hugged her back. "Doona be hasty, lass. I'm not rich like Sean or Arlen. Oh, I have enough. We'll not want for much, but there isn't a castle awaiting you back on the Isle of Lewis."

She nestled her face into the crook between his neck and shoulder. "I want you, not money. I've never had frilly things, and I don't need them now. Besides, what makes you think we have to return to Lewis? We can go anywhere. You were leaving there for a few months. I'll go with you. We'll wander through time and other worlds. Who knows? Maybe we'll find somewhere we want to stay for a while. Maybe not."

She laughed. "Christ, I'm babbling."

"I love to listen to you." He cradled the back of her head in one hand, appreciating how she felt in his arms. Birds flew overhead, singing to them. The raven cawed happily and brushed their faces with its wings.

Sorcha tipped her head back and locked gazes with him. "I can't quite believe Rhea is gone. I dreamed about her meeting a horrible end, but when it happened, it was so fast, I nearly missed it."

"Battles are like that. Ye plan and plot and strategize, but the critical parts are over in the blink of an eye."

"I hope Gloria was right about those other witches. We could have mown through them where they lay."

"My bloodthirsty darling."

She tilted her head to one side. "I am half demon. Still time to back out."

"Never." Gripping her head between his hands, he scooted close enough to kiss her. The angle was awkward, but the kiss was hot and sweet and urgent. He tipped them until they lay on the buttery soft leather couch.

Biting kisses alternated with deep tongue thrusts and nibbles that traveled from her mouth down her neck and back again. Tavin wasn't in a hurry. They had all the time in the world. She teased his mouth with hers, licked and suckled his lips.

Everywhere her mouth touched him set off a chain of sparks that rocketed right to his core. He was nuzzling the hollow in her neck now, following the stark line of collarbones out to her shoulder and back again. She shivered beneath his touch, and her nipples turned to smooth little points where they pressed against him.

He'd dreamed about touching her breasts and cupped a hand over one, luxuriating in the firm globe beneath his fingertips. The creamy fabric of her blouse warmed from his touch. Or maybe her breast was providing the heat that shot up his arm. He covered her mouth with his again. She tasted of smoke and magic and fire, and her wonderful scent eddied about them. Herbs and vanilla and pure Sorcha.

He raised his mouth from hers. "We have too many clothes on, lass."

"You think?" Her eyes sparkled with merriment. "I'd have tossed mine, but last time I came close to doing that, you ran like a scared bunny."

He snorted laugher. "I did not run."

"Not how I remember it." She rolled from side to side beneath him. "If you want my clothes off, you're going to have to move."

"I want to undress you. Unwrap you. Delight in every centimeter of skin."

"Oooh, sounds like a long process. Will I be old by the time you finally make love with me?"

"We're already old."

"Check." She giggled. "Thanks for the reminder, but I'll never be as old as you."

He kissed the tip of her nose and rose until he knelt over her. "Something to be said for mature men, darling."

"I'm waiting to find out."

He drew her to a sit and slipped her vest off her shoulders. The blouse had impossibly tiny buttons, but he undid every single one despite wanting to rip them apart. He pushed the garment open and reached behind her to undo her bra. He'd been planning to remove both shirt and underwear, but his hands had a different agenda. One cradled each breast.

He closed his eyes as he rubbed her nipples, delighting in them growing longer and harder and in the weight of her breasts in his hands. "Beautiful, lassie," he managed. Words were hard to come by, and his throat was drier than a month-long drought. Not that Scotland ever had those.

She shrugged out of her blouse. He let go of her breasts long enough to toss her bra aside. Before he dove into her high, full breasts again, he gazed at her naked torso. Broad shoulders were corded with muscle that wound down shapely arms. Her skin was a copper-gold shade, and her nipples the same color as ripe strawberries.

"Gods, ye're gorgeous."

Sorcha cupped a breast in each hand. "Look all you like. Later. They're feeling lonely."

He surged forward and fastened his mouth over a nipple. She shrieked her delight and threaded her fingers through his hair, snagging on braids that had mostly come unraveled. He moved to the other breast and then lashed his tongue back and forth. She rocked against him, surrounding them with magic that stoked the flames of his lust.

He looked up for a moment. Power shone around her, turning her beauty into something ethereal. He growled and undid the fastenings on her skirt. Far easier than the blouse buttons, the hook and eye and zipper fell aside, and he pulled the garment over her hips. On the way down, he ran into boots. It took all his self-control to unlace and remove them. Framed with spiky blonde curls, her pussy was centimeters away. Sorcha's back was arched in passion. Her legs edged apart.

He wanted to do everything all at once. Explore her with fingers and tongue and eyes, but his cock throbbed painfully against the front of his trousers. He ignored it and licked his way up the inside of her legs until he made it to the vee between them. Fastening his mouth over her nub, he sucked hard.

Her hips writhed and bucked beneath his touch. She grabbed his head and held it against her. He felt her arousal spiral as her clit hardened beneath his tongue. The magic she'd wrapped them in throbbed with sexual heat and added an entire other dimension to their lovemaking.

He slid fingers inside her, and her muscles tightened around him. His cock beat like a second heart between his legs. It wanted to be where his fingers were, but he'd be damned if he'd change anything before she came. He teased her clit, swirling his tongue around it as he fucked her with his fingers.

Her hips rose and fell. He tumbled headlong into her magic, threaded his with it, and willed her passion to crest. Sorcha cried out. Her pussy dissolved in rhythmic contractions, and he upped the ante moving both hand and mouth faster and harder until her body quieted.

She rolled upright from where she'd been splayed across the couch and kissed him. "Umm. I can taste myself on you. Makes me hot."

"If ye were any hotter, lass, ye'd burn down Sean's castle."

She laughed, silver bells of merriment that warmed his soul. "You still have all your clothes on."

"Observant. I've been a wee bit on the busy side."

"Let me." Sorcha knelt and unlaced his boots. He toed them off as she moved to his jacket, sliding it off his shoulders. A trail of magic made short work of his shirt buttons, and she tugged it off, tossing it in the vicinity of his jacket.

Rocking back, she ran her fingertips over his naked chest. "First time I saw you naked, I couldn't believe how gorgeous you were."

Delight coursed through him at the compliment. He thought back to when that might have been. "In the cave on South Ronaldsay?"

She nodded. "I've been plotting to separate you from your clothes ever since."

"I was naked on G4. Twice."

"I noticed, but we had other priorities." She pinched one of his nipples, and he yelped with pleasure. Bending forward, she swiped her tongue over first one and then the other.

Sorcha teased his nipples and stomach before moving lower. A quick flip of her wrist undid his belt and trousers. She grasped the waistband and levered them out of the way. They pooled at his feet, and he extricated one leg and pushed them aside.

His cock was clearly outlined against the fabric of his shorts. Sorcha ran her tongue over her lush lips and covered him with a hand. His cock jerked against her touch, hard as it ever got.

"Mmm," she purred. "I have an idea."

Before he could ask what she had in mind, magic surrounded his hips, and his underwear vanished. She straddled his lap and lowered herself onto him. The heat of her undid him. He wanted to know what magic ripped your clothes off, but he wanted to fuck her more. Knowledge could wait.

He settled his hands on her hips, needing to exert some control over her movements so he didn't come immediately. She leaned into him, breasts crushed against his chest, and closed her mouth over his. He sank his tongue inside her mouth while he moved her body upward, slow and easy, and then back down until he bottomed out.

He went slowly, letting her accommodate to his girth. She tightened around him; he twitched his cock.

They traded back and forth. Tighten. Twitch. Tighten, Twitch. Heat cascaded through him, leaving pure, unvarnished love in its wake.

He tore his mouth from hers. "I love you, lass. Ye've everything I've ever hoped for. Dreamed of. Strong. Gutsy. Gorgeous."

"Unprincipled." She laughed softly. "And you're ever so much more than I thought I'd find. I still can't quite believe we're together."

"Believe it, lass." His words were gruff because of the emotion roiling through him. "For now and forever more."

She steadied herself with her hands on his shoulders and rose until only the tip of him was encased within her. She sank slowly but rose again almost immediately. He understood. She couldn't wait any longer.

Neither could he.

Maintaining his hold on her hips, he upped the tempo of his strokes until he was driving into her. Her nails dug into his shoulders, and she slashed her mouth over his, biting and sucking his lips. The magic she'd summoned before closed around them until the only thing in the world was his cock in her pussy and their bodies straining together.

She melted around him in a blaze of heat and slickness. Semen that had pooled in his balls rushed forward. His cock spurted and spurted again. He came harder than he ever had, claiming the woman in his arms as his mate."

They collapsed against each other breathing in ragged gasps as their bodies quieted.

"For now and forever more," she said dreamily. "I like the sound of that."

"I meant every word."

"If what you said before about sex consecrating our magical bond is true, we're stuck with each other now," she teased.

"Och, surely a fate worse than death."

She sank her teeth into his shoulder. He ruffled her hair. "A wee secret ye forgot to tell me, lass? Ye've vampire blood mixed in with demon?"

"Would it matter?"

"Not at all."

She smiled. It softened her beauty, made her even more desirable. His cock was still hard, and he rotated it inside her.

"Lovely idea, but maybe we could find a shower? We can clean up and then have more sex." She crinkled her nose. "We both stink, but I was afraid if I suggested washing first, you'd bolt."

Tavin laughed. "Oh ye of little faith. There should be a bathroom a couple of doors down. I wonder why no one has come hunting us."

Sorcha lifted herself off his cock and stood over him. "Let's see. Arlen and Kat are probably doing exactly what we just did. So are Sean and Liliana. Leaves Morgan, and I bet she's rollicking in the lore she loves so much."

Tavin thought about it. "I bet they're either all back on South Ronaldsay or heading there. We have our fallen companions to honor." He got to his feet and swept her hair back over her shoulders. "Don't take this wrong, lass. I'd like naught better than to retire to a bed with you and never surface, but—"

She placed a hand over his mouth. "I understand. We'll clean up, find clothes, and pay our respects. If it weren't for those Druids' deaths, I might still be looking around every corner for Rhea."

"Ye're sure ye doona mind?"

"Of course I don't. We have our entire lives ahead of us."

Tavin smiled. "Aye, that we do. Once we've finished with the funerals, we'll map out what comes next."

The raven squawked, possibly in agreement and vanished in a flash of brilliant light. Sorcha tapped her breastbone. "My familiar is happy. Means a lot to me."

"Both of you being happy is my first priority, lassie."

"Pretty words from a pretty man."

"Except I've never meant anything more."

She leaned forward, resting her head on his chest before straightening. "Where did you say the bathroom was?"

He nodded. "Two doors down on the right. Thanks for understanding about joining the others."

"You don't have to thank me. I've gone from having nothing to having a mate and a family. I want to be there."

With an arm around her, he guided them through bird paraphernalia and out into the hall. Fierce protectiveness spilled through him. This was his woman. His mate. The partner he'd been waiting for all his long life. He sent a quick prayer to Danu winging forth. He'd leave an offering at her altar in the cave on South Ronaldsay.

"Tuppence for your thoughts?" She walked into a large bath decorated with cream-colored marble.

"I'm a lucky man."

Sorcha flipped the taps and hugged him while she waited for the water to warm. "We're both lucky. So long as we never forget that, we'll be just fine."

"Ye're wise as well as beautiful." He swatted her amazing ass. "Into the shower, wench."

"Bring that hairbrush with you. I'll comb out your braids before your hair develops terminal tangles."

Tavin joined her in the steam-filled glass enclosure. "What, exactly, is a terminal tangle?"

"It's a girl thing. It's where you give up and cut a chunk out."

It struck him as funny, and he started to laugh. She joined him. Soon they were howling like loons as they sluiced soap and water from their hair and bodies. He wasn't used to dissecting his feelings, but he was happy, and it felt incredible.

He was committed to getting them clean, dressed, and on their way, but he took a moment to kiss her as water pounded down on them. She fit perfectly in his arms as she molded her body to his.

"We belong together," he said, lifting his mouth from hers.

"Was there ever any doubt?"

"Nay, lass. None at all."

Two Years Later

Sorcha here. Tavin thought our story was tied up in a bow and done, but we demons always scramble to have the last word. And yeah, it took me a while to finish this up, but I've been busy.

Tav and I left after the funerals, but I'm getting ahead of myself. I'd never been to anything like a funeral before. For one thing, demons are damn near immortal. For another, anyone Satan rid Himself of never ended up having their life glorified.

I wasn't sure what to expect, but it was important to Tavin, and that was good enough for me. By the time everyone closest to the fallen Druids told stories about their lives, their bravery, and their good deeds, I felt I knew them. And I mourned their loss.

Didn't know I had it in me, but these last couple of years I've learned a lot about myself.

We remained in the sacred cave on South Ronaldsay for nearly a week. Druid rituals take time. Just preparing the bodies for the fire to take them into their afterlife was a two-day process. Before we left the island, I found Tavin kneeling over the shrine to Danu. He'd built a fire, added sweet incense, and was chanting in Gaelic.

I could follow the words, but wasn't familiar with the incantation, so I asked about it. He told me he was thanking the goddess for bringing me into his life. Really choked me up, and it still does. He's such an amazing man.

Anyway, I knelt next to him and did the best I could with my own thank-yous. Prayers aren't big in Satan's realm, so I'd never actually fashioned one. I'm not ashamed to admit it took me a while, and a lot of false starts. Tavin finally told me to stop worrying about it being perfect and to just tell Danu what was in my heart. So I did.

That man is full of good advice.

We left the next day. It was the middle of February, and we spent the next few months knocking around Indonesia. Tav has a small hut on one of the no-name islands west of New Guinea, so we used it for a base. He took his falcon form daily, and I loved watching him dip and dive from the skies. My familiar adored it too. I've never known it to be visible so much of the time.

When I asked Tav, he confirmed my raven was good friends with him when he was a peregrine falcon. They loved hunting together.

We left in late May and returned to Scotland for a while. Tav worked at his forge, and I puttered around his home on the Isle of Lewis. Eventually, though, I needed more. I'd digested all the magical scrolls and books and being idle never sat well.

Gloria was back in the States, so I teleported over there and visited with her. Tried to talk her into moving back to Scotland, but she wasn't interested. Not sure if I mentioned this, but she's a renowned geologist, and the Nevada mountains offered endless possibilities for her research.

After I got back to the UK, we visited Inverness. Turned out Liliana was having some of the same problems as me, what with needing more to do. She'd decided to open a clinic catering to the poor and asked if I wanted to help. At first, I thought she was joking. I've worked as a dancer, a barmaid, and a dishwasher.

Doctoring wasn't anywhere on the list.

She took me aside and pointed out magic was the best medicine of all. Since I had those bases covered in spades, I'd be perfect to work alongside her. She'd already sent her credentials off to the government offices in Edinburgh, and as soon as they issued her a medical license, we'd be off and running.

Since it was likely to take a month or two, Tav and I oohed and aahed over Arlen and Kat's young son, but then we left and bounced around through time for a bit. He took me to Leith, an early Leith a year or so before he'd been born. Such a sweet man. He wanted to show me the stone hut where his family had lived. Once I'd seen it in the past, we visited it in our current time.

I was surprised it was still standing, but it had been thoroughly modernized. Someone had built onto it, and pretty flowers grew in profusion around its walls. We stayed at an inn a couple of streets over. Reminded me of places I'd worked, and it was quite a change of pace to be a guest.

I offered to show Tavin my birthplace in Hell, even managed to keep a straight face while I did it. At first, he didn't know I was joking. You should have seen his expression as he hunted for a diplomatic way to refuse without hurting my feelings.

We had quite the laugh over that.

After a few more stops in the past, skirting Rhea and her ilk who were still very much alive and kicking, we poked our noses a few years into the future. It scared the bejesus out of us both. Every bad thing we'd suspected would happen to Earth was rolling forward unimpeded by anything like humans stepping in and altering their horrible practices.

One disadvantage of living nearly forever is we'd eventually make it to the future with rising oceans, red tides, out-of-control fires, and Class Six hurricanes. Tavin and the other Druids are working hard on a solution, but I told him it's a waste of time. Only true option is killing off half the human population.

Now that would make a dent in pollution and climate change.

He said my demon roots were showing.

Anyway, I've almost made it to where we are today. Kat and Arlen are pregnant again. They've made quite the names for themselves co-authoring anthropology research papers on the clans. Both are on staff at the University of Stirling but spend most of their work time digging in the dirt and unearthing bits and pieces of things that excite them and leave the rest of us cold. Their son, Dugan, is adorable, though. And I'm looking forward to their next baby, a daughter who's due in four months.

Sean is back at his cozy desk in the bank rattling pound notes. Liliana and I just finished our second month of clinic operation. By all accounts, it's been a great success and provided a desperately needed resource to augment the UK's national healthcare system. No one has to wait for care at our clinic. Not yet, anyway. She and I work long hours, and then I teleport back to Isle of Lewis and spend my evenings with Tavin.

Speaking of him, we're getting married next weekend in the Druids' cave on South Ronaldsay. Haven't been back there since we laid the fallen Druids to rest. I can see a few eyebrows twitching as you wonder why we're finally getting married.

He asked me back at the very beginning, but I put him off. Told him we had to make certain of things. The cold truth was I was petrified. Being bound by magic is one thing. Being bound by laws I've never respected, quite another.

Anyway, I, erm that is we, are expecting a child of our own. Damn but that was hard to choke out. I'm scared. What if it's a reincarnation of Rosemary's Baby?

Tavin assures me we'll love it to death no matter what it looks like, but I'm not so sure how I'll feel about an ongoing reminder of my years in Hell. You should have seen Tav when I told him, though. I'd have put it off longer, but it's tough when your partner has strong magic. He'd have sensed the extra life straightaway.

Liliana was as excited as Tavin. She did a magical version of an ultrasound and assures me the baby has ten fingers, ten toes, and no horns. I'll believe it when the little bugger is safe in my arms.

I think I've covered most everything. It's been grand sharing our journey with you. Now put the book down and go outside. Look at everything through fresh eyes. Magic is real, people. And your next door neighbor might be a whole lot more than you ever expected.

You've reached the end of *Time's Hostage,* and the end of the *Elemental Witch* series. Thanks for reading through to the end. If you enjoyed this series, you might also like my *Dragon Lore* books. A sample from *To Love a Highland Dragon* follows.

ABOUT THE AUTHOR

Ann Gimpel is a USA Today bestselling author. A lifelong aficionado of the unusual, she began writing speculative fiction a few years ago. Since then her short fiction has appeared in many webzines and anthologies. Her longer books run the gamut from urban fantasy to paranormal romance. Once upon a time, she nurtured clients. Now she nurtures dark, gritty fantasy stories that push hard against reality. When she's not writing, she's in the backcountry getting down and dirty with her camera. She's published over 70 books to date, with several more planned for 2019 and beyond. A husband, grown children, grandchildren, and wolf hybrids round out her family.

Keep up with her at www.anngimpel.com or http://anngimpel.blogspot.com

If you enjoyed what you read, get in line for special offers and pre-release special reads. Newsletter Signup!

Books in the Dragon Lore Series:
Highland Secrets, Prequel and Book One
To Love a Highland Dragon, Book Two
Dragon Maid, Book Three
Dragon's Dare, Book Four

A dragon shifter stirs and wakens in a cave beneath Inverness, deep in the Scottish Highlands. The cave's the same and his hoard intact, yet something's badly amiss. Determined to set whatever's gone wrong to rights, Lachlan Moncrieffe ventures above ground—and wishes he hadn't. His castle's gone, replaced by ungainly row houses. Men aren't wearing plaids, and women scarcely wear anything at all, particularly the woman who accosts him with unseemly banter. What manner of wench is she to dress so provocatively?

In Inverness for a year on a psychiatry fellowship, Dr. Maggie Hibbins watches an oddly dressed man pick his way out of a heather and gorse thicket. Even though it runs counter to her better judgment, she teases him about his strange attire. He looks so lost—and so unbelievably, knock-out gorgeous—she takes a chance and stands him a meal. Lachlan's shock when he picks up a local newspaper at a pub is so palpable, Maggie jumps in with both feet.

She knew something was off, but the hard-to-accept truth bashes gaping holes in her equilibrium. He looks odd, sounds odd, acts odd because he's a refugee from another era. Her half-baked seduction scheme takes a hike, but her carefully constructed life is still about to change forever. Born of powerful witches, Maggie runs headlong into the myth and magic that are her birthright.

Kheladin listened to the rush of blood as his multi-chambered heart pumped. After eons of nothingness, the unexpected sound surprised him. A cool, sandy floor pressed against his scaled haunches. One whirling eye flickered open, followed by the other.

Where am I?

He peered at his surroundings and blew out a sigh, followed by steam, smoke, and fire.

Thanks be to Dewi—Kheladin invoked the blood-red Celtic dragon goddess—*I'm still in my cave. It smelled right, but I wasna certain.*

He rotated his serpent's head atop his long, sinuous neck. Vertebrae cracked. Kheladin lowered his head and scanned the place he and Lachlan, his human bondmate, had barricaded themselves into. It might've only been days ago, but somehow, it didn't seem like days, or even months or a few years. His body felt rusty, as if he hadn't used it in centuries.

How long did I sleep?

He shook his head. Copper scales flew everywhere, clanking against a pile littered around him. More than anything, the glittery heap reinforced his belief he'd been asleep for a very long time. Dragons shed their scales annually. From the amount circling his body, he'd gone through hundreds of molt cycles. But how? The last thing he remembered was retreating to his cave far beneath Lachlan's castle and working with the mage to construct strong wards.

Had the black wyvern grown powerful enough to force his magic into the very heart of Kheladin's fortress?

If that's true—if we really were his prisoner, why'd I finally waken? Is Lachlan still within me?

Stop! I have to take things one at a time.

He returned his gaze to the nooks and crannies of his spacious cave. He'd have to take inventory, but it appeared his treasure hadn't been disturbed. Kheladin blew a plume of steam upward, followed by an experimental gout of fire. The black wyvern, his sworn enemy since before the Crusades, may have bested him, but he hadn't gotten his slimy talons on any of Kheladin's gold or jewels.

He shook out his back feet and shuffled to the pool

at one end of the cave where he dipped his snout and drank deeply. The water didn't taste right. It wasn't poisoned, but it held an undercurrent of metals that had never been there before. Kheladin rolled the liquid around in his mouth. He didn't recognize much of what he tasted, but he was thirsty and it seemed safe enough, so he drank some more.

The flavors aren't familiar because I've been asleep for so long. Aye, that must be it. Part of his mind recoiled; he suspected he was deluding himself.

"*We're awake.*" Lachlan's voice hummed in the dragon's mind.

"*Aye, that we are.*"

"*How long did we sleep?*"

"*I doona know.*" Water streamed down the dragon's snout and neck. He knew what would come next, and he didn't have to wait long.

"*Let's shift. We think better in my body.*" Lachlan urged Kheladin to cede ascendency.

"*I doona agree.*" Kheladin pushed back. "*I was figuring things out afore ye woke.*"

"*Aye, I'm certain ye were, but...*" But what? "*Och aye, my brain is thick and fuzzy, as if I havena used it for a verra long time.*"

"*Mine feels the same.*"

The bond allowed only one form at a time. Since they were in Kheladin's body, he had the upper hand.

Lachlan wasn't strong enough to force a shift without his help. There'd been a time when he could have but not now.

Was it safe to venture above ground?

Kheladin recalled the last day he'd seen the sun. After a vicious battle in the great room of Lachlan's castle, they'd retreated to his cave and taken their dragon form as a final resort. Rhukon, the black wyvern, pretended he wanted peace. He'd come with an envoy that turned out to be a retinue of heavily armed men.

Both he and Lachlan expected Rhukon to follow them underground. Kheladin's last thought, before nothingness descended, was disbelief because their enemy hadn't pursued them.

Humph. He did *come after us but with magic. Magic strong enough to penetrate our wards.*

"Aye, and I was thinking the same thing," Lachlan sniped in a vexed tone.

"We trusted him," Kheladin snarled. *"More the fools we were. We should've known."* Despite drinking, his throat was still raw. He sucked more water down and fought rising anger at himself for being gullible. Even if Lachlan hadn't known better, he should've. His stomach cramped from hunger.

Kheladin debated the wisdom of making his way through the warren of tunnels leading to the surface in dragon form. There were always far more humans than dragons. Mayhap it would be wiser to accede to Lachlan's wishes before they crept from their underground lair to rejoin the world of men.

"Grand idea." Lachlan's response was instantaneous, as was his first stab at shifting.

It took half a dozen attempts. Kheladin was far weaker than he imagined and Lachlan so feeble he was almost an impediment. Finally, once a shower of scales cleared, Lachlan's emaciated body stood barefoot and naked in the cave.

Lacking the sharp night vision he enjoyed as a dragon, because his magic was so diminished, Lachlan kindled a mage light and glanced down at himself. Ribs pressed against his flesh, and a full beard extended halfway down his chest. Turning his head to both sides, he saw shoulder blades so sharp he was surprised they didn't puncture his skin. Tawny hair fell in tangles past his waist. The only thing he couldn't see was his eyes. Absent a glass, he was certain they were the same crystal-clear emerald color they'd always been.

He stumbled across the cave to a chest where he kept clothing. Dragons didn't need such silly accoutrements; humans did. He sucked in a harsh breath. The wooden chest was falling to ruin. He tilted the lid against a wall, but it canted to one side. Many of his clothes had moldered into unusable rags, but items toward the bottom fared better. He found a cream-colored linen shirt with long, flowing sleeves, a black and green plaid embroidered with the insignia of his house—a dragon in flight—and soft, deerskin boots that laced to his knees.

He slid the shirt over his head and wrapped the plaid around himself, taking care to wind the tartan so its telltale insignia was hidden in its folds. Who knew if the black wyvern—or his agents—lurked near the mouth of the cave? Lachlan bent to lace his boots. A crimson cloak with only a few moth holes completed his outfit. He finger-combed his hair and smoothed his unruly beard.

"Good God, but I must look a fright," he muttered. "Mayhap I can sneak into the castle and set things aright afore anyone sees me. Surely my kinsmen will be glad the master of the house has finally returned."

Lachlan worked on bolstering a confidence he was far from feeling. He'd nearly made it to the end of the cave, where a rock-strewn path led upward, when he doubled back to get a sword and scabbard—just in case things weren't as sanguine as he hoped. He located a thigh sheath and a short dagger as well, fumbling to attach them beneath his kilt. Underway once again, he hadn't made it very far along the upward-sloping tunnel that ended at a well-hidden opening not far from the postern gate of his castle, when he ran into rocks littering the way.

He worked his way around progressively larger boulders until he came to a huge one that totally blocked the passageway. Lachlan stared at it in disbelief. When had that happened? In all the time he'd been using these paths, they'd never been blocked by rock fall. If he weren't so weak, summoning magic to shove the rock over enough to allow him to pass wouldn't be a problem. As it was, simply walking uphill proved a challenge.

He pinched the bridge of his nose between a grimy thumb and forefinger. His mage light weakened.

If I can't even keep a light going, how in the goddess's name will I be able to move that rock?

Lachlan hunkered next to the boulder and let his light die while he ran possibilities through his head. His stomach growled and clenched in hunger. Had he come through however much time had passed to cower like a dog in his own cave?

"No, by God." He slammed a fist against the boulder, and it went right on through. The air sizzled. Magic. The rock was illusion. Not real.

Counter spell. I need a counter spell.

Mayhap not.

He stood and took a deep breath before walking into the huge rock. The air did more than sizzle. It flamed. If he'd been human, it would've burned him to ashes, but dragons were impervious to fire, as were dragon shifters. Lachlan waltzed through the rock, cursing Rhukon as he went. Five more boulders blocked his tunnel, each more charged with magic than the last.

Finally, sweating and cursing, he rounded the last curve, and the air ahead grew brighter. He wanted to throw himself on the ground and screech his triumph.

Not a good idea.

"Let me out. Ye have no idea what we'll find."

Kheladin's voice in his mind was welcome but the idea wasn't. *"Ye're right. Because we have no idea what's out there, we stay in my skin until we're certain. We can hide in this form far more easily than we can in yours."*

"Since when did we take to hiding?" The dragon sounded outraged.

"Our magic is weak." Lachlan adopted a placating tone. *"'Tis prudent to be cautious until it fully recovers."*

"No dragon would ever say such a thing." Deep, fiery frustration rolled off Kheladin.

Steam belched from Lachlan's mouth. *"Stop that,"*

he hissed, but his mind voice was all but obliterated by wry dragon laughter.

"Why? I find it amusing ye think an eight foot tall dragon with elegant copper scales and handsome, green eyes would be difficult to sequester." Kheladin paused a beat. *"And infuriating we need to conceal ourselves at all. Need I remind you we're warriors?"*

"Of course we're warriors," Lachlan said affably, sidestepping the issue of hiding. He didn't want to risk being goaded into something unwise. Kheladin chuckled and pushed more steam through Lachlan's mouth, punctuated by a few flames.

Lost in a sudden rush of memories, Lachlan slowed his pace. As a mage, he would've lived hundreds of years, but bonded to a dragon, he'd live forever. In preparation, he'd studied long years with Aether, a wizard and dragon shifter himself. Along the way, Lachlan forsook much—a wife and bairns, for starters, for what woman would put up with a husband so rarely at home?—to bond with a dragon, forming their partnership. Once Lachlan's magic was finally strong enough, there'd been the niggling problem of locating that special dragon willing to join its life with his.

Because the bond conferred immortality on both the dragon and their human partner, dragons were notoriously picky. After all, dragon and mage would be welded through eternity. The magic could be undone, but the price was high. Mages were stripped of power, and their dragon mates lost much of theirs too, as the bond unraveled. Rumor suggested that mages who became dragon-less risked madness—an additional stumbling block and strong incentive to choose wisely.

Lachlan hunted for over a hundred years before finding Kheladin. The pairing was instantaneous on both sides. He'd just settled in with his dragon, and was about to chase down a wife to grace his castle, when the black wyvern attacked.

Rhukon had approached Kheladin long before Lachlan did, but the dragon rejected the bond, spawning long-standing animosity. That Rhukon finally acquired a dragon of his own hadn't lessened his ill will one whit.

"*What are ye waiting for?*" Kheladin sounded testy. "*Daydreaming is a worthless pursuit. My grandmother is two thousand years old, and she moves faster than you.*"

Lachlan snorted. He didn't bother to explain there wasn't much point in jumping right into Rhukon's arms through the opening in the gorse and thistle bushes growing at the mouth of the cave. An unusual whirring filled the air, like the noisiest beehive he'd ever heard. His heart sped up, but the sound receded.

"What in the nine hells was that?" he muttered

and made his way closer to the world outside Kheladin's cave.

Lachlan shoved some overgrown bushes out of the way and peered through. What he saw was so unbelievable, he squeezed his eyes shut tight before opening them and looking again. Unfortunately, nothing had changed. Worse, an ungainly, shiny cylinder roared past, making the same whirring noise he'd puzzled over moments before. He fell backward into the cave, breath harsh in his throat, and landed on his rump.

Lachlan shook his head and balled his hands into fists. Frustration and disbelief battered him, making him wonder if he'd died only to waken in Hell. Not only was the postern gate no longer there, neither was his castle. A long, unattractive row of attached structures stood in its stead.

"Holy godhead. What do we do now?"

"*Go out there and hunt down something to eat,*" the dragon growled.

Lachlan gritted his teeth until his jaw ached. Kheladin had a good point. It was hard to think on an empty stomach.

"*Here I was worried about Rhukon. At least I understood him. I fear whatever lies in wait for us will require all our skill.*"

"Ye were never a coward. 'Tis why I allowed the bond. Get moving."

The dragon's words settled him. Ashamed of his indecisiveness, Lachlan got to his feet. He brushed dirt off his plaid and worked his way through bushes hiding the cave's entrance. As he untangled stickers from the finely spun wool of his cloak and his plaid, he gawked at a very different world from the one he'd left. There wasn't a field—or an animal—in sight. Roadways paved with something other than dirt and stones were punctuated by structures so numerous, they made him dizzy. The hideous incursion onto his lands stretched in every direction.

Lachlan curled his hands into fists again. He'd find out what had happened, by God. When he did, he'd make whoever erected all those abominations take them down.

An occasional person walked by in the distance. They shocked him even more than the buildings and roads. For starters, the males weren't wearing plaids, so there was no way to tell their clan. Females were immodestly covered. Many sported bare legs and breeks so tight he saw the separation between their ass cheeks. Lachlan's groin stirred, his cock hardening. Were the lassies no longer engaging in modesty or subterfuge and simply asking to be fucked? Or was this some new garb that befit a new era?

He detached the last thorn, finally clear of the thicket of sticker bushes. Where could he find a market with vendors? Did market day still exist in this strange environment?

"Holy crap! A kilt, and an old-fashioned one at that. Tad bit early in the day for a costume ball, isn't it?" A rich female voice laced with amusement sounded behind him.

Lachlan spun with his hands raised to call magic. He stopped dead once his gaze settled on a lass nearly as tall as himself, which meant she was close to six feet. She turned so she faced him squarely. Bare legs emerged from torn fabric that stopped just south of her female parts. Full breasts strained against scraps of material attached to strings tied around her neck and back. Her feet were encased in a few straps of leather. Long, blonde hair eddied around her, the color of sheaves of summer wheat.

His cock jumped to attention. He itched to make a grab for her breasts or her ass. She had an amazing ass: round and high and tight. What was expected of him? The lass was dressed in such a way as to invite him to simply tear what passed for breeks aside and enter her. Had the world changed so drastically that women provoked men into public sex? He glanced about, half expecting to see couples having it off with one another willy-nilly.

"Well," she urged. "Cat got your tongue?" She placed her hands on her hips. The motion stretched the tiny bits of flowered fabric that barely covered her nipples still further.

Lachlan bowed formally. He straightened and waited for her to hold out a hand for him to kiss. "I'm Lachlan Moncrieffe, Laird of Clan Moncrieffe, my lady. 'Tis a pleasure to—"

She erupted into laughter—and didn't hold out her hand. "I'm Maggie," she managed between gouts of mirth. "What are you? A throwback to medieval times? You can drop the Sir Galahad routine."

Lachlan felt his face heat. "I fear I doona understand the cause of your merriment...my lady."

Maggie rolled midnight blue eyes. "Oh, brother. Did you escape from a mental hospital? Nah, you'd be in pajamas then, not those fancy duds." She dropped her hands to her sides and started to walk past him.

"No. Wait. Please, wait." Lachlan cringed at the whining tone in his voice. The dragon was correct that the Moncrieffe was a proud house. They bowed to no one.

She eyed him askance. "What?"

"I'm a stranger in this town." He winced at the lie. Once upon a time, he'd been master of these lands. Apparently that time had long since passed. "I'm footsore and hungry. Where might I find victuals and ale?"

Her eyes widened. Finely arched blonde brows drew together over a straight nose dotted by a few freckles. "Victuals and ale," she repeated disbelievingly.

"Aye. Food and drink, in the common vernacular."

"Oh, I understood you well enough," Maggie murmured. "Your words, anyway. Your accent's a bit off."

His stomach growled again, embarrassingly loud.

"Guess you weren't kidding about being hungry." She eyed him appraisingly. "Do you have any money?"

Money. Too late he thought of the piles of gold coins and priceless gems lying on the floor of Kheladin's cave. In the world he'd left, his word was as good as his gold. He opened his mouth, but she waved him to silence. "I'll stand you for a pint and some fish and chips. You can treat me next time."

He heard her mutter, "Yeah right," under her breath as she curled a hand around his arm and tugged. "Come on. I have a couple hours, and then I've got to go to work. I'm due in at three today."

Lachlan trotted along next to her. She let go of him like he was a viper when he tried to close a hand over the one she'd laid so casually on his person. He cleared his throat and wondered what he could safely ask that wouldn't give his secrets away. He could scarcely believe this alien landscape was Scotland, but if he asked what country they were in, or what year it was, she'd think him mad.

Had the black wyvern used some diabolical dark magic to transport Kheladin's cave to another locale? Probably not. Even Rhukon wasn't that powerful.

"In here." She pointed to a door beneath a flashing sigil.

He gawked at it. One minute it was red, the next blue, the next green, illuminating the word *Open*. What manner of magic was this?

"Don't tell me you have temporal lobe epilepsy." She stared at him. "It's only a neon sign. It doesn't bite. Move through the door. There's food on the other side," she added slyly.

Feeling like a rube, Lachlan searched for a latch. When he didn't find one, he pushed his shoulder against the door. It opened, and he held it with a hand so Maggie could enter first. "After you, my lady," he murmured.

"Stop that." She directed the words toward his ear as she went past. "No more *my ladies*. Got it?"

"Aye. Got it." He followed her into a low ceilinged room lined with wooden planks. It was the first thing that looked familiar. Parts of it, anyway. Men—kilt-less men—sat at the bar, hefting glasses and chatting. The tables were empty.

"What'll it be, Mags?" a man with a towel tied around his waist called from behind the bar.

"Couple of pints and two of today's special. Come to think of it…" She eyed Lachlan so intently it made him squirm. "Make that three of the special."

"May I inquire what the special is?" Lachlan asked, thinking he might want to order something different.

Maggie waved a hand at a black board suspended over the bar. "It's right there. If you can't read it—"

"Of course, I can read." He resented the inference he might be uneducated but swallowed back harsh words.

"Excellent. Then move."

She shoved her body into his in a distressingly familiar way for such a communal location. Not that he wouldn't have enjoyed the contact if they were alone, and he were free to take advantage of it.

"All the way to the back," she hissed into his ear. "That way if you slip up, no one will hear."

He bristled. Lachlan Moncrieffe did *not* sit in the back of any establishment. He was always given a choice table near the center of things. He opened his mouth to protest but thought better of it.

She scooped an armful of flattened scrolls off the bar

before following him to the back of the room. Once there, she dumped them on the table between them. He wanted to ask what they were but decided he should pretend to know. He turned the top sheaf of papers toward him and scanned the close-spaced print. Many of the words were unfamiliar, but what leapt off the page was *The Inverness Courier* and presumably the current date: June 10, 2012.

His heart thudded in his ears, deafening him with the roar of rushing blood, as he stared at the date.

It had been 1683 when Rhukon chivied him into the dragon's cave. Three hundred twenty-nine years ago, give or take a month or two. At least he was still in Inverness—for all the good it did him.

"You look as if you just saw a ghost." Maggie spoke quietly.

"Nay. I'm quite fine. Thank you for inquiring...my, er..." Lachlan shut up. Anything he said was bound to be wrong.

"Good." She nodded approvingly. "You're learning." The bartender slapped two mugs of ale on the scarred wooden table.

"On your tab, Mags?" he asked.

She nodded. "Except you owe me so much, you'll never catch up."

Still shell-shocked by the realization hundreds of years had slipped past while he and Kheladin slept, Lachlan took a sip of what turned out to be weak ale. It wasn't half bad but could've stood an infusion of bitters. Because it was easier than thinking about his problems, he puzzled over what Maggie meant about the barkeep *owing her so much he'd never catch up.* Why would the barkeep owe her? His nostrils flared. She must work for the establishment—probably as a damsel of ill repute from the looks of her. Mayhap, she hadn't been paid her share of whatever she earned in quite some time.

Protectiveness flared deep inside him. Maggie shouldn't have to earn her way lying on her back. He'd see to it she had a more seemly position.

Aye, once I find my way around this bizarre new world.

Money wouldn't be a problem but changing three-hundred-year-old gold coins into today's tender might prove challenging. Surely banks existed that could accomplish something like that.

One thing at a time.

"So." She skewered him with her blue gaze—Norse eyes if he'd ever seen a set—and took a sip from her mug. "What did you see in the newspaper that upset you so much?"

"Nothing." He tried for an offhand tone.

"Bullshit," she said succinctly. "I'm a doctor. A psychiatrist. I read people's faces quite well, and you look as if you're perilously close to going into shock."

Witch's Bane

Witches Rule

Dragon Lore

Highland Secrets

To Love a Highland Dragon

Dragon Maid

Dragon's Dare

Earth Reclaimed

Earth's Requiem

Earth's Blood

Earth's Hope

Elemental Witch

Timespell

Time's Curse

Time's Hostage

GenTech Rebellion

Winning Glory

Honor Bound

Claiming Charity

Loving Hope

Keeping Faith

Rubicon International

Garen

Lars

Soul Dance

Tarnished Beginnings

Tarnished Legacy

Tarnished Prophecy

Tarnished Journey

Soul Storm

Dark Prophecy

Dark Pursuit

Dark Promise

Underground Heat

Roman's Gold

Wolf Born

Blood Bond

Wolf Clan Shifters

Alice's Alphas

Megan's Mates

Sophie's Shifters

Wylde Magick

Gemstone

Lion's Lair

Unbalanced

STANDALONE BOOKS

Branded, That Old Black Magic Romance (paranormal romance)

Edge of Night (short story collection, paranormal and horror)

Grit is a 4-Letter Word (nonfiction)

Heart's Flame (post-apocalyptic romance)

Icy Passage (science fiction romance)

Marked by Fortune (post-apocalyptic coming of age story)

Melis's Gambit (historical paranormal romance)

Midnight Magic (paranormal romance)

Red Dawn (post-apocalyptic paranormal romance)

Shadow Play (historical paranormal romance)

Shadows in Time (Highland time travel romance)

Since We Fell (contemporary romance)

Warin's War (paranormal romance)